Praise for the Bod

M000306953

MARKED

"Once again I have to hold on to my hat while we zip around Europe and land in lovely Florence where author Ritter Ames lures me in with her delightful vignette of Italian life seen through the eyes of an art expert."

– Maria Grazia Swan,
Author of the Lella York Mysteries

"Ames, with her great writing and brilliant story, has created a masterpiece of her own in *Marked Masters*. She leaves her readers doing their own research between the pages. Like Laurel, Ritter keeps the story with its rightful owner—the reader."

– *Crimespree Magazine*

"Boasting a great cast of characters, good conversations and the global background, this was a very enjoyable read and I look forward to the third book in this exciting series."

– *Dru's Book Musing*

"Well-plotted and will keep you guessing until the very end...The action is nonstop and you will find that you can't put this book down. Mystery readers will enjoy the chase and be pleased with the outcome. I can't wait to read the next in the delightful series. If you like your mystery filled with hunky spies, then you should be reading *Marked Masters*."

– Cheryl Green, *MyShelf Reviews*

COUNTERFEIT CONSPIRACIES (#1)

"An intricately woven tale with plenty of action and suspense. The story is crafted in such a way to keep readers guessing. The characters are well-written with smart and witty dialogue. An enjoyable read."

– *A Cozy Book Nook*

"Funny, fast paced and just a smidge of romance. What more could you ask for? Bring on the next one!"

— T. Sue Versteeg,
Author of *My Ex-Boyfriend's Wedding*

"A high-octane, fast-paced thrill ride of a mystery adventure that will definitely leave you anxious for the next installment."

— *Girl with Book Lungs*

"This fast-paced mystery had me reading far past my usual time for bed. I simply couldn't put it down because I was so drawn into the story. It's simply wonderful!"

— Dianne Harman,
Author of the Cedar Bay Cozy Mysteries

"The book takes you on car chases, shooting, great locations around the world all in the hopes of finding a missing friend and lost artifact. I read the book three times enjoying each time."

— *Book Him Danno*

"To save the day, Laurel takes you with her every step of the way on subways, planes, fast cars, and motorcycles all while being in danger. This book is truly a keeper, jump in and go for a ride!"

— *Destiny's Book Reviews*

"Incredible attention to detail. The author creates a world that you truly can get lost in. The book is also a fast-paced, fun read. I'm looking forward to reading book two."

— *A Girl and Her ebook*

"This fast-paced, action-filled whodunit was enjoyable and hard to put down...it was fun to watch the pieces come together in this well-written drama. I'm looking forward to the next book in this series."

— *Dru's Book Musings*

ABSTRACT
aliases

**The Bodies of Art Mystery Series
by Ritter Ames**

ABSTRACT
aliases

A BODIES OF ART MYSTERY

RITTER
AMES

HENERY PRESS

ABSTRACT ALIASES
A Bodies of Art Mystery
Part of the Henery Press Mystery Collection

First Edition | October 2016

Henery Press, LLC
www.henerypress.com

All rights reserved. No part of this book may be used or reproduced in any manner whatsoever, including internet usage, without written permission from Henery Press, LLC, except in the case of brief quotations embodied in critical articles and reviews.

Copyright © 2016 by Ritter Ames

This is a work of fiction. Any references to historical events, real people, or real locales are used fictitiously. Other names, characters, places, and incidents are the product of the author's imagination, and any resemblance to actual events or locales or persons, living or dead, is entirely coincidental.

Trade Paperback ISBN-13: 978-1-63511-073-9
Digital epub ISBN-13: 978-1-63511-074-6
Kindle ISBN-13: 978-1-63511-075-3
Hardcover Paperback ISBN-13: 978-1-63511-076-0

Printed in the United States of America

This book would have never been finished without the help of my husband and my dog—because they always forgave me when I said, "Just a minute. I'm almost done with this scene," but I kept writing for hours. Every author needs that kind of unconditional support.

After that, I need to mention all the terrific teachers through the years who not only taught me a love for writing, but also for reading, history, research, and how to organize my thoughts onto a page.

Last, but certainly not least, my late-father for not only introducing me to mysteries, but also for sharing his love of James Bond movies. A girl couldn't ask for a better childhood.

ACKNOWLEDGMENTS

I've mentioned this before, but it really sums up all the people on this Acknowledgments page, so it bears repeating: One of the quotes on the wall of my writing corner is by Goethe, "Be bold...and mighty forces will come to your aid." I've given Laurel Beacham a fictional team any art recovery expert would be proud of, and who she can always count on to come to her aid. But in writing these books, I've discovered I've gained my own version of mighty forces. Here are only a few:

I'll start this time with Dianne Wallace, because she's been a stalwart supporter of this series long before I even knew her name, and she was the key person who gave me the idea of how Laurel could lose her luggage this time. Not as easy as it sounds when it happens every book.

Jeanie Jackson may be retired from library work, but she's still the biggest supporter of authors and readers that I know. Not just my books—but every author lucky enough to catch her attention. Dru Ann Love is someone else who took a chance on me when my first book came out, gave me a spot on her blog, and has supported this series ever since. Honestly, authors cannot survive without the lovely people who write reviews and let us blog on their sites. Jenna Czaplewski and Joanne Kocourek are in this same class—lovely ladies who make sure readers always hear about good books and authors. They're also terrific critiquers when I'm looking for ways to write really short ad copy.

A number of people who started out as readers on my books have become friends, literary confidants, and cheering sections for me. This isn't supposed to be in any particular order, but the names just came out this way as I wrote them. Gale Sroelov might be even more dedicated to this series than I am, but more importantly she is someone whose friendship I appreciate because she always tells me what I Need to Know—not just what I Want to Hear. Kelly Hobbs wrote my first review—yes, I remember—and her posts on Facebook give me smiles every week. Helga Thompson is someone who absolutely keeps me on-task with this series, and I'm a better and faster writer because of it. Kay Hutcherson is another librarian who not only supports this mystery series, but supports books and readers and authors everywhere. More people who are always there to spread the news about Laurel's & Jack's adventures are: Heidi Wimmer, Maria Grazia Swan, T. Sue Versteeg, Susann Hughey, Andrea Stoeckel, Penniann Milan, Shannon Binegar-Foster, Mary Allen and Carrie Azurza.

Beyond the names above, I must recognize the greatest street team in the world—a group of women whom I'm so happy to say are just as committed to my books as I am. Thank you ladies for all you do to help me in my work as a mystery author.

Finally, and equally important, I have to thank all the wonderful people at Henery Press. This is a small but mighty force of professional people who do the best for their authors *Every Single Day*. From the editing team to those wearing the marketing hats to make sure everyone has the physical books they need, and all the other gracious Henery authors who welcomed me into the Hen House and answer all my questions—I truly want to thank you all.

ONE

We stood across the wide moonlit river from Big Ben, in the prime spot for viewing London's New Year's fireworks extravaganza. The jubilant crowd jostled and shouldered its way to fill every inch along the Thames, more than a half-million people crowding into every open space around us this clear cold night. All waiting for the countdown to start. Even with the event tickets Jack had snagged, we shared our roped-off space with about a hundred thousand fellow revelers. Central London bridges began shutting down just after noon, readying for the standing-room-only masses, and many of the streets were closed all day in preparation for the night's event and the hordes of people looking for a place to catch the stunning pyrotechnic performance. Rock music pulsed through the PA system, but the constant babble of the voices around us, most raised so their words could be heard by the people standing next to them, made all sound flow into a nearly incomprehensible rumble.

"Have you been here for the Lord Mayor's event before?" Jack Hawkes leaned down and shouted into my ear.

"Not for a while," I returned, equally loud. I'd been in Sydney the last couple of years, enjoying the milder weather during their January summers. Though the temps in Oz were nice and the people definitely fun, it didn't have the same electric feel for me as a frosty New Year's Eve in New York or the U.K. The brisk wind off the water zigzagged through the crowd, blowing my long hair across my face. I used a hand to brush away the blond curls, then hunkered down in my champagne-colored leather coat as I added,

"This is all much as I remember, though it is kind of weird getting a priority spot."

"But worth it," Jack said. "The special ticketing for the event only happened a couple of years ago. From the crowd control standpoint alone it offers a lot of advantages."

Safety, naturally, had created an even greater need for knowing who might be in a crowded world capital during something as well-attended as this public party. The thought made me take another glance around the crushing public. Not that I thought I would spot criminal activity—or even could in this throng—but it seemed the thing to do. When my sweeping gaze returned to Jack, I saw he was doing exactly the same thing. As an art recovery expert, observation skills are my chief tools of the trade. Jack's talents were even better developed than mine, though I hadn't yet learned why he was such a pro at doing a job he never talked about.

I moved closer and tugged his collar. When I wore heels he stood nearly a head taller than me, but the walking boots I'd donned for the occasion kept me much closer to the ground. I wasn't worried about being overheard in this cacophony, but I wanted him to actually hear my words when I asked, "Nico told me he sent you a tracking app. Did you get it?"

My wonder geek, Nico, usually kept tabs on me via the GPS in my phone, but Jack had rather unconventional ways of doing so. Ways we'd argued about. Often.

Jack cocked a dark eyebrow. "Yes, he said it was to track you more easily. I was surprised you didn't argue."

"So you didn't say anything because...?"

He shrugged and had the grace to look a little sheepish.

"Nico got inventive after Tony B kidnapped me in Miami. When his thugs broke my phone and I disappeared from everyone's radar, he decided we needed a backup method for GPS." I held up my left hand to show off my newest piece of jewelry. A lovely charm bracelet. "The camera charm disguises a tiny transmitter."

The app Nico sent to Jack keyed into the charm's frequency.

"You're okay with that?" he asked.

"Nico asked permission."

"Like he wouldn't have done it regardless."

"Still, he asked."

"I feel privileged to be in the inner circle. To know *where you are* at all times."

I caught the sarcasm in his tone and matched it. "I didn't want you to keep working so hard behind the scenes. You might use up too many favors with MI-5 and the Met police."

Jack gave me a crooked grin, then fingered the tiny silver camera. "At least I'll know where your bracelet is at all times."

I got the dig. He knew I'd slip my leash whenever I wanted, but his steady gaze told me he understood I took the continued threat seriously. We didn't know why I had become particularly interesting to criminals during the previous months, but until we identified the reason or captured all the players, I was ready to accept a little electronic help from one of Nico's gizmos.

We'd had our rocky starts, Jack and I, not the least of which due to both of us wanting to always be in charge and neither really trusting the other. With reason. He knew everything about me—well, all about the "public Laurel Beacham" at least—and told me little about himself. Jack's reason for not always trusting me was...well, I play by my own rules. Some of those rules have gotten me into trouble lately. When finding lost art is the objective, trouble can happen more often than one would think. Being able to always track me had become a priority, whether I liked it or not.

He looked at his Silberstein. "Minutes away from the countdown. Are you getting cold?"

Only my face felt the freezing temps off the river. I knew he was changing the subject. The bundled crowd around us was more than enough body heat to keep us warm. "I'm toasty. Does the Eye signal the start again?"

He nodded. "The lights begin flashing about ten seconds before."

Next, the glorious twelve-count strikes of Big Ben would sound and fireworks soar thundering to the heavens and usher in new beginnings, new promise, and a new year. It didn't matter how many times I witnessed an event like this, the kid in me always got antsy. I wanted it all—pronto.

"There's the kissing at midnight, remember," Jack said, his gaze never leaving mine.

"I think in a crowd this size we should have no trouble finding a friend to pair up with." I smiled.

"Did you think I was sugges—"

His teasing response was interrupted by a slurred shout. "Oy! Jack Hawkes. How the devil are you?"

A thirties-something man stumbled into us. He was rail thin, even in his long gray greatcoat, but his momentum almost made us lose our footing. The man was also familiar.

"Hamish." Jack bolstered the tipsy friend. "Never expected to see you here tonight, mate."

The interloper turned to me, weaving a bit and slurring, "Can't forget this pretty lady...Laurel Beacham, correct?"

I smiled and nodded, realizing the obnoxious drunk was an old school chum Jack introduced me to when we were in Florence last fall chasing criminals. Hamish taught art history at the university level there, and I'd had Nico check him out. Nothing overly suspicious came up on his background, nor anything to imply involvement in the prospective heist we currently worried over. We struck him from our list of suspects when no big payoffs appeared in his bank accounts. Though he was likely in town for Christmas visiting, I did find it interesting he was in London and materialized beside us at this event.

"Here on winter break," he said, confirming my suspicion as he gave Jack a friendly slap on the back. Knowing the man had no biceps, I doubted Jack felt a thing. Hamish continued, "Have to leave tomorrow to return to teaching the dil-et-tante rabble."

Despite his stutter over dilettante, I began to think he wasn't as buzzed as he appeared. He couldn't be truly drunk, or one of the roving bobbies would have moved him through the crowd and out the gates. Was it an act for us? Or had he simply been super-careful until he spotted his old friend, Jack? Just the same, I wondered how much alcohol was actually in that skinny body.

"Is Milli here?" I asked, stretching tall to pretend to look for his pretty wife.

Hamish waved a crazy hand as if brushing something aside. "No crowds for our tight-assed Mills. She's afraid someone will trod on her fancy shoes."

She was from money and held the purse strings. Was this a drunk's loose-tongued revelation, or an admission of trouble in paradise? For Hamish's sake, I hoped not the latter. His personal paycheck could not provide the lifestyle he'd grown accustomed to with his marriage to Millicent and her daddy's money.

Suddenly, a raised voice on the loud speakers cried, "One minute, everyone!" The air charged. The crowd shifted. Everyone turned toward the London Eye.

"Forty-nine, forty-eight—"

A half-million voices counted down in unison with the speaker on the PA. I looked at Jack and he grinned at me. I felt eight again—and twenty-eight at the same time. I raised my voice with the others.

Hamish stayed silent beside me. Maybe he was too drunk to be able to count backward. As we hit twelve, I turned and saw he was staring off in the distance. Away from the flashing wheel keeping us on track with the countdown.

"Ten, nine—"

I kept in time with everyone else, smiling up at Jack before watching the lights again.

"Three, two, one—"

The bell in Big Ben gave a decisive first gong as the lights strobed around the Eye. I turned to Jack as he moved toward me.

Then I was whirled around and smashed into the worst slobbery, beery kiss of all time.

Jack roared, "What the bloody hell?"

I tried desperately to escape Hamish's determined embrace. I finally broke free and pushed away from the intoxicated boor. Jack's fist was already in play.

He had obviously been aiming for the side of Hamish's ear. When I pushed the fool, my chin ended up in the trajectory instead. Quick reflexes and a bit of luck allowed Jack to pull back a little, making it a glancing blow. Nonetheless, the brief contact with the side of his fist knocked me off my feet.

"Oh my god, Laurel. I'm sorry. I saw at the last second, but I could only—"

I waved a hand at the distraught almost-white knight kneeling beside me. "I'm alright." I wiggled my jaw a couple of times to be sure. Yep, I'd be sore, but it wasn't anything I hadn't experienced before. "At least you didn't strangle me this time." I smiled as best I could to show I was teasing, but Jack's face immediately grew more thunderous at something behind me.

Turning, I realized we had more trouble.

"Laurel, *mon dieu,* I will call an ambulance." It was Rollie, the grandson of Devin Moran, the master criminal we presumed was in charge of the premier heist Jack and my team were trying to stop. All of Moran's confederates were on our most wanted list, and Rollie in particular because he may have been connected with Tony B due to video evidence of a couple of recent events. While we'd been working feverishly since October to find the hole he and everyone else was hiding in, I definitely didn't need him there. At that moment.

The last time we'd seen Rollie he was walking down an Italian sidewalk with an international felon. Now he was in London, apparently attempting to get Jack to throw another punch as they set me back on my feet. They were more successful at playing tug of war with me as the presumed prize.

"Stop!" I jerked my arms free and pulled my cuffs back down to my wrists. "I'm fine. Thanks, both of you."

"I saw him hit you." Rollie got ahead of me and bent down, trying to look closer at my chin. "We will call the *gendarme.* I will swear—"

"I didn't mean to hit her," Jack growled and tried to pull me away. Rollie made another grab for my arm.

A far too interested crowd had formed around us, and the fireworks were proceeding without anyone in our vicinity paying the slightest attention. Why should they when the ground entertainment rivaled any top ten reality show?

Hamish did the smart thing and disappeared. I needed to get Rollie to do the same. Especially once I saw we'd caught the attention of a uniformed bobby. The officer was making his way down from the edge of the crowd. Time to work fast.

"Guys, please." I smiled at Jack, then turned to Rollie. "I appreciate your help, but Jack's chivalry simply backfired. It was an accident. Please, go back and join your friends, Rollie, and don't worry about me."

"*Non*, I will stay here, I will—"

"No." I shook my head and reached up to pat his chest with my hands, effectively pushing Rollie away as my fingers touched the fine leather I recognized from this year's Versace line. "I'm going to call it a night, and Jack will take me home."

"This barbarian—"

Jack pushed in closer. "I didn't—" he started.

I interrupted my Hulks before they rumbled. "It's all right. Thanks so much for your help, Rollie." The bobby was close enough to see my smile. I gave him a "don't worry about it" wave and pulled on Jack's arm. "Let's go."

I didn't see which direction Rollie headed. I hoped seeing me turn my back on him and going away with Jack would end further discussion.

Roman candles burn at temperatures exceeding twenty-five-hundred degrees centigrade. I'm not sure Jack's temper wasn't beyond this range as we worked our way through the crowd. He likely could have talked his way out of any trouble with the constable, but we didn't need the attention.

"Damn that bastard Hamish," Jack cursed. "All the times I saved his bloody arse in school."

"He was drunk tonight and mad at his wife," I said. After the awful kiss I knew he'd had his share of alcohol, but I did wonder what he was looking at moments before the big blowup.

Jack growled something under his breath, before saying louder, "Then that arse Rollie shows up and acts like I did it on purpose."

"Well, you did mean to throw the punch."

"I didn't mean to hit you!" He pulled me nearer a street light and looked closely at my jawline. "Laurel, I'll make this up to you, I promise."

"You certainly will," I said, trying to keep from wincing when he touched a tender spot. "You're taking me dancing, buster. Dinner too. That's how you'll make it up to me."

He finally grinned. "Dancing with you doesn't exactly sound like punishment."

"You've only worked with me a few months. You have no idea how long I can dance."

He laughed. I'd completed my objective. "Really, I'm okay." I gave him a hug.

I kept my arms around him but leaned back to see his face, right as another symphony of light splashed across the sky in every imaginable color. The noise was ear-shattering, and I could already smell the gunpowder riding the air currents, but the effect was magnificent. "Oh, my."

"Let's stand over there and watch."

I nodded, and we moved along the fringe. He kept his arm around my shoulders, and I let him. As the music swelled and the heavenly display reached its climax, his body relaxed a little, and I thought everything was back in balance again.

Until he said, "Really, you didn't have to flirt with the jerk to keep him from reporting me to the police. I do have resources, you know."

"I do know." I looked up at him. "So do I. What you thought was me flirting to get him to go quietly away actually served a higher purpose. It allowed me to leave a small remembrance of this evening in the breast pocket of his jacket. The kind of pocket in leather coats men likely never use. Or look into."

At Jack's puzzled expression I held up my left arm, making sure my charm bracelet glowed in the light. The bracelet no longer displaying a tiny silver camera.

"When you straightened your cuffs," Jack said, wonder filling his voice.

"When I straightened my cuffs."

"We can track him."

"You can. I don't have the app."

"I could kiss you."

"First, pull out your phone and start tracking."

TWO

The app told us Rollie was still in the midst of the crowd, but at the other end from where we'd all been at midnight. As we went one way to exit, he'd gone the opposite direction. Deeper into the crowd. How did he happen across us unless it had been with intent? Was he following me, or both of us? Or had he been tipped off by someone who knew our plans this evening?

Standing in a space filled with a hundred thousand other ticketed gawkers, I simply couldn't believe it coincidence.

"How do you think Hamish and Rollie both lucked into us in the masses of people?" I asked.

Jack looked up from the screen and stared off across the Thames. "I've been wondering the very same thing. Have you noticed any shadows lately?"

"I haven't really been looking."

"Nor have I."

Lazy. Both of us. We counted on someone at Interpol or Scotland Yard to notify us if Rollie stepped through any customs points. Hamish Ravensdale, however, had never been a person of interest.

"You know Hamish from years ago. What do you know about him lately?"

He looked me in the eye. "He's someone who's always been afraid of any kind of pain. He can be cunning, and in school he stayed one step ahead of everyone else so he could duck behind someone like me when a situation called for caution. What did Nico find out in the background check? Or did you do it?"

Of course he knew. "I outlined my suspicions and Nico looked for verification."

"What did he find?"

"Hamish needs to stay married or live like a pauper."

"His family had money—"

"Not anymore."

"Interesting." He took my hand and guided me down the sidewalk in the direction of the car, all the while keeping watch over the little dot on his phone screen. He stayed too quiet not to be up to something.

"Where are we going?" I asked.

"To the car." He picked up his pace as we crossed an intersection. Traffic was lighter than usual, but still busy. People lined the curb hoping to hail a taxi. Several occupied cabs zipped by, never slowing.

I caught a glimpse of Jack's cell screen and saw the dot moving again. "You think it would be easier for us to follow him in the car?"

"No. I'm going to follow him. You're going to drive my car back to your hotel."

"You've decided all of this by yourself—"

"I have the app on my phone. It only takes one person to follow the blinking dot."

I was certain "blinking" wasn't the word he actually wanted to say. I shoved my fists into my coat pockets and hugged the leather around my body. "I'd be there for backup if necessary."

"It won't be necessary."

He sped up as the crowd opened a bit. I wasn't wearing heels and had no problem keeping up. When we were stopped by the light at the corner, I glared at him. He glared right back.

Jack knew exactly what he was doing, and my argument sounded weak even to my ears, but I didn't like him making unilateral decisions. And he knew it. "We're supposed to be a team."

He blew out a long breath. The light changed, and he caught my elbow to hurry me through the crosswalk.

"I'm only following him, Laurel. I want to see if he'll lead to Moran or anyone else we've been trying to find. Nothing challenging."

Like I hadn't heard that before. "How are you going to get around?"

"On foot as long as he is. I'll grab a cab or take the Tube if I need to go faster."

Two more taxis drove by us, both with their top lights turned off.

"A number of the Tube stations are closed, and some of the trains aren't running," I reminded him. "You might have trouble getting a cab."

We maneuvered around crowds of people who had clustered outside the ticketed area to watch the fireworks display. The show was over, and everyone was leaving en masse. A minute later, we reached the lot where Jack had parked the car. He hit his fob and the black Audi S5 beeped and flashed its lights.

"Everything you say is entirely possible," he said when we were finally away from the mob. "Until I know how we were stumbled upon in the crowd tonight, you're getting safely tucked in behind your doorman and your trusted desk clerk. You must understand this makes the most sense."

I did, but I didn't have to like it. Or tell him I agreed. Reluctantly.

As he opened the driver's side door for me, I asked, "What if you were the one tracked with your car?"

Jack stared at me, his eyes widening for a moment. This was something he hadn't considered. "Bloody hell."

He turned toward the road, then looked back at me. He scratched his forehead. "We didn't pass an empty cab the whole way. Not an option." He ran a hand along the bumpers and into the wheel wells and said, "Take the car. If anyone tries to stop you for any reason, there's a Walther PPK in a holster attached to the bottom of the driver's seat. Reach down with your right hand. It has a full clip."

I swallowed. The idea of my leaving with his gun made me want to repeat the argument we should stay together, but the laser look he shot my way said any idea to the contrary wouldn't fly. I didn't have my tracking charm any longer either. If I did go with him and we got separated...

Instead of arguing, I slid into the seat and felt for the gun's grip. It was right where Jack said. "Do you want me to park on the street and leave your keys with the front desk?"

"You have valet parking, right?"

"Yes. There's a parking garage."

He nodded. "Pull up to the front door and use the valet. I'll get the car tomorrow."

"Be careful. I don't like you doing this alone."

"I'm only going to see where he goes. No heroics, I promise."

I raised an eyebrow. "No fists either. And don't look for Hamish. You're liable to beat any information out of him."

"It wouldn't take much."

"Jack..."

He held up his hands. "I promise. Now go. Be sure to get some ice on your chin."

"Call me when you get home."

He looked at his screen. "He's moving faster. Gotta go. Keep my car in one piece." He slammed the door and hurried back in the direction we'd come. Doing everything his way, of course.

I'd argued about being sent home, but I was tired. Despite the holiday, I also had a morning appointment with museum officials and didn't really have time for a scavenger hunt if the objective was to only follow Rollie, rather than have him arrested.

Besides not having the least hope Moran would be discovered during Jack's reconnaissance, I wanted to follow orders and get ice on my chin. I could feel the tight muscles around my jaw and worried the skin might be several unattractive shades before long. It wasn't the best practice for the head of the London office of Beacham Ltd. to arrive anywhere looking like she'd just gone a round in the ring.

Life is definitely on a risky path when a person feels gratitude over having the ability to use a Walther PPK—unless it's trivia night in a bar and the question is what model firearm James Bond employs.

The Audi and I made it to the hotel without incident. However, I didn't like the idea of leaving his gun in a car headed for valet parking either. As I pulled up to the front door of the hotel, I slid the gun from the holster and inside my coat. I'd have to remember to give it back to Jack later.

The guys in valet livery were still on duty, and one opened my door before I had the chance. I popped the trunk—okay, the boot—and pulled my big Fendi bag from the dark recesses. Leaving it there earlier to deter pickpockets and purse snatchers during the revelry had seemed the best idea. Given what happened I was glad I'd taken the precaution. The doorman ushered me into the lobby as the valet-driven Audi roared off. On the way to the elevator, I detoured into the hotel bar and got a large cup of ice.

I checked for messages as I entered my room. There were four calls from Cassie, my personal assistant. From the voicemails I learned she'd returned to London early from her Christmas travels to the States and would meet me at the office in the morning. Before she left, I'd had her working on forgeries potentially tied to the bigger heist, and something over the holiday made her think she might have spotted new information. Between her cryptic messages and Rollie reappearing, I hoped it meant an imminent breakthrough on the case.

I texted Nico asking for a new charm to replace the silver camera. He was in Italy for Christmas a few more days, and though I didn't know what resources he had at his disposal, past experience said he would get on the task as quickly as possible, regardless of the holiday. Business completed at the moment, I put ice into a washcloth and checked my face in the mirror.

A heavier hand with makeup should do the trick, I thought after a careful examination. I finished up my nightly routine and headed for bed. My phone sat charging on the nightstand. If Jack didn't call, I hoped he would at least text. But he operated under his own counsel and whim, so I counted on nothing.

Next morning, I hadn't heard from him when I finished my shower. I sent a text telling him I removed the gun from the car. He texted back a minute later: *OK, but leave it next time. You are not in the U.S. anymore and can get arrested with it in the U.K.*

Sheesh. That was gratitude. I kept him from getting his gun confiscated or stolen by the valet service and received a lecture for my trouble. I already knew the long reach of the Prevention of Crime Act, which is why I'd had to give up carrying my beloved telescoping baton. In the back of my mind I wondered if his response was merely to irritate me enough so I wouldn't ask for more info on his reconnaissance. I almost sent another text to call his bluff, but it was irritating to have to push. I shoved my phone into my pocket and headed to the office, stopping on the way for coffee and a cruller.

Even with my late night I was at my desk half an hour early. Messages checked, phone calls returned, and a note written for Cassie filled the time until I needed to leave for my National Gallery appointment. I was delivering an Old English masterpiece I'd recovered through a combination of unorthodox networking and some pseudo-hostage negotiating. The painting leaned against the wall by my office door, wrapped in plain brown paper, awaiting its return to the museum.

A couple of generations ago, the Beacham Foundation started out as a fundraising liaison for museums and artistic organizations, helping match up funders with fundees during my grandfather's reign. After my father lost control about a decade ago, things evolved to a greater degree in recovering missing masterpieces and shoring up exhibit security.

My boss, Max, had been one of my grandfather's protégés, and when he assumed responsibility over the foundation, he recognized it sometimes required unconventional thinking and practices to ensure art stayed in the public realm. Given this usually meant less was paid out in ransom for stolen pieces, these ideas made us very popular with the insurance sector and museum board members.

We kept our fingers in art circle fundraising, even as our mission expanded, and I personally attended several dozen posh pledging events annually. No one wanted to pay twice or three times for the same painting or sculpture, which happened when pieces were stolen and ransomed back. Add in the fact many museums didn't have the funds to insure most of their pieces, and ransom was often not an option anyway. For those who did insure, the insurance companies put their own pressure on the administration and wealthy art patrons, frequently employing corporate bounty hunters to mitigate losses to stockholders. It was easy to see why recovering a national favorite, like this painting, made me a person to call when masterpieces went missing.

I was almost out the door when Cassie finally got into the office. I'd expected her at nine, but she was more than an hour late. The shadows under her eyes said she had a major case of jet lag.

"I left you a note," I said, pointing to her desk. "I have an appointment, but I'll be back by early afternoon. Can you work without me?"

She'd already moved automatically to her white board. From her leather tote, she pulled a stack of Post-It Notes she'd probably scribbled up during the plane ride back. "Sure. Go ahead. I need to check some files and make a couple of calls."

"You do remember it's a holiday?"

"I know. I'm good at leaving voicemails."

"Yes, I know," I said, pulling open the office door. "I listened to four about one thirty this morning."

She stared at my face. "Why did you change your makeup?"

"Jack slugged me last night."

"What?"

"He aimed for Hamish. I got in the way."

"Hamish Ravensdale?"

"The very same."

"Why was he in London, and why did Jack try to hit him?"

"He was visiting for the holidays. Jack threw the punch

because it was midnight, and Hamish pulled me away from Jack so he could kiss me instead. Then Jack tried to slug him, hit me, and as Hamish ran away Rollie showed up."

"Rollie? What kind of New Year's party did you attend last night?"

"Good question. As far as I know Jack's still trying to figure it out."

Cassie gave me her worried mother look. "Your makeup is good. I wouldn't even know if you hadn't told me. Does it hurt much?"

I laughed. "Don't worry. Jack kissed the pain away soon after."

"Damn it, Laurel!" She dropped her pastel notes. "You can't leave until I get details."

"A joke, Cassie. I promise I'll tell you everything later." I slung my purse on my shoulder, gripped the top edge of the package guaranteed to be the star of the meeting, and zipped out the door.

THREE

My late-morning and early-afternoon hours were spent in reserved celebration with the curators at the National Gallery. As a collective body in that sweeping institution, they were thrilled in reticent British fashion—broad smiles, dignified but relieved handshakes, and the offer of tea and toast when I entered the conference room with my flat brown-paper-wrapped package. Moments later, one of the more senior members ordered up champagne flutes and the tea was forgotten.

"A toast to the woman of the hour, Laurel Beacham," the director proclaimed. "A lovely lady, and the world's foremost art recovery expert."

My face felt the heat of a blush, but I smiled broadly and played the role I was born to. I clinked glasses with the guy beside me, who'd been paying more attention to my attributes than to those of the painting I'd recovered. One more time I told myself it was not my fault I was an almost thirty-year-old leggy blonde who had more brains than many people gave me credit for. I moved to the other side of the room when I saw the media person, Megan Jenkins, motion for me to join her and a board member.

The media woman nodded toward the silver-haired gentleman in the Savile Row suit as she said in her lovely Irish accent, "Laurel, I was just telling Lord Singleton how the BBC is intrigued about this story."

Our gathering celebrated the return of a lesser-known but beloved British masterpiece I'd recovered the morning before.

Immediately ahead of authorities collaring the thief. The work had disappeared in a sleight of hand maneuver the thief employed in a lucky moment, and he planned to use the treasure in a vain attempt to win back the woman of his dreams. Bad luck for him, the act turned into his personal nightmare. Scotland Yard is good, but more intent on getting their man. Art is my area of expertise, and catching the thief remains paramount, but secondary to retrieving items like a fifteenth-century original oil painting.

Success came after a few days of reconnaissance, as well as calling in favors from all corners of my personal intelligence network of sticky-fingered pickpockets, cunning grifters, and less-than-forthright fences. All of those bits and pieces of finagled information culminated in a long session of strategic negotiations with the thief in question, and finally resulted in my liberating the work of art from captivity. Leaving the perpetrator to once more reside as a guest at one of Her Majesty's historic penal establishments. Nothing had been heard of the girlfriend.

This kind of success buoyed me, when I knew I'd pulled off a feat others in my trade only dreamed of accomplishing. I appreciated why the story caught the attention of media outlets, but I wasn't going to spill my secrets on television.

"Wonderful, Megan. Let me know when the story airs and I'll try to catch it."

"No," she said. "They want to interview you."

As I feared. "Really, I don't want to take the emphasis off this valued institution, and I especially don't want to play a part in sensationalizing a crime. If they want to do a piece highlighting how this brilliant work of art is back in the collection where it belongs, for instance, and interview the curator, I'd be happy to play second chair. But I have no interest in a one-on-one interview."

"I understand and concur," Megan said.

"We were hoping your response would run along those lines," Lord Singleton said in his cultured baritone.

"We'll have to give a more detailed response than the press

release I sent out earlier," Megan said, frown line forming above her tawny brows. "However, I am glad we all agree."

"You have my number," I replied. "My assistant, Cassie, keeps my schedule. Let us know what you work out. Email any copy you want me to stick to in my responses."

"Thanks very much, Laurel."

For the next hour or so I circled the room chit-chatting, picking a few brains about missing art works I had a particular interest in, and making sure to connect with everyone for the sake of keeping contacts while we all had the museum to ourselves. Constant gratitude is wearying after a while, however, and I eventually ran out of original ways to say "it was my pleasure." But this came with the job and was the way I got my name on more private-ticket guest lists than the average art recovery pro.

The museum crew continued marveling over the recovered painting and worrying to seek out any new scratch as I said my goodbyes and headed back to the office. Almost everyone tried to get me to stay longer, but I resisted. I wanted to learn why Cassie cut her holiday trip short by two days. I also knew she'd kill me if I waited much longer before explaining what I'd teased her about when I left.

As I saw the museum's exit in the distance and picked up my pace, I planned what I would and would not say on the record if the interview ended up being a go. All I knew for certain was I would say as little as I could get away with and try to put as much attention as possible on the museum and its professional staff.

It would be good press for the Beacham Foundation, sure, which was how Max, my boss, would view things, no matter how many ways I petitioned for a low profile. It was hard enough outsmarting art thieves. My job would be made doubly difficult if the more competitive criminal element of society decided to test my mettle simply because I got primetime press.

I hurried through the museum's public areas, smiling when the lone guard stood up to let me out of the building. The bleak gray skies showed through the huge windows. I cinched my leather coat a bit tighter and slowed as I hit the building's outer paved apron. Before leaving the protection of the Gallery's portico, I pulled out my phone. Buried in the middle of the missed calls and messages was a text from Nico. He had a new charm ordered and warned me to keep my phone on at all times until I received it. I texted back for him to tell them to expedite the damn thing to me and stop nagging.

The evening before had been glorious for the celebration, but today everything was damp and dark—from the coats on the pedestrians to the mottled clouds above. Last night, clear skies offered the perfect venue for the Mayor's New Year's fireworks. Twelve hours later, all the energy was spent in getting to the next sheltered location. I had another stop nearby and planned to briskly walk the long mile and ruminate over possibilities while I gained a little high-heeled exercise to make my Fitbit happy.

Trafalgar Square, steps from the National Gallery, remained one of my favorite places to people watch, but the drizzly weather eliminated the possibility. I hurried down the stairs and across Trafalgar. As I rounded the sidewalk past Nelson's Column, I reached up to stroke a front paw on a huge brass lion reclining at the base. For luck, if nothing else. Then I struck off in the direction of the office.

My phone rang. It was Jack. Any other time, I'd think he was calling about the case we were working together as unofficial partners. The one which sent him tailing Rollie on his midnight run. After last night, though, I figured he was calling to see if my chin was black and blue. I answered, saying, "You don't have to worry. I look fine."

"Good. Where are you?"

I started to tease him about his habit of answering my question with a question. His tone of voice changed my mind. "Left the National Gallery a minute ago and on my way to the office after a quick errand. Why? Where are you?"

"I'm in Rome. Tony B was attacked early this morning in prison. The outlook is bloody dicey."

Now I understood Jack not calling earlier to give an update. He knew I'd have wanted to tag along. Tony B was a thug whose allegiance to man and country was determined by whichever best payday he could receive. After his arrest in October, we'd been trying to ascertain who the felon worked for, but he wasn't talking. In the meantime, the U.S. attempted to extradite him for a murder in Miami that occurred the same day he'd had me kidnapped. Italian authorities, on the other hand, wanted him chiefly for major art crimes. I could only imagine the number of people who might want him dead. Jack and myself included—after he answered our questions, of course.

"He's alive though?" I asked, looking around to check no one was nearby. I hunkered down close to the statue and shivered. I blamed the cold, but wouldn't have sworn to it.

"Barely. In ICU. I have a mate on the military side who's attempting to get me in to see him." Jack blew out a long breath. "The DNA evidence finally came through matching the true killer to the murder, but not Tony B, and a deal was struck yesterday. He was going to talk and get a lighter sentence with no extradition if he testified via video against Tina in the Florida murder trial."

Tina Schroeder was someone I thought was a longtime friend, but who had learned from her mother to play every angle of opportunity without any scruples. She'd changed her identity and thrown in with Tony B until they both got caught. Then they turned on each other. Before the attack in prison, it sounded like Tony B was gaining the best outcome.

"Don't tell me Italy and the U.S. were going to let him go."

"No, but he would have had a chance to get out much earlier than any of us would like. With no evidence to tie him to the killing, the kidnapping charge against you likely remained the strongest thing the U.S. could hold him on. Here in Italy, they had a gun charge and a stretch toward attempted murder with you testifying and Nico backing you up, but they're more inclined to pursue the art and antiquities charges. Thus, they were better open to dealing."

Which led me to wonder if this murder attempt was mounted

by the bad guys who didn't want Tony B talking about them or the good guys who preferred he didn't get out with little more than a slap on the wrist. "Who do you think did it?"

"My money is on his employer," Jack said. "If we could find out who it is, of course. After discovering Rollie in London, I can't decide if it makes a stronger case for Moran to be Tony B's boss, or a reason why he likely isn't."

"What's your plan?"

"If I'm allowed to go in with the prosecutor, we hope to get some of the names promised as part of the deal. All assuming, of course, Tony B is alive and conscious when we arrive."

"How far away are you?"

"Five minutes from the hospital. I'll have to turn my mobile off inside. I wanted to give you this information while I could. I was just briefed a minute ago."

A minute ago, my ass. He ran off without me, like last night. Nevertheless, this phone call was a big step for Jack. Admitting he was letting me know current info almost as soon as he learned it was not a practice he did easily.

We both suffered from a driving desire to be the solitary point person with the lion's share of the data. A pivotal point in our relationship happened about a week earlier when I demanded Jack not keep me in the dark about himself and our respective jobs. Even when he won't admit anything concrete about his job, it pretty much has to be something in law enforcement and have a tangible connection to art. Or he's an excellent con man who is superb at running the long game. I was trusting him more, but the jury was out until I received a definitive answer—and I told him so. This new about-face for him tied to my requirement. Probably a little guilt from last night too. Of course, acknowledging the act meant I was obligated as well to start being equally open. Or appear a hypocrite.

"Thank you, Jack," I said, ignoring the stress gathering around my shoulder blades.

He mumbled something I didn't catch, then said, "We're here. I have to go."

"Are you still tracking Rollie?"

"The tracker isn't moving, so he's not wearing his coat. I do know where he spent the night."

"That would be?"

"The same Mayfair address we already knew about."

At least we had confirmation the address remained an active one for Moran's group. We'd spent time watching the residence over the past couple of months, waiting for anyone but the regular maids and tradesmen to enter. Two weeks ago Nico learned the place had changed ownership, purchased by a German conglomerate, and we assumed Moran decided the location was too hot to hold on to.

"The German corporation didn't appear to have ties to Moran. Do you think it's covering for him, or Rollie kept a key and a copy of the alarm codes?"

"Either or both, it doesn't matter. I notified Scotland Yard last night, and they tell me he was spotted leaving by taxi before six this morning."

"I'm assuming this was about the same time you were contacted by Rome."

"Yes. I don't know what it all means, but keep your mobile on and I'll call back as soon as I know something," Jack said. His tone grew quieter when he added, "Please be careful. You're on your own."

"Don't worry. Cassie's back, and we plan to spend the day in the office. We'll be safe."

"I'll try to catch a return flight tonight."

"Okay. Good luck." I hung up.

More to ponder. An attempt to kill Tony B before he could talk. Why wait this long if it was related to someone who employed him to do the dirty work? He'd been in prison for months. Plenty of time to take him out if his death was the objective.

"He finally had a deal," I mused aloud as I returned my phone to my Fendi and brushed at a scuffmark on the bag's silver-gray side.

Had they waited, hoping he would get out without turning traitor? Or had they counted on him keeping his mouth shut?

On a personal note, I wrestled with myself about calling Jack again and asking him to try to find out what Tony B did with *The Portrait of Three.* The trio of masterpieces had last been in the criminal's office in Miami when he'd held me captive there. After his arrest in Italy, the Miami detective involved in the takedown got a search warrant based on my testimony. By the time the team hit the building, Tony B's office was empty, including the two connecting gallery rooms where at least four stolen paintings had hung on the walls. I silently mourned the fact I hadn't been able to take the priceless works with me when I made my escape.

Too much to do and think about. I needed to get my last errand run and return to the office to see if Cassie had some good news or had figured out what puzzle pieces went together. Knowing my focused assistant, she'd spent the past few hours madly rearranging her colored notes on the white board, trying to see a pattern some part of her brain assured her was there if she looked closely enough.

I hoped she'd discovered a clue to the art threat which started as a simple pickup job of a snuffbox at a Lake Como party in September, but quickly gathered steam and villains and forgeries. The snuffbox played a role in how Jack got involved in my life too, as I'd thought it was a simple sixteenth-century object, while he wanted it for an intelligence micro-drive supposedly secreted inside. We were both wrong—or we'd been outmaneuvered when the person who was supposed to deliver the snuffbox to me was murdered before I found him. The next time we saw the snuffbox it not only didn't have any digital intel, but was found to be a fake that led us to Florence and an even grander-scale forgery factory than anyone imagined. In the interim, I'd tasked Cassie with tracking the tangibly-related forgeries uncovered to date, while Jack and I tried to track the forgers. All of this would have been much easier if someone wasn't killing forgers at the same time. Seriously limiting our abilities to interrogate sources.

Until Rollie showed up last night, the players in this farce and most of our leads kept disappearing like smoke in the night. Despite everything, Tony B stayed tight-lipped, apparently even at the point of near death. If someone tried to kill me on orders of someone else—someone who wanted me to keep my mouth shut to help them—it's an easy bet I'd be singing to every guard, doctor, nurse, or janitor about who was behind the attack. But then, I wasn't working on making a deal for my freedom.

Quickening my steps, I detoured for a necessary stop on the way back to the office. The errand was to check on a restoration promised for an exhibit starting the next day. The address was nearby, and in less than ten minutes I was talking to the usually perky brunette who always made me think of a pixie.

"Another hour or so, Laurel," the restorer, Nelly, promised. She worked from her second floor flat.

London's second floor, so it was a third floor for me. All those stairs.

I wished her a happy new year, and she responded in kind, though a bit distractedly—not at all the upbeat personality I usually encountered. She showed me the tapestry, pulling at her corkscrew curls while pointing out the final section she wanted to spend more time on. "A tiny bit more refining is all. I promise. I want to do it right."

The work already looked brilliant, but I didn't argue. Her perfectionist tendencies were why I hired her. "Okay, great. Shall I come by on my way home?"

"I have an appointment later tonight, and I need to leave before five. Can you come back about four?" she asked. She continued running a hand nervously through her hair. "Or I could have it sent to your office by messenger in the morning."

"I'll come and get it. No problem. Or if I can't make it I'll send Cassie."

We spent a few more minutes talking mutual friends and events before I left her to her expert craft work. I wondered who she was meeting later, and if perhaps the appointment was the reason this normally calm bohemian artist, who was a wizard with textiles and thread, suddenly turned into a most nervous Nelly.

"Not your problem, Beacham," I muttered as I waited curbside in front of her flat, trying to hail a cab. I had enough dragons to slay. If Nelly wanted my help about something she would have said so.

FOUR

The black cab let me out at the address of Beacham Ltd., and I walked down the half-dozen steps from street level to reenter the foundation's London office. I pressed the brass latch lever of the solid black enameled door and brushed the kick plate with the toe of one high heel as I pushed inside. My promotion came several months ago, yet the fact I was in charge of the European arm of this venerable organization never ceased to amaze me. The Beacham Foundation had been a constant in my life since birth, and a constant in my family for generations before me. The New York office had been where I'd played and grown up, going to work with Grandfather whenever I had the chance. Even after Grandfather passed on and my father sold out for the cash he'd already spent, I hadn't realized it would be my calling and passion too.

My promotion to head of the U.K. branch came after I uncovered the extensive criminal wrongdoings of the previous person who held the position. Some likely felt the upgrade was my just reward; others thought I was too inexperienced for the responsibility. In part, I sided with the latter—after all, I hadn't successfully brought the criminal, Simon Babbage, to justice. Only hobbled him somewhat. Our foundation director and chief penny-pinching officer, Max, let me know privately he wanted Simon caught at any cost. No minor thing, believe me. Cost was always uppermost in the mind of my cheapskate boss.

However, Max did not have to challenge me on this. Catching Simon remained my first thought on awakening every morning, and prosecuting him for selling out the foundation while he worked as a double agent for Moran—and finding out if he'd absconded with a priceless artifact and left me with a well-made fake—kept me channeled on this goal without my superior's prodding. We weren't sure there was a true sixth-century sword, or if the fake I returned with was always the treasure. If Simon did steal a priceless relic, I wanted to be the one who brought it in. Optimally, without running the blade through the bastard first.

"Wow! Welcome back. I didn't think they'd let you leave this early," Cassie said as I entered our cream-on-beige reception area. This was a nice space. Her elongated wooden desk and well-lighted worktable sat positioned in one half, perpendicular to the long bank of windows set high along the outer wall.

"The champagne was gone by the time I left, but the staff continued reveling," I said. "A few of the directors made noises about leaving, and I took my cue from them."

Cassie motioned toward the printer. "They sent a copy of a previously faxed page to you a second ago. Looks like a press release with additional handwritten instructions."

The printed text was the updated press release Megan mentioned earlier, and scrawled in the margin was a note about getting a quick interview set up that evening to head off more questions. It was a good idea. The more time until the press got what they wanted, the more time they had to think of questions we didn't want to answer. Plus, the holiday increased the probability it was a slow news day, making reporters nosier about a full scoop. I pulled out my phone and texted her I was free after four p.m. In doing this, I remembered to give Cassie notice about the other change in plan.

"I went by Nelly's on the way back here, but the tapestry wasn't up to her standards yet. I said I'd pick it up before the end of the business day, as she needs to get away for an after-work engagement." I tapped the paper. "Now I have a television interview scheduled this evening, a taped affair coordinated by the grateful board at the National Gallery." I sighed. I might agree with

Megan's reasoning, but it didn't mean I had to like it. "While I can probably make both, if anything comes up I need you to go by and get the tapestry by four o'clock."

She handed me a notepad and pen. "Write down the address for me."

As I complied, she asked, "The interview tonight, is it you solo? Or you and someone else?"

I handed back the notepad and watched her add the time for the pickup and Nelly's name. My cell pinged to report a text from Megan saying she would be sending talking points momentarily. "It will be me, a head curator, and a conscientious BBC reporter intent on getting the story behind the story. Which will not be completely forthcoming." Another text alert sounded. "Megan says she has me scheduled with a makeup artist who wants me in her chair at five thirty sharp."

"Max will love the exposure for the foundation." Cassie gave me her Cheshire cat grin.

"At least one of us will." I took off my coat, held the collar and gave a quick shake above the tiled part of the floor, and hung the garment on a coat hook to dry. Our rainy day towel sat in its typical place behind the door, and I corralled it under one ebony Louboutin to swipe at the water. "Anything new crop up this afternoon?"

"A delivery service tried to drop off a package marked 'personal.' I wasn't sure when you'd be back, and it wasn't for the foundation, so I got him to deliver it to your hotel instead."

"Thanks." While I would prefer more permanent digs, between trying to save the art world from counterfeits and heists and having to work with trans-Atlantic moving professionals in an effort to get my possessions transported from New York, finding a flat of my own stayed sidelined for temporary digs. The hotel did its best to keep me comfortable, and given I typically stayed in some hotel somewhere two hundred or more days a year for my job, it felt enough like home for the moment.

Cassie walked around to the front of her desk, leaning on the top and crossing her arms. "I've waited long enough. Tell me what happened between you and Jack."

I laughed and gave her most of what she'd missed while she was away, and how our midnight adventure ended. One thing I didn't tell her about was Jack and my having dinner together the night she left for America, nor about the brief dossier he'd sent on himself to convince me to go to Ireland with him over Christmas. The information was a start. I'd learned he grew up with a single mom and went to an exclusive prep school thanks to a number of wealthy patrons. Whose names were not listed in the dossier, by the way. His mother died of breast cancer mere days after his twenty-first birthday, and he entered the Royal Navy a week following his graduation from Oxford. I found nothing in the file detailing facts after his military stint. It wasn't everything I'd hoped for, but it was a start. At my insistence, he did provide a copy of the dossier he had on me. It was illuminating...and irritating.

After some late night reading, I did accept his olive branch—and plane ticket—to join him in Ireland for a couple of days of sightseeing and relaxation.

We went there purely as friends, but having a few days away let us see each other in a different light. Well, maybe more clearly. I'd spent enough time reminding myself of how much he irritated me that I found it surprising to let down my guard and simply enjoy him being charming.

But I had no desire to tell Cassie any of this. She'd make more of it than I preferred. And I wasn't completely sure what I preferred. For now, hearing about Rollie's appearance was enough to send her into a tizzy.

"Thank goodness Jack was there! Do you think he was trying to kidnap you again?"

"We aren't certain Rollie knew about Tony B kidnapping me last time. All we know for sure is he was in the museum the day it happened."

"We need to get you some protection."

"No, I don't think it's necessary and would make life more

difficult. I've already messaged Nico for a new tracking charm and he monitors me 24/7 on my phone. I'm covered."

When I'd left earlier in the morning, the pink spikes in Cassie's blonde hair formed a uniform 'do all over her head. In the intervening hours the left side had evolved into intermittent patches of pink squashed against her skull and random spikes taking on a drunken air after having been pulled and clenched in her fist while she worked. "Your hair tells me you haven't made much progress in your project."

"Oh, is it bad?" She circled the desk and pulled a mirror from the top drawer.

"Needs evening out, is all," I said as I cranked the deadbolt. Twisting strong locks tightly closed had become a way of life for me. As late as early fall, my life was my own; I was even on my way to my first vacation in four years. Only to be sidetracked by the recovery job which ended way off course and gained me Jack Hawkes as an enigmatic sidekick. Well, less enigmatic all the time, but still a bit shadowy. I contemplated telling Cassie about his call from Rome, but decided not to send things down a new side path until I'd heard what she came up with while I was gone.

As I crossed the carpet, I said, "You've moved away from Post-Its on the whiteboard, I see, leaving me to assume you've been playing with computer files again. Bring whatever you have into my office and we'll brainstorm. Maybe you need to hear your ideas out loud."

"Worth a shot."

In about thirty seconds she pushed in, carrying her laptop and a couple of file folders, and sat down in one of the visitors' chairs. My office was my sanctuary, though despite my protests it continued to look more like Simon's old office than I wanted. Cassie held to the belief everything must be restored whenever possible. I had wainscoting and a wallpaper pattern she saved from destruction, rather than ordering the fresh look I'd requested. Not that I should expect anything less. Her background was art history and restoration after all. Wherever possible, I made changes, though not as quickly as I wished. At the same time, I continued to wonder who was really in charge.

"Where should we start?" I asked, pushing aside a couple of reports and my Fendi. She centered the laptop, making the screen visible to both of us.

"My brilliant idea didn't really pan out like I'd hoped," she said. "But I know there's something...I'll see it eventually." She sighed and punched a couple of buttons on the keyboard to load a carousel of photos. "I printed copies of recent stories surfacing about faux religious icons showing up and the supposed originals subsequently deemed fakes. Nothing new, but no sign of the true masterworks either. I forwarded the name of another dead forger to Nico, since you made this a priority before we left for Christmas."

"Good. We need to find someone who can talk to us about who the forgers had been working for. At first I thought it was Moran, but he's used forgers for years without their life expectancy suddenly tumbling. If he's employing these victims, we need to learn why the dynamic changed the last year or so. If it's someone besides Moran, we have to learn who and figure out a plan of attack. I'm no fan of forgers, but I'd prefer they ended up behind bars instead of inside coffins."

She slapped a folder atop my chrome and glass desk. One of those changes I mentioned. Simon's had been a carved rosewood behemoth. The new desk was a contrary move on my part. I really favored antique over modern, but I needed to make the office feel different. I had too much negative history with the old furnishings. Cassie understood, but hadn't forgiven me yet for the switch. She sent Simon's desk to a storage warehouse somewhere in Chelsea, along with other items we didn't need or currently use. Nothing was said, but I knew she hoped I'd change my mind and retrieve the antique soon.

I opened the slim folder to find the stories she'd mentioned, as well as a cornucopia of art masterpiece prints, from paintings to statues to jeweled items and lithographs. "Each has a forger's mark?"

"Yes. Some the same Florentine forgers' marks which started all of this, and some different forgers' marks to investigate next."

"Why mark the fakes as fakes?"

"Not all of the forgeries are marked, remember. Could matching the forgers' marks with the dead forgers be a way to..." Cassie shook her head. "I don't know. See a means of pointing to why any of this is happening?"

I pulled a map from my desk drawer we used to highlight the locations of murdered forgers in the past twelve to fifteen months. So far, no pattern emerged. "Nico and I discussed an idea similar to this before he left for Italy. I'll remind him when we talk again. He had a few ideas about databases to check and might have come up with something new while he's been away."

"Do you want me to work on the database angle? Try to match the marks and the dead forgers through computer files?"

"No. It's better if you work on the art angle. Copies versus originals are more your specialty. Leave the hacking potential to Nico." Most of our information on the murders—usually muggings—came via Nico tiptoeing through law enforcement databases without leaving behind footprints. Jack had sources he wouldn't talk about, but he was able to produce needed information at critical times. However, the need for warrants and jurisdictions made it more difficult when other countries were involved and was where Nico's talents shined.

"And leave the meetings with shady informants to you?" she asked, raising a thin brown eyebrow.

"I'll only meet with known quantities," I promised. "But yes, I've sent out a few cautious queries and hope for information in the coming days."

She tapped a fingernail twice on a second file. "Don't want to change the subject, but here's additional data on the painting you asked about from the yacht in Miami. I found it accidentally when I worked on the other stuff."

"*Woman Dressing Her Hair*?" I almost snatched the file from her hand. The painting was a forgery hanging in the saloon of an incredible mega-yacht Jack and I stayed on a few months back. My geek extraordinaire, Nico, worked on the yacht ownership angle, and Cassie was tasked with the art research. Despite best efforts, we had nothing more than the memories I brought home from Florida. No, correction. We had discovered the original work disappeared almost thirty-five years ago from a secure location while repair work was being done to the piece. The trail went cold immediately afterward.

Inside the file were two printed pages. One, a book excerpt referencing when the painting was included in a major museum fundraising exhibit held a month before the work vanished. The other page showed a grainy security photo of two men walking away with framed canvases. The one in the lead carried the likely original of *Woman Dressing Her Hair*.

"More than we had before. I'm assuming the repair we already knew about was from a mishap during the exhibit."

"I assume the same. That's going to be my next avenue of investigation when I get time. Find out what other paintings disappeared in the same robbery. We can see from the photo several others left with the thieves."

"You never know." I sighed and secured the pages again in the folder. "Wish this told us who copied the work and when."

"Are you thinking the forgery has something to do with what we're working on?"

I shook my head. "Probably a coincidence. We didn't even have an idea this forgery ring was in operation when I saw the *Woman Dressing Her Hair*."

"Why the interest then?"

"Good question." I looked away for a moment, trying to recapture the scene of the painting in its place of prominence on the yacht's wall. "It was something about the brushstrokes, I think. Though there could have been something more hitting my subconscious, but it hasn't yet come to mind. I thought I recognized the brushstrokes, or the technique. Or the copyist was someone mimicking someone else's. I don't know. We have forgers using the marks of other forgers. This may be a continuation of the same puzzle."

Cassie sat back in the lovely reproduction Chippendale I'd purchased to create a counterbalance to the modern desk. She asked, "Did you think about the mimicking at the time? Or only after the forgery ring was uncovered?"

"Everything happened so fast those few days, I'm not completely sure anymore. I think at the time I was interested in why elements of the painting were familiar to me. My subconscious hinted at something. Maybe a previous case. We're looking at forgeries anyway, and I didn't think it would take much extra effort. If it does, though, let me know."

Returning my attention to the slightly thicker heist data file, I said, "Running along the same lines, what started you thinking you had a fresh angle on the forgeries? Think back. What different elements led you into a new direction?"

"I'm not sure if it's a new direction, or a detour," she said, her hands resting on the chair's carved arms. "We were at my aunt's for dinner. She had an art book on the coffee table and pointed it out to me. The copyright date was two years ago, but when I looked through some of the sections I noticed one picture showed what looked like part of a forger's mark we've been watching for." She pulled back the file and shuffled through the pages, displaying a photo she'd printed off. Pointing to a lower corner, she explained, "I took this shot with my phone. You can see the picture in the book cut off the lower part of the painting, and the mark only shows up as half what we normally see. Yet, since they're always slightly camouflaged, I couldn't be sure if this was an abbreviated one, or just an imperfection on the print."

I stared at the photo. She was right as far as it went. The impression could be part of one of the forger's marks. Or something entirely different. We'd spent the intervening months following a myriad of clues, looking for trails leading away from the forgeries Jack and I saw in Florence. After Nico and Cassie's early research turned up dead forgers, we'd combed all available police files on suspicious deaths and muggings of anyone across Europe rumored to be related to counterfeiting art. Jack worked with U.K. officials highlighting why all the players in this case needed to set off alerts if they tried to cross borders. None of those analyses or safeguards pointed to an absolute or pivotal direction to move into. For the moment we kept with the necessary detail work that was tedious but offered the most likely means of poking a hole in the bubble covering this evolving crime syndicate.

"Most people at the publishing house are likely gone—"

"I emailed the Beacham New York office asking them to send a query," Cassie interrupted. "Figured they'd get answers before we would. Don't worry. I didn't say what I wanted to know and why. Simply asked if there was a full print of the painting showing an image out to the edges. If we find it warrants our attention, we can try to talk to the photographer who did this photo shoot. To find out when and where it was displayed for photographing."

"Excellent." I rose from my desk to pace. "New York publishers work pretty slowly on books of this type...especially if it involves a large amount of photographs...The photo could have been shot as much as four years ago."

Cassie agreed and swiveled to keep me in sight as I moved. "Exactly what originally got me thinking along these lines. We've been looking at this thing as some organization sending forgeries out slowly over the past year or so. Ideas validated by the bills of lading and museum data we quietly collected. If this mark does pan out—"

"They were making quiet inroads much further back than we've imagined."

"Like they were test driving their system." She typed for a second and several articles and art book prints appeared in a stacked checkerboard on the screen. "I've been looking for more possible instances, checking out online editions of recent art books to see if I can spot any of the marks, but I haven't found any." Cassie bit her lip. "Maybe I'm imagining it."

I picked up the print and studied it. "No. This could easily be a forger's mark. The fact the painting was not shown clear to the edge makes me wonder more about it. Such as who might have cut the mark in the edits to hide its forgery status."

"If it is a forgery."

"Of course," I said. She was right. We needed to keep this in perspective until any hypothesis panned out. "Did you notice other pictures in your aunt's book where the edges were cut off as well?"

"A few. One I recognized as a work known for having been damaged and badly repaired, and I assumed was the reason the photograph was incomplete. The others I noticed may have been cut down for space in the pages, allowing the finer details to be kept as large as possible. I made a list of those works, but I can't find any record online suggesting they may be forgeries or prints showing a mark of the type we're following."

Our offices were partway below street level, with Cassie's space enjoying most of the windows. My office made do with a kind of round porthole-inspired affair in a cutaway alcove behind the door. The bottom of the window hit me at shoulder level as I took in the scene outside, lower legs walking along the sidewalk past the iron fencing, car and bus wheels turning. I gazed out as I pondered her words, seething a little over the injustice of it all. When I looked back, Cassie sat squeezing her hands tightly together as she chewed her lower lip. My recent nearly fatal escapes kept her constantly vigilant about my safety. One more reason I wished all our bad guys hadn't gone to ground and we could halt whatever was on the horizon. I prayed Rollie's resurface offered a new direction. Not simply a brand new worry.

"Sorry. I'll step away from the window," I said.

Maybe Cassie's palpable fear heightened my own senses, or maybe I'd been through too much to not act instinctively. About a minute after I returned to my desk, a tremendous thud pounded the front door. We barely looked at one another before running to exit out the back way through the bathroom.

Cassie ran with her laptop clasped to her chest. I'd scooped up the papers on my desk and gripped my Fendi. We moved quickly and with such synchronization it was almost as if the hidden door in the back of the bathroom opened of its own accord.

The latch clicked closed, and I turned the key in the lock. I stopped Cassie as she tried to hurry me out of the janitor's closet constituting my office's "back foyer."

"Come on, Laurel!"

"Shh, no," I whispered as I clicked my phone app to gain eyes on the video feed from the security camera in my office. The audio picked up several additional heavy thumps, then I heard a tremendous *crack*. Either the solid front door gave way, or they attacked the doorframe and beat the lock. Regardless, the front entry was breached. Light reflected from the outside and into the full image of my office, streaming in as a broad ray into the room and brightening the dark wainscoting that circled the lower walls. I started to switch over to the feed in Cassie's reception area when I heard the jumble of several unrecognizable voices. Before I had a chance to switch feeds, my phone screen showed the leader striding into my office carrying a cricket bat. His face came into range, and I gasped as the focus sharpened. He swung the bat and the image—and likely the whole camera—disappeared. I choked back a scream.

"What?"

"We have to go!" I threw brooms and buckets against our side of the door to add obstructions. The new deadbolt needed a key on either side, making it necessary for them to battle through this door as well. The additional gauntlet we created with cleaning items wouldn't stop anyone for long, but might slow them down if they tried to leave the office via this route.

"That's what I've been telling y—"

"Cassie! It's Simon!"

"Oh my god!"

Between us we quickly blocked the door with everything portable. When she started to leave through the hall entrance I stopped her, shoving the folders and papers into my shoulder bag as I whispered, "Simon knows about this back exit. Someone is probably stationed outside the door to catch us."

Footsteps on the bathroom tile behind us echoed through the connecting door. I wanted to panic but didn't have the time. My gaze traveled over the shelves, and I grabbed a couple of aerosol cans with ingredients particularly irritating to skin and eyes. At the same time, my brilliant assistant began pouring liquid soap onto the floor. As the gallon jug ran empty, she threw it aside and caught the propellant I tossed her way. I used a broom handle and smashed the exposed light bulb in the ceiling center, plunging us into almost total darkness. My hand was on the knob when I heard the pounding start. Simon and crew wanted access into our getaway closet.

The only light came from the space between the painted door and the marble floor. We couldn't see anything else. I had to trust Cassie was ready.

I whipped open the door. And stopped. Blocking the way was a dark-haired thug who towered nearly a foot taller than me and my heels. One hand held a wicked-looking knife. The other curled into a fist the size of a small car. We channeled our sprays into his craggy face. He screamed, scrabbled at his eyes with his free hand, and hulked blindly toward us. My first kick hit him in the groin. Hard.

He groaned and dropped to his knees. Cassie got a two-handed grip on her can and slammed into his knife hand, knocking the weapon out of reach. He groped for the knife. I jumped over his head to escape. As he moved blindly toward his right, Cassie tried to do a run around on his left. He anticipated the move and caught her ankle.

I heard a satisfying crunch when I stomped his wrist. He cursed as I grasped Cassie's hand and pulled her with me down the hall to freedom. My heels slid a bit on the marble tiles, and she helped keep me on my feet as we ran.

"Any idea where we're going?" Cassie yelled.

My legs worked independently of my brain as the adrenalin coursed through me. "Not sure yet, but we'll know when we get there," I replied.

FIVE

First, I called Scotland Yard and was relieved to immediately get connected with Superintendent Whatley, who was in charge of Simon's case. He and his team were working backup along the New Year's Day parade route and had just returned to the Yard. After I said Simon was back, he covered the phone, but I could hear him yell to a colleague to coordinate with the Met to dispatch units to our office. With typical British courtesy he asked, "Are you safe?"

"We're on the run. We took out one man, but we're okay."

"Out?"

"He's in pain. Not dead."

"Leave this mobile on and we'll track you. Get out of the area as quickly as possible. They may be anticipating you'll head here to the Yard. I think it might be preferable if you stay on the move."

Like I needed him to tell me. I ended the call, and Cassie and I slid across the lobby's marbled floor as we veered toward the interior entrance of our landlord, the trust company. As our feet hit carpeting, we doubled our speed to exit out the street doors. I'm sure we caught people's attention. No one usually ran out of a financial institution at the speed we employed unless they wore a mask and carried a big sack of money. Thankfully, the security guard recognized us and hurried to open the glass door to the sidewalk.

The rain had stopped. Small mercy. Both of us left our coats in the office. But the sky continued to look grumpy. A double-decker bus idled at the corner, nearly loaded. Cassie and I jumped on at the last second.

"Ohmigod! You don't have your Oyster card," I cried, pulling mine from my purse, ready to bribe the driver to wait while she jumped off to get a ticket from the machine outside.

"Yes, I do." She pulled a slim wallet from the pocket of her blazer.

We made our way up top, to gain any kind of view of our assailants and the destruction they may have caused to the front of the office. The bus traveled in a westward direction, and as we passed the corner toward our side of the building, we couldn't see what must have been a gaping hole where the heavy brass-trimmed black door once stood. The be-bop of police sirens sounded off in the distance. A second later a silver Vauxhall Astra decorated with an orange Metropolitan Police stripe screamed past the bus, screeching as the car slid around the corner as first on the scene.

I turned back in my seat, face forward again, and relished the sudden feeling of safety and anonymity. Whether I truly was safe or not. Relaxing and swaying with the lumbering gait of the bus, I wanted to pretend there was no need to do what really should be done. In the end, however, my professionalism took over, and I pulled out my phone. I hid the screen for a moment by laying a hand atop the glass. Leaving it active, as the superintendent asked, was one thing. Using it to make the call I knew I should make but didn't want to was something else entirely.

"Aren't you going to call Jack?"

I shook my head. "He called as I was leaving the National Gallery. He's in Rome, and his phone is off at the moment." I explained the current Tony B dilemma. Her eyes got a little bigger with each sentence. In the distance, I could see the dome of St. Paul's Cathedral and wished I could go and sit in there for an hour or six.

"Do you think the murder attempt on Tony B and the break-in by Simon are connected?" she asked.

"Hard not to believe so." I tapped a fingernail on my phone, wishing desperately I could talk to Jack and find out if he'd learned anything yet. "We know Simon works for Moran. If it isn't a coincidence, it has to mean Moran has something in play."

"Extending your line of supposition, it means we can assume Tony B wasn't working for Moran if Moran put a contract out on him in prison," Cassie replied.

"Or he was working for Moran, and the attempt was made to silence Tony B from revealing information he was trying to use as leverage for his deal."

Cassie frowned. "Oh, yeah. Makes more sense."

"No, nothing about this thing makes sense. Another round of whack-a-moles popping up all the time."

I couldn't talk to Jack, but in the interest of the fair-play angle he'd obviously instigated with his call, I needed to give him a heads-up about the current situation here. The connection went immediately to voicemail, as expected, and I told him to call me. I could have left a detailed message of the recent events, but I knew Jack would stop listening three seconds in and phone back. This way I wouldn't have to repeat myself.

"You need to let Max know," Cassie said as I ended the call.

"Shh." Time to make the call I really didn't want to dial. My boss had two volumes, loud and silent. I knew exactly which one I would get.

"Laurel—"

"Give me a minute." I watched a little girl at the front of the upper deck holding onto the windowsill and ogling the sights and people at street level. Beside her, the patient but careful mother held the child at the shoulder, keeping her safely seated despite her jack-in-the-box impulses. I could see the energy radiating off the young girl and remembered my own first ride on a red double-decker bus, back when they were open to the elements. I wanted that innocence again. I didn't want to be the adult. But Cassie was playing parent this time and holding me down to do what was necessary.

As I swept a finger over my call list, I passed Max's name three times, but eventually the screen stopped at the right spot. Damned smartphone.

My boss's long-suffering executive assistant, Doris, answered on the first ring. "I'm sorry, Laurel, but he's presently in a meeting." No, she is a *secretary*, and will not respond to the term executive assistant. I don't understand the logic, but it was likely one of her self-preservation techniques to tame our bombastic boss. She said, "I'll slip a note in for him to call you."

"Please, just a message. Simon broke into the office, and I've called Scotland Yard—"

"Oh, no, no, no! I must get him right away. Hang on."

I put the cell face down in my lap. "Crap!"

"What's wrong?"

"Doris went to get Max. He was in a meeting. I thought I was going to avoid talking to him."

"Laurel! What's happening?"

Even with the device upside down and pressed against my leg, I heard him roar. I held the phone to my ear. "Max, we're on a bus. Calm down."

"Doris said Simon surfaced and broke into the office!"

"Yes." I tried to keep my volume lower, fruitlessly hoping he'd follow suit. "He brought some muscle with him. He only had one guard on the back door, which helped us get away."

"What did he want? Did you slow him down until the police arrived?"

"We don't know what he wanted. He entered by battering down the door. He came with some big helpers. We ran." In my mind's eye, I could see the lethal glint of the blade Cassie knocked out of our adversary's hand. "We called Scotland Yard as soon as we could, and we're riding around on a double-decker bus until we can figure out where to land next. We aren't going back to the office."

By the way, we're unhurt, Max. Thanks so much for asking.

The little girl in the front turned and looked at us with wide eyes. I wondered what she made of the screaming man's voice coming through my phone.

"I'll order up a guard. We can—"

"Stop, Max, and lower your voice. You're scaring a child at the front of the bus."

His volume went a smidgeon quieter when he asked, "Did you talk to Simon at all? What about the sword? Did you learn if he's working for Moran like we believe, or is he trying to work undercover?"

Was the man daft? Or had he been watching too many spy thrillers again? I knew he remained fixated on the sword, but I needed him to focus on the here and now.

"Simon is not working on behalf of Beacham, undercover or otherwise. Get that idea out of your head this minute. And no, I didn't offer him tea and conversation. Max, he made an entrance using shock and awe tactics. Not a smile and a handshake, for heaven's sake." I heard my boss start to bluster. I charged on, "Granted, I wish I had been able to talk to him, but Cassie and I instinctively ran when we heard the first blow hit the door. The kind of sound to either make you flee or scare you into standing stock still. We ran. I didn't know it was Simon waving a cricket bat until I saw him on my cell screen via the security feed, and going back in the office then didn't seem like a prizewinning idea."

"No need for sarcasm, Laurel."

"You're right, I apologize. I obviously didn't make it clear enough how he chose to forgo knocking and assaulted the door instead. Had we stayed in the office, who knows what would have happened to us?"

Silence told me Max was trying to determine the next best approach. I waited.

"Why do you think he chose to break down the door? Because the door was locked?"

He wondered why I resorted to sarcasm.

"No, he would have knocked if the locked door was a problem for him. He wanted to get something and wanted it fast. Obviously, he also wanted to catch anyone inside unaware until he was physically in the building." I rubbed my forehead, feeling a headache coming, and was surprised it had taken this long. Probably a hangover from all the adrenalin. "I don't know if he wants data, an art object, or...well, Cassie and me. Whatever it was, he posted a back door guard to keep whatever he wanted from leaving, and tried to use the back door exit after he recognized we had escaped. You can draw your own conclusions."

"All your high-tech security—"

"Quiet down, you're getting loud again."

"What about the cameras?" he said, modulating his tone slightly.

"I watched Simon break the camera in my office with a cricket bat. I doubt we'll get much information about their search on video. The silent alarm notified the Met police. We saw a car pull up as we left the area and heard several more police cars seconds later. When I talk to Superintendent Whatley I presume he'll tell me if they collared any of the gang."

"Which means we wait."

"You wait." I didn't have time to sit quietly until others contacted me. "Simon worked over a decade in our office. He knew precisely how long it takes for police to respond to an alarm call from our system. My assumption is whether he left with anything or not, he was gone before the police got there. We'll find a place to hide, and Cassie will call and give you the particulars." My assistant was an unexpected pro at calming the Max-monster. I would have let her handle this mandatory call except it really was my responsibility. "It's too late for a guard. If there was something in the office, Simon has it. If there wasn't and he's after me to try to find it...hiding is a better idea. When we have a plan together, we'll pass the details along to you through Doris. I'll check back with Whatley, get his take on the situation, and have him coordinate with you as well." I sent up a mental apology to the superintendent.

"Very well." Max was calmer, but not much quieter. "I'll be expecting a call this evening as plans and details are better known."

"A call or an email. I can't promise the superintendent has the time or budget to phone you directly. Simon's reappearance may make this move very quickly."

"Oh, yes, right. Exactly right. Let me know how I can help."

While I had an opportunity..."I could use some funds.

Whatever we do, we're going to require additional cash outlays."

"Laurel—"

"You asked. What did you expect—I would pay for repairs and a temporary office out of my own bank account?" Like it could happen with my redlined credit. Max's control issues and my proclivity toward spending money were the reasons I didn't have a corporate credit card.

Our bus continued lumbering in a westward direction. I heard him release a long sigh. "Okay. I'll issue funds to a corporate account and have a credit card overnighted to you."

"Thank you." I tried to put as much humility in my voice as I dared. This was a huge move for him. "Please have it sent to the U.S. Embassy and I'll pick it up there. I'm not sure where I'll be staying tonight."

"I understand," he said. Then he couldn't help himself and added, "You know, it's your job as management to be fiscally responsible. The London office's budget must be safeguarded."

"You do recall the reason I have to make repairs is the last office head you appointed tore up the place today. This following the fact he absconded with the historic item you asked me to bring back in September. You also remember I not only missed out on my vacation due to that job, but I was injured—shot at, choked, and almost shot again when I finally found Simon." Cassie sent me a warning look. After one long breath, I continued, calmer and quieter, "I'm being displaced personally and professionally due to the actions of the same former office head. Did you have this identical conversation with him, Max, when he was in charge of the London branch? Perhaps he forgot your mentoring pep talk."

"Laurel, I mean—"

"I think we need to stop talking so you can get back to your meeting. Maybe you could spend a few moments remembering which *current* employees you should be backing up. Afterward you might want to carefully consider what you want to say to me once you've fully comprehended the kind of day I've had."

"Oh, the meeting, yes—" the cowardly bastard said.

"Talk to you later. Don't forget to send the credit card with a decent balance."

I heard him hollering for Doris as I ended the call. I turned and saw Cassie wore her worried face again. "What?" I asked.

"You were kind of hard on him."

My jaw dropped. I couldn't help it. The bus slowed to make a stop. I rose from my seat and said, "I think we need to walk awhile."

When we were safely on the sidewalk, Cassie suddenly shrieked. "Laurel! The package!"

"What?"

People stared at us. I pulled her along to a small park area down the block.

"What if it was from Simon?" she asked, after we were a reasonable distance from anyone.

I shook my head. "There's no point, and Simon is always logical. If he sent the package to see if I was in the office, he would have known I wasn't when you sent the deliveryman away. If he did it to see if the office was open, he wouldn't have brought the battering ram and all the assembled muscle along when he came to call unless he had a man stationed outside to hear me throw the deadbolt."

"I gave the deliveryman your address. Told him the name of the hotel where you're staying."

"If he wanted to know how to find me off-site, he would have planted a bug or found a way to hack into my phone or Max's. He could not have known you'd send the delivery guy to my hotel. However—"

"Better safe than sorry," Cassie finished for me.

"Yeah." I dialed the number for the concierge in my boutique hotel. Within a few minutes, I had him briefed on my security problems—the sanitized PR version—and he promised to have my things packed and sent to a similar hotel with which they shared a reciprocal relationship. It was farther from the Beacham Ltd. location, but no matter. I didn't intend to work in the office for a while. If ever again.

"One more thing," I added before ending the call. "There should have been a package delivery for me today at the front desk." I looked at Cassie. "Maybe a few hours ago." She nodded.

I heard the clicking of a keyboard, and the concierge spoke again. "A suite of rooms is reserved for you at the hotel on Manchester. I will text the address and confirmation number to your mobile. One moment while I check for the package." More clicking. "Ah, yes. Something came addressed to you this afternoon. I'll make sure it is put with any mail and sent with your property."

"No. I want the package left at your hotel." I didn't have the time or inclination to apprise him of my concerns about the package. Despite my assurances to Cassie it hadn't likely been used by Simon for clandestine purposes, we didn't have the luxury of taking chances. "I'll have the package picked up at the front desk tonight or tomorrow. I'll call and give the front desk the name of the party doing the retrieval. They can check ID."

"Very good, Miss Beacham. As you prefer." I knew he was probably curious, but like a consummate hotel professional, he let it go.

"It is. You've been a tremendous help. Thank you."

When we disconnected, Cassie pounced. "We need to find out what's in the package. It might be important."

"It might be a bomb."

Her eyes grew huge, and I laughed. "Seriously, Cassie, don't worry. I'm kidding. It's probably some piece of art someone wants my opinion on, or something needing a restoration and the owner is looking for a recommendation."

"You never know—"

"If it makes you feel any better, I'll contact Superintendent Whatley later, give him the details and see if he'll retrieve it."

I contemplated the busy city around us. I adored London. Knew a lot of its secrets. Loved to watch its people move around on the crowded streets. However, at that moment I wished I knew if we were being watched. Suddenly feeling vulnerable, I whispered, "Regardless of what we think, I can't be sure the package doesn't contain some kind of tracking device. Letting it stay in the hotel I'm leaving—even for a night—is a good precautionary measure until it can be checked."

Another deep breath and I was ready to move again. "So much for melodrama." I looked around to get my bearings. "I haven't had anything since breakfast but a flute of champagne," I made a circle with my index finger and thumb, "and a couple of rounds of toast with something creamy on top."

Cassie grinned and looked at her watch. "No wonder you're cranky."

"Yep, time flies when you're running for your life."

"You don't have to be at the television thing for a while—"

"I'm not going." I used a finger to swipe my screen and locate Megan's number. "Granted, the television station has security. However, until we know who is in Simon's pocket we have to assume he could have contacts at the BBC."

Megan answered and I explained I had to bail on the interview. When she asked about a reschedule, I hedged and said I'd have to get back to her. I needed to talk to the Scotland Yard superintendent before I moved forward on the interview, but I didn't want Megan to know all my reasons. "I'll try to call you in the coming days and let you know if my schedule changes. Feel free to replace me with someone else from the museum."

Her flat tone told me she wasn't satisfied, but she thanked me and I ended the call.

Cassie had apparently been in a holding pattern for the previous few minutes and immediately reminded me, "We have less than an hour and a half before your deadline at Nelly's."

"Damn. The day's almost gone."

I looked at my watch, then turned to look down the cross streets and between buildings. The dark tips of wintering trees in Hyde Park appeared close by. I loved the park and the very English names and types of trees found there, like the sweet chestnut and horse chestnut, the Queen Elizabeth oak, and something like two hundred and fifty other varieties carefully architected into the landscape. Even better, this sighting meant we weren't far from Harrods. They were on shorter hours for the holiday but should be open for business. And for eating. As good a spot as any to find food and a place to hide in a crowd. "Follow me. I hear a food hall calling my name."

SIX

To put it simply, it's true the Harrods Food Hall is expensive and expansive. Beyond a place to hide, Cassie and I needed a way to soothe our souls and restore a little sugar in our systems to replace what we'd burned during our flight. "Good food in the current situation is a necessity. Not simply because I'm starving," I said. "Before you chew me out for strong-arming Max, remember we've both had massive shocks today."

"No, I've decided you were right." Cassie shook her head, her pink spiky cut looking normal again after a side trip to the amazing store's restroom—a surprisingly understated powder room for such a unique retailer. "Max should have made security a priority weeks ago. He didn't, which was bad enough, but he also didn't acknowledge right away the threat we'd experienced when he got on the call. He was too busy trying to minimize losses and find a better outcome for his purposes. He's clueless, and you called him on it."

Yikes. I hoped I hadn't lost the Max Whisperer to whatever personality Cassie currently channeled. I considered rethinking which of us would communicate updates to our boss.

At the moment, however, almost indescribably beautiful food, all freshly prepared and as tasty to the eye as the palate, beckoned us from nearly endless display cases positioned under fabulous custom ceilings and specialty lighting. The large rectangular rooms with their elegant grid pattern allowed us to easily zero in on our favorites. Even more enticing than magazine food porn and available right in front of us. We contemplated one of the restaurants, but decided to build our own smorgasbord instead. The noodle bar came first and neither of us hesitated.

"Carbs are good food for shock," Cassie said.

"Save room for truffles from the candy room. Also good for shock," I replied.

We cruised the glass cases like connoisseurs. The delicacies were presented in exactly that kind of spectacular manner. Pricey, sure, but it was "food art" after all. And Cassie and I recognized the price of admission. We pointed to salmon pinwheels, followed by a small crate of raspberries, washed and ready for devouring. An avocado salad for me, and a chicken salad for my friend, along with several kinds of cheese to share. We both ordered Harrods Moroccan Mint tea. Sure our meal was eclectic, but it was the best way to forget about an awful afternoon.

Everything was savory and fabulous on the tongue. I couldn't wait to add the receipt to my expense report. Max might blow another fuse.

A couple of empty chairs along a wall beckoned us, and we pulled them closer together. Anything we said would be lost in the steady hum of conversations and exclamations around us. Nothing like fabulous food to keep attention off the quiet folks who prefer a little privacy within the public. I people-watched and bit into my first pinwheel, marveling at the different tastes bursting into my mouth with the seasoned salmon. The food was tempting, but it didn't stop me from keeping an eye out for faces in the crowd who seemed to have more than cuisine on their minds.

Much as I wanted to be lost in the food, I couldn't stop thinking about what had happened—and most importantly, why.

"He posted a rear guard," I mused, sipping my tea and letting the lovely mint taste settle over my tongue. "If he was only coming to do a smash and grab for something he'd left behind and needed, why leave the knife-wielding bully guarding the back hall? Did he even know if we were in the place? From where we sat in my office, a recon through the windows in the reception area wouldn't have shown us at all."

"They could have seen you briefly in the window."

"Except they came equipped with the battering ram, and the man in the hall would already be stationed at his post." I knew she meant well, reminding me to be careful, but I had to show her there wasn't a bogeyman around every corner. Attacks required pre-planning. "Besides, you had your laptop. If they looked in the windows there weren't even signs on your desk of someone in the office and working. This is a holiday, after all."

"Why the dramatics of the battering ram and phalanx of thugs?" Cassie added. "Though I guess phalanx might be over the top when talking about three or four guys."

I smiled at her words. "Your point meshes with my own thoughts. He had guys with him we didn't know and wouldn't have recognized. I totally get the idea of trying to move in quickly to snatch what he needed before we had a chance to stop him or call the police. Why not send his crew to knock on the door and muscle in if we said no entry?"

"He knew the office had a silent alarm too."

Something else to ponder. During the time of the shakeup, when Simon disappeared and before I'd learned he'd gone over to Moran's side, I went to his office—now my office—and found an auburn-haired Amazon inside pretending to be Simon's secretary while she actually ransacked the place. I found out later she hadn't breached security, but apparently entered with the code or a way to bypass it. At the time I'd thought she worked for the opposition. Learning Simon was the opposition made me wonder if she worked for him as well. Aloud, I said, "For some reason, he believed he needed to be on the scene today. A significant risk when everyone is looking for him. Simon was kind of a control freak, but..."

"Maybe he didn't trust his men to bring back what he wanted?" Cassie set down her fork and wiped her mouth with a Harrods napkin.

"Could be." This ran along my idea of his potentially sending in the Amazon before. I added, "He most definitely became a control freak when someone wasn't around to remind him to loosen up. I can't imagine the past few months of running and hiding has done anything to relax him."

"What could he need enough to go to such desperate lengths?"

"The Amazon left the place in a state of utter destruction. If it was in the office when he worked there, you would have found it in the cleanup stage," I said. After Simon's escape, my agenda and flight plan didn't allow room to schedule time to clear up the mess left behind by the redhead's search, or put the office back into business. There was also the matter of a huge saltwater aquarium that had flooded everything in its immediate area and was kind of my fault. Well, yes, all my fault.

Upon my return to London from France, Cassie and I met for dinner and I learned her internship at the Victoria and Albert Museum would not be renewed. She was at loose ends and didn't want to go home to the States, and I desperately needed someone I could trust. We struck a quick agreement, and she accepted the position of my assistant to keep the office operating and get everything back up and running. Her background in restoration served her well in the role. Except her tendency toward keeping historic places in as much of a status quo state as possible made her resistant to changes in interior design, no matter how much I preferred to step away from Simon's décor. Besides, she was a frugal wiz at all things restoration-oriented—office or otherwise—leaving Max to agree with whatever she suggested.

Even more important, her art history and practical application degrees aided her in the analysis and tracking of art forgeries. Teaming her with Nico generated me more leads on the possible heist threat which continued to grow exponentially with each new revelation. It might even be worth sending Nico to New York to take a field trip to the publisher's office to ask about the book and photos Cassie uncovered.

Cassie broke my train of thought. "Maybe Simon was trying to kidnap you. That's why he posted the rear guard."

I dragged myself back to the present and shook my head. "It doesn't make sense. He could have posted a kidnapper outside to grab me before I came in one morning. I watched on my phone as he broke the camera with a cricket bat. He was already identifiable when I checked my phone app. Breaking the camera couldn't have been to avoid evidence of his being there. Whapping the camera had to be a measure to keep anyone from seeing what he was taking. Or where it was hidden."

"Makes sense. Except someone almost immediately came after you as we ran."

"No. Someone tried to come through the secret door. We don't know they even saw who slipped out the back way, nor do we know if they saw one person or two. The guard with the broken knife hand can tell them now, but he wouldn't have known until we opened the door to the hall." The more I considered the facts, the clearer it all became to me. "They couldn't have known I was even in the office unless they were watching when I entered, but already prepared to go in by force. Leaving this line of thought to bring us back to the question of why they didn't kidnap me on the street and shove me into a vehicle. No, it had to be something in the office. Whatever it was, it had to be something they could realize wasn't there seconds after Simon broke the camera, and *that's* why they came after whomever ran out the back door. To see if we carried it with us."

"Yeah, okay, it makes sense. But what could have equaled the risk of coming himself? There are a lot of people who want to talk to Simon."

Or do worse to him. Well, maybe I'm the only one who wanted to physically hurt him at the moment, but several branches of law enforcement from multiple countries were looking for Mr. Babbage, and it wasn't to invite him to dinner.

Did they immediately discover what they came for was gone, and followed us to get whatever it was from us? Or did Simon grab what he wanted right after he broke the camera, then sent his goons to grab us "just in case?" Which was why his posting a rear guard bothered me. Too many ways planned to catch us if he simply wanted a hidden item.

"Did you notice anything during the reconstruction efforts to make you wonder why it was in the office? Even something left in pieces? Granted, Simon has to believe whatever he wants remains accessible. It's the only explanation for him to take a chance coming in. I just can't figure why he would have waited this long to try to grab anything important."

Cassie chewed her lip and raised her right hand to rub her neck. In anyone else, I would have assumed both actions tipped the scales toward nervousness or lying, but I'd known Cassie too long and this didn't fit. I waited to see what she would say.

She turned to look me straight in the eye when she spoke. "Nothing. I simply cannot think of anything."

I'd been holding my breath. This job was getting to me, and not in a good way. Relief returned when she continued and I recognized I had been reading the body language correctly—I simply hadn't fathomed the nuances.

"I feel so guilty," she said. "Obviously I missed something. What you say dovetails perfectly with the facts. His actions run counter to logic unless there was something hidden in the office he needed to retrieve. What? And why? I'm sorry. I should have found it—whatever it is. I'll keep thinking."

I patted her arm. "Don't beat yourself up. It could have been a file completely destroyed and tossed out with all the rubbish the Amazon made of the office when she blew through it. She made such an ungodly mess. Even now, I can't decide if she was looking for data or attempting to destroy it."

"We went through papers for weeks trying to salvage whatever we could from the files. I saved everything for you to look through. Every effort was made. Simon had already hit the cloud server and erased those files, leaving us without the option there either. I really think it has to be something besides a file."

"All good points," I said. What could he have been looking for? This was going to bug me until I knew, but I didn't want Cassie obsessing over it. "Give it a rest. We already have enough to work on with this case."

"I'll keep thinking. You never know what might suddenly appear differently when I let my mind wander a little."

I hid a smile behind my napkin. There was no point in arguing with her. She could be as immoveable as a brick wall when she felt it necessary. We'd been college roommates and she was the one person in my life who never changed.

College had been a proving ground for me. My father lost the family fortune by my first semester at Cornell. By the end of my second semester he had skied off the side of his favorite Alp, leaving behind gold diggers' broken hearts and black-hearted mob bosses trying to find ways to lessen their losses. And how was I? Well, when I wasn't dealing with shadowy men who held markers they were ready to strong-arm to get paid on, and who didn't particularly like it when I said I was desperately looking for any leftover signs of the family fortune myself, my emotions vacillated the short distance between grief and anger.

Naturally, the tracking needle stayed much, much longer on the anger end of the scale than it did for grief. Add in a few self-destructive tendencies, and by the time I started my sophomore year I was on the verge of getting kicked out.

Until Cassie wandered lost into my coed dorm hall, carting a duffle bag half her weight and a laptop with a browser bookmarked to every art history and restoration site known to man. I batted away the two male letches who homed in on her and hurried her into my dorm room. She'd been my conscience ever since.

Now she obsessed about something she probably couldn't have accomplished anyway, while I needed her to stay on the same task she'd come back to London to solve.

"Let me be the one who mulls over how Simon thinks. You only met him once, when I was in London and we all went to dinner to celebrate your internship at the V and A. A night when he was on his best behavior. You have no real clue to his personality quirks. I've worked with him more than most, and spent almost a year thinking we were in a committed transatlantic relationship. Simon had fooled all of us, but I have to believe I have a little more insight—and less charity—when considering his possible actions. If there's something in the office, I'll figure it out, like I found the thumb drive he hid in his aquarium." I finished off the last of my tea. I'd learned the best way with Simon was to act on instinct—not to overthink. Given time, something would trigger the answer for me. If there was one. I put a hand on her arm. "You need to stay on the forgeries. See if some of the trails you've already found lead anywhere."

One thing I learned in the eight months we were together was the private Simon could be much different from the public one. He'd always been keen on shaking things up in unconventional ways, making the break-in less surprising.

My watch said a quarter past three. Our impromptu lunch and brainstorming session had gone quickly. Time to move on. I slung my purse on my shoulder and said, "I don't know about you, but I have enough room for a red velvet cupcake if we share it. Are you game?"

"Absolutely."

Less than five minutes later we'd finished off one of the luscious mini-cakes, made from a recipe unlike any I'd tasted back home. Our final impulse buy meant purchasing Charbonnel et Walker truffles on our way out. We were almost giggly by the time we bade the doorman good day.

"I feel like a kid playing hooky," Cassie said. "We haven't had this much fun in ages."

"Hard to call it hooky when we've been working on our day off, but I get your point." I finished my truffle and had chocolate on two fingers. Grandmamma would have glared at me if she'd been alive, but I licked them. Harrods chocolate was worth the social faux pas. "We need to do stuff like this more often. Not just when we're on the run and mad at Max. We used to have fun. Remember?"

The days had been crazy since Cassie joined Beacham Ltd., and we'd jumped from one frustrating conundrum to another. Though we'd made some headway, especially when she was able to tag-team the research with Nico, we hadn't actually closed any part of the case starting from the ill-fated trip to Italy to handle the "easy pickup" of the antique snuffbox. Where I met Jack. Which was why we continued piecing together clues.

My phone rang. "It's the superintendent." I pointed to the window wall on that side of the building. "Let's move over there." We walked toward a place along Harrods, out of the way of the pedestrians, and I answered the call. "Hello, Superintendent Whatley. Do you have any news?"

"No one was there when the first car arrived," he said. "We did, however, find something puzzling. The crime tech discovered several sets of fingerprints, including a good set on an abandoned cricket bat."

"Simon left the cricket bat?"

"There was one positioned squarely in the middle of the glass desk."

My desk. Simon had to know it was my desk too. What kind of message was he leaving me? "Definitely puzzling. Hearing you say it makes me realize the guard who tried to stop us in our escape wasn't wearing gloves either. He had a knife, but no gloves."

I closed my eyes and tried to remember seeing the thugs who entered my office behind Simon. "The security video file would confirm this for sure, but I think the other guys who came in with Simon were wearing dark gloves."

"Unfortunately, it appears they left with the hard drive to your security cameras. Your impressions are important, as the gloves may mean their fingerprints are documented in the Scotland Yard or Interpol systems. We didn't have a record of Babbage's prints, and those of the man in the public hallway would be difficult to isolate."

I had the speaker positioned to allow Cassie to hear, and she asked, "Why would Simon leave the cricket bat with his fingerprints if he knew you didn't have them before?"

"He probably didn't think about Laurel watching the video feed when you both ran away. He didn't realize she could give evidence to prove he was the one holding the bat."

Good for me. I did an irresponsible thing by letting my curiosity make me stop to watch, but doing so gave us a good bit of definitive evidence Scotland Yard needed. Oh, wait a minute— "Is his apartment still sealed? You could verify the fingerprints there."

"When we arrived at his address in late September the place was empty," Whatley said. "The entire flat had been wiped down completely, and we couldn't find any fingerprints or DNA trace evidence. My team couldn't even find partial prints on normally forgotten places."

"What kind of places do people forget about?" I asked.

"Sorry, confidential information." We heard papers shuffled, then he said, "I'd like to meet with the two of you. I have some snaps I'd like to bring out to see if anyone looks familiar."

"The package," Cassie reminded.

I nodded. "Superintendent, we might have something else you need to follow up on first." I briefed him on the mysterious delivery. "I was hoping you could get the package picked up at the hotel, to make sure it wasn't something with a tracker or worse."

"Absolutely. I'll go by and pick it up myself and take one of the portable X-ray machines. Are you on the way to your new hotel?"

"We have one stop to make before heading to the hotel on Manchester. I'll forward the text of the address and my room number. Or we'll be happy to come into Scotland Yard."

"No, I don't really want to bring you in here and run the risk of someone keeping eyes on you both as you leave."

Cassie gasped. I jumped in, saying, "Okay, we're a ten-minute walk from the place where we need to pick up a tapestry. We'll catch a cab to the hotel."

"I believe it might be better if you take a cab to both places," Whatley said. "A little less opportunity for someone to spot you along the way. On second thought, why don't I meet you at your appointment and take you to the new hotel myself?"

"Good point." I gave him Nelly's address. "We have to pick up a tapestry she's been working on. We'll stand in her building's lobby and watch for you to drive up."

"Very good. I'll leave here momentarily, fetch your package, and meet you at the place of your appointment."

"I'll call the concierge at the hotel and make sure you have no difficulty there," I promised.

"Capital," he said. "Be sure to tell them to check for ID. I'll have mine ready, but I don't want anyone to arrive ahead of me and get the package first."

Neither did I.

SEVEN

Cassie glanced at her watch. "We need to get moving if we're going to catch a cab," she said.

She was right. I hadn't planned to walk to Nelly's for purely the exercise. With traffic thickening by the minute, two feet could easily beat four wheels.

The superintendent's words of warning resonated as I noticed all the people passing back and forth on the busy sidewalk in front of Harrods. Before the phone call it seemed like a good idea to hide in a crowd, but second thoughts ran through my head. I felt even more exposed when someone called my name. A good-looking guy resembling a young George Clooney headed our way. His smile widened. "It is you. You are Laurel, right?"

Dylan had some kind of financial position in the City, and the last time I saw him—which was also when I met him—he left me in Jack's care and protection, despite my reservations and attempts at protest. To Dylan's credit, I didn't protest too adamantly at the time because I was trying to figure out who or what Jack was, and we were in public. A Beacham is taught at an early age not to make a public spectacle of oneself if it can in any way be avoided. This was following my escape from two of Moran's henchmen by stomping on the foot of Dylan's friend, Jeremy, to create a diversion while we exited the Tube, making for one "mini-scene" already on my record for that day. Plus, by then I was kind of getting used to Jack popping up unexpectedly.

"Yes, Dylan, Laurel Beacham." I walked forward, extending a

hand. We needed to get moving, but it seemed prudent to at least be friendly. His lovely brown eyes crinkled at the corners with his grin. Something about them reminded me of someone else, but I couldn't remember who. "Good to see you. Does Jeremy still have a contract out on me?" We both laughed, but Cassie didn't. I took a moment to smile at her and make a quick introduction. I asked him, "What are you doing here?"

"Using the bank holiday to do a little shopping." He leaned close and whispered, "The only way they let me loose on the city." We moved out of sidewalk traffic and he continued, "Need to get away from family, and I hoped to hide within the tourist crowds in Harrods. Less chance of running into someone who knows me."

I looked at his empty hands. "You didn't find anything you liked?"

He shrugged and gave a chuckle. "Found a million things, but my wallet pled poverty. Some of it I'll buy online later at a price loads cheaper. Others, like the gorgeous sports car over there..." He pointed to a gold Bugatti parked at the curb. "Gives me something to work toward for the future. What do you think? A million-pound price tag?"

Actually, I knew the MSRP had been exactly two million euros. The Saudi prince who owned the beauty invited me for a joy ride early in the summer. We were in Monte Carlo at the time, and the sweet baby handled those seaside curves like a supercharged mountain goat. The prince apparently liked it enough to have the car transported afterward, given it sat twenty feet away. Or maybe he had one garaged in every country. "I'd heard Knightsbridge has a bit of a problem with rich residents and their toys. Good to know there's a basis to the rumors."

"I'd really love to drive that baby."

"I did. It's a high-octane dream."

His eyes widened. A second later, he roared in laughter. "You're joking!"

"I never kid about driving expensive cars I'll never be able to own."

Dylan's face held a dazed look. He turned to Cassie as if for confirmation. She smiled and nodded.

"I am impressed," he said. "Look, can I buy you both a drink?"

"Actually, we'd love to, but we need to go," Cassie said. "We have an appointment."

"She's right. But it was nice seeing you."

"How about a rain check?" He pulled a couple of business cards from a case. "I'll be leaving for Milan soon to meet with boring bankers there. I'd love a chance to catch up sometime." He handed a card to me. "Get to know you both better," he said as he slipped the other into Cassie's hand.

This was awkward. The logical response would be to give him one of our cards. Except our office was in ruins, and I was having second and third thoughts of ever going back there. "Our office—"

"We're doing some redecorating," Cassie cut in, removing one of the embossed Beacham Ltd. cards from her wallet. "You won't be able to find us at this address at the moment, but the business line is forwarded to my cell when we're away. I always know Laurel's schedule."

God, she's brilliant.

"We'll see each other again soon," he said, giving us a smile as he walked off. We moved to the curb to try flagging down a cab.

Cassie turned to watch Dylan's departing figure. "He seemed like a nice guy."

"He is," I replied.

With public transportation reduced for the holiday, vehicle traffic was horrible. A dozen or more occupied taxis zoomed by in the first few minutes. Finally, a black cab stopped on my signal. The driver reached out of his window to twist the handle and open the back door for us, and we scrambled inside. Cassie gave the driver the address as I slammed the door. Traffic was stop and go, but eventually we got to Nelly's building. We had five minutes to spare.

My cell buzzed with a text as we hit the sidewalk. The superintendent reported his car was a few minutes away and said the package was "safe."

"What do you think it is?" Cassie asked.

"We'll find out soon. Probably some art item like we'd talked about."

The outer door of the building was ajar. I frowned. The door had always been closed before, and Nelly released the lock electronically. I motioned for Cassie to follow me, and we moved up the stairs. I rapped on Nelly's dark green door. Cassie and I waited. And waited.

"Think she's already left?"

"No. She said she was leaving a bit before five, but it's not yet straight up four o'clock."

I knocked harder. Again, no answer.

"You're sure she's expecting you back here? She wasn't going to courier it to the office?"

"Of course I'm sure. She suggested using a messenger, but I told her one of us would be back to pick up the parcel."

I was about to knock again when the sound of something moving came faintly through the door. I stepped closer and put my ear to the wood.

Then we heard the crash.

The doorknob turned in my hand. Inside, the room was trashed. I pushed Cassie back into the hall. "Go to the street to meet the superintendent. Call and tell him to hurry," I said, turning her toward the stairs and urging her on. "Tell him to bring medical help too."

She looked at me, chewing her lower lip.

"Go on!" I shoved my own cell into her hand and waved my hands urgently. "I'll stay here and wait."

She was convinced and flew down the stairs, the phone at her ear. I waited until she got past the outer door and slipped into the loft flat.

A straight chair with a broken back barred my way, and I stepped over it, careful not to turn an ankle from the rest of the debris scattered throughout the space. The other end of the open room was equally disastrous, but deserted. It was Nelly's workspace. The heavy table she used was shoved aside, and two floor lamps lay on the carpet, the bulb burning in one and the other in pieces. The chest holding her thread and supplies was ransacked, the specialty trays from inside tossed around the room and the work materials unspooled and unrolled. A piece of linen had a man's boot print nearly covering the square of fabric. He had to be huge.

I spotted a pair of scissors near the back of an overturned chair. I scooped up the sharp shears and held the handles tightly in my fist.

A short staircase alongside the far wall led up to a sleeping alcove. On the back wall was a door leading to her kitchen. A glittery blue high heel held the door open a few inches.

With my first thought for Nelly's safety, I automatically rushed to open the kitchen door—and stopped. Instinctively, I knew I had to take stock before going forward. I looked through the gap held open by what I presumed was my friend's shoe, though there was no foot in the heel. I couldn't see anything from the angle but one wall and counter. The door resisted as I tried to push it farther into the kitchen. I was afraid to put my shoulder into it and possibly hurt Nelly or mess up evidence. I heard a moan, and the soft cry decided things for me.

It took all my strength, but I was able to move the door enough to get my head through the opening. Nelly was curled up by one of the cabinets, her dark hair haloing her head. She'd changed to a dressier outfit and wore the mate to the blue shoe. She whimpered as I tried to take in the scene. I craned my neck to see behind the door. Along the door and wall lay one of the largest men I'd ever seen. His head was next to Nelly's bare foot, half his skull caved in and bloody. He didn't appear to be breathing. His massive black-shirted chest was motionless. A large-blade knife was just out of reach. On the floor beside Nelly's right hand sat a large meat mallet.

What appeared to be glass from a broken vase littered the floor. Presumably, the cause for the smashing sound I'd heard when we were at the flat's door.

"Nelly?" I squeezed through the gap and hurried to kneel beside her. There was blood at her neck; he'd started slitting her throat. Her pulse was weak, but gave me hope. I yanked a towel hanging on the wall and pressed it against the wound.

The wailing be-bop of a siren sounded in the distance. I heard the clatter below of the entrance door getting flung open and banging against the wall. Boots pounded up the stairs. I heard more sirens coming closer.

"In here," I shouted.

Whatley blasted in first. An emergency tech with a medical tool case followed close behind.

"She's alive," I cried, looking through the opening. "But her assailant isn't. He's blocking this door. Do you want me to move him?"

Two more men entered the flat and the superintendent motioned them to come and help. They slowly pushed the door until they displaced the dead man's body enough to get through.

Superintendent Whatley roughly pulled me back into the workroom area of the loft. His face was a mottled red. "You should have stayed downstairs with your friend."

"In case I could help Nel—"

He pointed to a step stool near the closet. "Sit there."

"I tried not to contaminate the scene, but I had to put pressure on the wound. Nelly was bleed—"

A voice called out from the kitchen, "She's alive, but the bloke is dead. Looks like she brained him good with the mallet at his temple. Lucky strike."

Whatley grasped my arm and we moved to make room for the empty gurney bumping into the room.

"I understand," Whatley said. "You were only trying to help. I'll talk to you in a moment."

"Would you prefer I go downstairs?"

He shot me a harried look. A lock of his blond-grey hair flopped onto his forehead. "Actually, with the day you've been having, I think I'd like to keep you in sight." He motioned for a uniformed officer. "Go downstairs and stay with Miss Beacham's assistant. I'd like to keep them separate until I have a chance to interview everyone. Her assistant is the blonde with the..." He mimicked making points of his hair.

"Got it." The uniform turned on his heel and left. Whatley entered the kitchen, and I made myself semi-comfortable on the hard plastic stool.

A couple of crime scene techs came in with tool chests of supplies. One poked his head into the kitchen and told Whatley they were going to work. They each gave me nods and brief smiles before starting on the other side of the space. I looked around at the upended sofa and chairs. The worktable I'd already noticed. Nelly had a small roll-top desk in one corner. One of the techs began working there.

"I can't imagine her opening the door for anyone she didn't know or didn't have an appointment with," I called out to the techs. "She needed to leave before five and would have been in a hurry to get ready. She was squeezing me in for a pickup. Her calendar probably has a clue where she was headed tonight, and maybe—"

Oh, good lord, I was dithering. I apologized, "I'm sorry. I'll let you get back to work."

"Very good, miss," the tech at the desk replied. "All good information for us to know."

He was being nice about it, but I redoubled my efforts to keep quiet.

A large rectangular dress-sized box, wrapped in packing paper, lay crushed under the arm of an overturned chair. I had the feeling my tapestry was inside.

Ready to go as soon as I got there. My hands itched to move the chair and open the box to make sure my treasure was safe, but I knew I wouldn't win any points with Whatley or the two techs if I did.

Minutes later, the door was pushed open and held wide by one of the EMTs. I jumped to my feet. Nelly was strapped to the gurney. She was so pale. The emergency crew had applied a thick gauze pad to her neck, but in my mind's eye I could see the gash and imagined she was likely bleeding into the white bandage. They moved quickly through the room. I heard some banging as they carried the gurney down the narrow stairs.

Whatley came through the kitchen door next and walked over to me. "They're not sure she'll make it, but you adding pressure right away helped. I don't want to recommend you start running into violent situations, but your instincts may have saved her life."

"Thank you." The frown lines in his forehead told me I was dangerously close to a lecture. I changed the subject. "You have some questions for me?"

"Yes, you said you came by earlier. Why did you come back?"

I explained Nelly's perfectionist tendencies, and how I needed to come back in time for her to leave for her appointment. I added my impressions about her nervousness, and my fears her assailant was the person she was supposed to meet later in the evening. "If so, you might find a calendar with the name in her desk. She keeps a desk calendar book. Blue leather cover. I've seen her use it when I've been here."

"How long have you known her?"

"About four years. We're not close friends, but we have friends in common. I learned about her through a colleague, though I don't remember at the moment who originally referred her. She's excellent at her craft."

He walked closer to the working techs and told the one at the desk to look for the calendar, then he returned to my spot. "Do you know where she received her training? To help us learn how she gets her clients."

"No, I haven't a clue. Cassie might know. A lot of their individual expertise had influences in common, and they may have talked when Cassie first brought the tapestry by."

"You're saying the victim only worked with your assistant before today?"

"No, I phoned initially to hire Nelly. I always do. I've used her several times in the past. We talked about the tapestry, what work needed to be done. I was busy at the time Nelly said to bring it by. I asked Cassie to instead."

"And that was..."

"Four weeks ago."

Whatley scratched his ear. "This was a big job, I take it?"

"Not particularly. A medium-sized work, but Nelly is meticulous, which is why I hire her. These are irreplaceable items that have been damaged. With the right expert touch, the repairs are practically impossible to spot. A perfect repair is what we're always hoping for." I motioned toward the chair and the box. "I believe the smashed box is the package I came to pick up tonight. I would really appreciate being able to leave with it. I don't want to disappoint the owners by telling them the priceless tapestry they plan to lend for an upcoming exhibit is in an evidence lockup."

He got one of the techs' attention. "When you get the chance to work the area around the chair there, see if you can get things to the point where we can release the box to Miss Beacham."

The tech nodded, aimed the camera and took a few pictures of the box *in situ*. At the same time, Whatley motioned for me to follow him to the kitchen.

"I realize this is pretty grisly, but I wondered if you had a good look at the man. In case you saw him hanging around when you were here earlier." He looked embarrassed to be asking.

"I didn't really take a good look at his face after I saw he wasn't breathing. I can look now."

"We'll be taking him out in a few minutes," Whatley said.

"I can handle it," I assured him as we stepped through the doorway. A collapsed gurney waited alongside the body which had been moved to free up the entrance. The lone tech working on collecting the kitchen evidence rose from his crouched position and pressed against the counter to give us space to get in closer. I saw the coagulated blood all over the side of his head. The man's face was turned away. When I noticed the bandaged wrist, I felt my knees weaken.

Whatley caught me before I fell.

"Here, we can show you a photo later. Let's get you back—"

"No." My voice didn't sound as strong as I wanted it to. I tried again. "No. I want to see his face. It's important."

Whatley supported me as we neared the body. The tech leaned down to turn the face up, to get me a better look. It was who I'd feared.

I looked around. "Where's the knife he had?"

The tech stood again and grabbed an evidence bag. The knife was a different one, but the man was the same.

"He was the guard Simon posted in the hallway of our building. The one who tried to keep Cassie and me from escaping out the back."

"Are you sure?" Whatley asked.

I nodded. "Pull back his bandage and I promise you'll find a broken wrist." I suddenly felt sick to my stomach. "I need to sit down."

"Certainly."

Whatley helped me back into the main room, and one of the techs brought over a straight-backed chair. Too many thoughts ricocheted through my brain. I shook my head to try to clear it.

"I don't know how he could have found her by following us. He had to have gotten here ahead of time to attack her, but how? Could he have overheard me giving you the address over the phone?"

"Sit here and collect your thoughts. I'm going to go and talk to your assistant. I'll be back. Would you like some water?"

"No, thank you. I only need a minute here."

Thinking didn't help, however. Nothing made sense. The only way he could have known I was coming back this evening was if he followed me earlier and overheard Nelly giving me the return time. If so, was he following me to report when I would be in the office?

The tech in the kitchen called for one of the others to help him. Seconds later, they moved out another gurney. Though this time the body strapped to the bed was zipped into a body bag.

Cassie cried out. I jumped to follow the men downstairs and see what was wrong. As I finally reached the ground floor lobby,

Whatley was holding my sobbing assistant and looking very uncomfortable.

"What's wrong?" I pulled her into my arms and received a relieved smile from the superintendent.

"The note..." she sobbed. "I...I..." Another cry swallowed up any of her words.

Whatley spoke, "I believe she left a note back at your office with the address. At least it's what I've put together."

She nodded and the pieces fell together for me. "Yes, the time and address were written on a notepad on her desk. I said she might have to do the pickup. She has trouble remembering London addresses." I smoothed her hair as she started to hiccup, trying to stop her tears. "It's not your fault. You didn't do anything wrong."

"I feel horrible," she wailed, and the tears began fresh.

The tech who had been working on the desk thundered down the stairs and sidled up to Whatley. I could see he carried the calendar, as well as something much smaller. The two men shared a whispered conversation. Whatley asked me, "Would you have any idea why she has three passports in three different names?"

My eyebrows shot toward my hairline, and the question even shocked Cassie enough for her crying to stop.

"No, Superintendent, I do not. Given the business she and I are in, the only reason I could imagine would not bode well for Nelly's honesty. I prefer not to assume anything."

"Understood."

As the coroner's van pulled away, another Met sedan drew to the curb. Whatley held up a finger to signal everyone to wait and stepped out to talk to the officer. He came back and said, "I think you've answered enough questions at the moment. You've both had a succession of shocks today. This car will take you home. I'll contact you tomorrow."

"The tapestry—"

"I'll try to have it in a state to release to you then as well, if the tapestry is what we find packed into the box under the chair."

I wondered about him suddenly wanting to get rid of us, but

he was right. I felt wiped out and Cassie was upset. I had nothing else to tell him. Until I remembered my package from the hotel. "Superintendent, the package you picked up for me—"

"Oh, right." He opened the outer door and stepped back, allowing us to leave first. He walked past us to his vehicle and opened the passenger door. "Here it is. The X-ray shows what appears to be a jewelry box. If you like, you can open the package here before you leave."

"No, it's fine." I shook my head. "I feel silly having asked you to retrieve it. But with this afternoon...I...well..."

"Absolutely fine. If I hadn't gone to fetch it, I might not have been as close when you called me from here."

I shivered, though not from the cold.

"Let's get you into the car and on your way." Whatley herded us into the patrolman's car, handing over the heavy box.

Before he shut the door, I asked, "Didn't you have some pictures you wanted us to see?"

He shook his head. "Now that you've identified the victim as the guard in the back hall, there's really no need. You said Babbage was the only one you could identify on the screen. The rest of the group you only heard, correct?"

"Yes," I said. "I saw some arms and backs, but nothing to help me identify any of the others."

"Very good. Try to relax tonight and get some rest," Whatley said. He stepped back to close the vehicle's door.

I squeezed Cassie's hand and gave the uniformed officer the address of my new hideaway hotel.

EIGHT

My latest hotel home was slightly larger than my former abode. A little brighter, with a corner location and more windows. More neutrals in the furnishings. However, I regretted being farther from the city center. The old hotel was much handier, and cozier with its light mauve-y décor. I'd get used to the change, I told myself. Or the differences would force me to finally make a flat search a priority.

While Cassie wandered through the amenities, rubbing a hand along the fabric and woodwork in her tactile fashion, I pulled my cases and checked everything had been packed and transferred. Especially the not-so-public gadgets I used to get into places where I didn't exactly have an invite.

Most of my smaller super-secret tools and gizmos stayed stashed in my Fendi for ready access. Larger things, like my climbing gear and the electronic wonders I got from a wizard in Zürich, waited patiently in a hard-sided case with a complicated keypad entry. I checked anyway. Everything seemed present and accounted for.

I sat down on the eggshell and beige bedspread and turned my attention to the box Whatley handed over as we left Nelly's.

The wrapping showed no return address, just my name and the foundation's address. A sticker on the wrapping showed the time of pickup—nine a.m. Greenwich—and the delivery service—Speedy Joe's. My eyebrows raised a little. The name sounded more like a fast food enterprise than one bonded to deliver packages like an antique jewelry case.

At least, I assumed it was antique. The superintendent told me the X-ray appeared to show such a box. No age implied about the piece. But my line of work made it reasonable to assume the item was centuries old. The package was heavy.

I tore through the brown wrapping, keeping an eye out for any kind of business card or note attached to the paper. Cassie finally finished her tour and took a chair nearby to watch my progress. The jewelry case was well packed inside a cardboard shipping container. I pushed aside packing peanuts and unwound a final layer of flannel protecting the finish. The item was semi-vintage and made of some kind of blue marble. A white filigree design chased across the top and around the sides, and a brass lock on the front panel held the top tightly closed. The matching brass key was taped to the bottom of the box. Well-made, and obviously expensive, it measured approximately ten inches long by eight wide and about four inches tall.

"Oh, lovely," Cassie said.

"Pretty, but seemingly contemporary and anonymous." I checked out the bottom for marks and found one by an Italian artisan whose heyday was in the 1950s and 1960s. I hoped there was a letter or something inside to point toward the owner of the piece. The outside looked pristine. Whoever sent it likely wasn't looking for restoration work. Maybe they needed authentication. I turned the key and lifted the lid.

Luckily, I was sitting down with the jewelry case on my lap. I might have dropped it otherwise. There wasn't any kind of letter of introduction or instruction. There was, however, a large photograph positioned over the jewelry pieces in the two compartments. It was a picture of two people, one of whom was my mother.

Taken in an unguarded moment, the photo showed love radiating from her face. She looked exactly the way I remembered. Her hair and dress pointed to fashion shortly ahead of my birth, by maybe two or three years. No more than that. But the man to the side, the one looking back at her and whose expression matched the emotion on my mother's face, was not my father. It was the same man who appeared in the smaller shot with my mother and her friend Margarite—the mysterious photo slipped into my purse at the October event in Florence.

I lifted the picture away to see inside, but kept the photo pinched tightly between my right index finger and thumb. In the two long velvet-lined compartments I found the kind of big eighties earrings my mother adored. There was a pair of aquamarine and diamond ones I knew had matched her eyes, along with a necklace and bracelet to match. A separate compartment held a pair of diamond chandelier-style earrings sharing space with a diamond choker and bracelet. There were more, but I was feeling overwhelmed.

"Laurel, what—"

I raised a hand to stop Cassie's words. No way I could put voice to any of the questions running through my mind at the moment. Without a jeweler's loupe I couldn't be sure, but everything looked real. Real expensive. If these were my mother's, where had they been stored? Why were they sent to me nearly twenty-five years after her death?

Returning the photograph to its place atop the jewelry, I looked closer at the man's image. As with the previous picture, my thoughts as I gazed on it were how beautiful my mother looked, how much I looked like her—and how the man looked remarkably like Rollie, Devin Moran's grandson and heir apparent to the criminal mastermind's empire. Rollie, the same young man Jack and I had been trying to find for months, and who suddenly appeared before us during the fireworks display.

I wasn't sure what this photo and jewelry box meant. The man in the picture would have to be in his sixties if he was still alive. Was he Moran's son or a younger brother? Had to be some relative. I'd looked under every digital rug I could find but still didn't know all the names Moran even used, and which was truly his family surname. Jack and Nico had helped with the task, but I hadn't told them about the picture I received in Florence with this anonymous man in the frame of the shot. So they hadn't been looking for another Moran heir. In time sequence, the first photo I received was taken almost a decade ahead of the one I now held.

Guilt and fear made me wish I had told Cassie and the guys. We could maybe have known who this mystery man was by this point. Guilt and fear were also the reasons I held back the information all these months. Fear of what I might learn about my mother, and guilt I was even thinking there was a connection between her and Moran's family. She was my mother; I shouldn't even be considering a connection with this criminal element. Yet my eyes told me otherwise. The gaze they shared in the shot was too intimate to ignore.

From research we'd successfully gained over the past couple of months, we knew Rollie was the son of Moran's daughter. I'd never seen verified photos of Moran at this age, and I wouldn't have been certain of a family resemblance between him and this mystery man if I hadn't met Rollie during the first phase of this operation.

Rollie was a few years under thirty, and this man looked late thirties. I had to believe they were connected. Especially since each time one of these "presents" got delivered, Rollie turned up wherever I happened to be.

What was my mother's relationship to this man in the photo and his family? Besides the fact I tried constantly to put Moran, the patriarch of the family, behind bars every chance I could?

I wasn't sure what this photo and the jewelry box meant, but I knew one thing—I was sick of getting blindsided by someone determined to play mind games with me.

"Do you know her?" Cassie asked.

"She was my mother." I brushed the photo softly with a finger, then passed it to Cassie.

Cassie studied the shot and said, "Of course. She could be your older sister, the two of you look so much alike. What's she, five years older than you at the time of this shot?"

"Sounds about right. I'm thinking a couple of years before I was born."

I delved into the treasure chest. Also inside was a pearl necklace matching a pair of earrings I'd been given from my late mother's estate for my twelfth birthday. If I'd needed any more confirmation—which I didn't—the necklace offered final proof to my hypothesis about the case and the jewels. Covered up by everything else, I found some bangles I was sure were hers simply because such bracelets were one of the strongest memories I carried in my heart about my mother. Her hand hanging onto mine and a cascade of thin gold, silver, and jewel-toned bangles tinging and dinging anytime she moved her arm. My mother loved bangle bracelets and left dozens behind after she died.

As a grieving four-year-old, I tried to wear them for a while, moving them past my elbow in a futile effort to keep them from falling off. My father confiscated them, saying he couldn't take the sound. It reminded him too much of her. I wanted to protest, to say the sound was what I loved about them, and how the bracelets' music made me feel she was yet with us. Except, I comprehended the pain of loss and didn't want my father to grieve any more than he had to. I was young enough at the time to care about his happiness—I hadn't been sufficiently hurt yet by his excesses and narcissism.

The bangles disappeared completely soon after my mother's funeral. I never knew what happened to them. Whenever I brought up the subject I was told, "The topic will not be discussed."

Fingers trembling, I caught each bracelet and ran the cool metal over the squeezed fingers of my right hand and up to my wrist. I couldn't stop myself from making the bangles dance.

"This came from Rollie. I know it did," I said. I set the jewelry case on the bed and got up to pace. Emotions and adrenalin were fighting for control, and I had to move or spontaneously combust. The previous "gift" I'd discovered secreted in my purse in Florence, a compact and picture of my mother before she married my father, had all the earmarks of being planted by Rollie at the black-tie event. I couldn't be sure as others had equal opportunity.

After what happened last night—or rather, early this

morning—and this anonymous delivery...Well, I wasn't feeling puzzled any more. In fact, I was feeling righteously nosy.

I called Nico. He picked up immediately. "*Pronto!*"

"Can't you say 'ciao' like other Italians?" I said.

"Other Italians say 'pronto' too," Nico said, his accent making his words sound like a grumble. "I cannot help it if the English misuse the word. I expected you to call sooner. The Scotland Yard superintendent telephoned Jack about Simon's little stunt, and the dead man you found a few hours later."

The irritation in his voice came through clearly. Though I'd left a message for Jack to return my call, I hadn't specifically mentioned the attack, and Nico's testiness made sense. "I knew you and Jack had your hands full with the Tony B situation. I didn't want you sidetracked, and Scotland Yard leapt right in as soon as I notified Whatley." He gave a kind of soft snort, and I assumed it meant all was forgiven. I pushed on. "There's more though, Nico. I want your help, but I don't want Jack to know what I'm going to ask you."

"Unfortunately, this will be *problematico*."

Almost as clear as Nico's voice, I heard Jack growl, "Let me speak to her."

"I don't want to talk to—"

"Not an option." Jack had apparently liberated Nico's phone and was speaking directly to me. "What don't you want me to know?"

I chewed my lip. In order to break into Moran's Mayfair address to see if there was anything inside pointing to this jewelry cache or my mother, I needed Nico. But I wouldn't get to talk to Nico until I told Jack what I planned. Or lied my way out of the current predicament. It was already past six o'clock. No time to spare. "Okay, the truth is, I want to get into the Mayfair address you said Rollie stayed at last night. I want to see inside."

Jack's voice filled the speaker. "Why would you even consider such a foolhardy thing? We know he's fled the scene."

"He left something behind, and I want to see if there are any more surprises that may come my way." I filled him in about the jewelry box, my mother's picture, and her probable gems inside. "I didn't tell you about a picture and compact I received the night of the Florence event. I wasn't sure it was Rollie who slipped it into my purse at the time, but this delivery makes me certain. The reason I want to get into the Mayfair house is because Nico did a recon through it in September, the night you and I found the Welshman at the docks. He already knows the setup, and I figured he could help me get in tonight without getting caught. I'm going to wear the special computer glasses he gave me. He can see and hear everything I encounter along the way and talk me through any obstacles."

Jack blew out a long breath. "Do you want to know the status of Tony B?"

"Well, sure. I was going to ask in a minute."

"He's dead."

"From the assault in prison?"

"He was stabbed by an inmate," Jack said. "The injury wasn't what killed him, however. He'd been to surgery. The doctors thought he had every chance of recovery."

"What do you mean?"

Cassie walked closer, trying to hear, and I activated the speaker option.

"Less than an hour ago, he was wheeled out of recovery and given a strong painkiller when he was put into his bed in intensive care," Jack replied. "We were able to talk to him for a minute. He still suffered the effects of the anesthetic, but he repeated one sentence three times when he saw me."

"What was it?"

"'Get Beacham.'"

"That's it?" Too many things were hitting me at the same time, and Cassie's eyes grew wider by the second.

"Yes." Jack sighed. "We've learned nothing else. You can see why—"

"Back up a second," I interrupted. "You said Tony B is dead, but the doctors had thought he would recover. Are there some missing details?"

"As we left his area of intensive care, the doctor came to do a follow-up exam. Tony B was mostly out of it, so Nico and I and my friend in Italian law enforcement went downstairs for coffee. When we came back, the floor was a madhouse. Code blues were being shouted in Italian, and Tony B had flat-lined. Despite best efforts, no one could revive him."

"What happened?" I had a sinking feeling I wouldn't like the answer.

Jack spoke almost mechanically, like he was reading from a bulleted page of notes. "The guard told my friend everything went downhill once a redheaded nurse went into the room. She entered a few minutes after the doctor left. She had the proper IDs to get past the guard, and had a filled syringe on the metal tray she carried. She was in the room less than a minute and smiled at the guard as she left, hurrying down the hall toward the next wing. Seconds later, Tony B's alarm sounded, and everyone came running. Everyone *except* the very tall redheaded nurse."

"It was the Amazon," I said.

"Our conclusion as well."

"Did you get pictures off the security cameras?"

"We did," Jack said. "She managed to turn most of her face away each time. Not enough to get an identification with recognition software. The last camera caught her leaving the building and jumping into a waiting Fiat 500 with obscured plates."

"Damn!"

"The guard did get a good look at her," Jack said. "Meaning there's a chance of making an ID after he works with the police sketch artist."

"I'm guessing she wore latex gloves the whole time."

"No fake nurse and real assassin would be without them," he quipped.

"Why can't something ever be easy on this case?"

"What? Take out all the challenge?"

I started pacing again, trying to figure out what I needed to say. "I get why you don't want me taking off on rabbit trails."

"Yeah, breaking and entering a criminal mastermind's former residence is a *rabbit trail* you should avoid," Jack said wryly. I appreciated the sarcasm in place of his usual lecture—but my relief was short-lived. "I told you, Rollie is gone. When I talked to Whatley about your afternoon's activities he admitted they'd had someone watching the place all day and it's still empty." His voice softened. "I realize you've had a second emotional shock tonight. I agree with your assumption Rollie and/or Moran is behind it by the way, but you could definitely be in danger based on what's happened in the last twenty hours or so. Plus, breaking and entering is illegal."

Like it's ever stopped you, I thought, but kept the smartass remark to myself. There was no use arguing. I'd never get Nico to help me after this turn of events.

Rollie was back, Simon broke in, Cassie and I escaped, the man who tried to capture us tried to kill one of my art restorers and was killed instead, and she clung to life while law enforcement worked to find out why she possessed a handful of phony passports. Following an attempt on Tony B's life that sent him to the hospital, he warned Jack about me, and the Amazon surfaced after an almost four-month hiatus and finished the job the inmate in the Italian prison started. Wow. All in less than a day. Did Rollie head for Rome? Or was he starting something new? And where did Simon go into hiding this time?

"Have any of your Home Office sources found a trace of how Rollie or Simon got into the country, or if they've left again?" I asked Jack.

"No, nothing yet." Weariness came through in his voice, and I understood it. He'd gotten even less sleep than me. Maybe none at all. I looked over at Cassie and saw her eyes at half-mast too.

"Rollie is gone," I said. "You and Nico are in Rome, the Amazon is in Rome, and Tony B is dead in Rome. Sounds like all the action has been moved to your venue."

"Yes, exactly why I'm thinking it might be better if you're here with us until this thing is settled somehow. I don't know when I can get back to London, and with what Tony B said, I'd feel more comfortable if Nico and I had eyes on you all the time."

"We can't leave. After the crime scene team is through, we have to go to the office tomorrow to check out everything. To see if we can figure out what Simon wanted or stole. I have to get the tapestry back—"

"Simon may have been after you. Tony B said, 'Get Beacham.' Who's to say Simon hadn't already received the same message? He may have been trying to protect you or planning to deliver you to whomever might have a bounty on your head."

"Seems a little melodramatic."

"I'm serious, Laurel."

I knew he was. I didn't want to think about where his mind was going. "Are you thinking Tony B worked for Moran or Simon, given we know the latter two were in collusion for the past year or more? Or do you believe it's more likely he worked for the mysterious second criminal organization everyone whispers about? The one we're assuming is tied to Ermo Colle?"

With an abstract gesture, I raked back the top of my hair with my fingers to keep the curls out of my eyes. I needed to think. This was too frustrating. The only known facts on the mysterious Ermo Colle was the organization functioned as an Italian importer/exporter who bankrolled the October event in Florence. With the many layers in place, we couldn't even be sure yet if Ermo Colle was a person or group.

In Florence we found—for lack of a better term—a forgery factory in one of the palazzos near the Duomo. Nico eventually connected it superficially to Moran through outdated titles, but could not find anything proving he'd recently used it. Nothing connecting to Ermo Colle either.

However, we spotted Rollie leaving the area, and likely the palazzo, shortly before Jack and I broke in to check out the contents. Then Tony B pulled a coup and Jack was apprehended.

Unfortunately, law enforcement celebrated by arresting Jack, and no one saw the truly dangerous contraband on the roof he and I found earlier.

So many pieces to the puzzle. No provable connections.

"I know nothing," Jack replied. "But we can't rule out anything."

We were stymied and frustrated.

"Cassie has a new idea. I'll let her tell you."

While my assistant took over the conversation, I thought about every option. Another quick search of my possessions told me I likely had everything needed for any contingency. Jack's Walther PPK was in the hidden pocket of my luggage. I moved it to my room safe. I removed the bangle bracelets, returned half of them to the jewelry box, and put everything in the safe and reset the combination. I didn't want to risk losing them, but I wasn't ready to temporarily give up all of the beloved touchstones either. I found a clamshell necklace box the remaining bracelets fit into and added it to my Fendi.

Cassie's words pulled me back into the conversation. "Jack, I think you're right. Laurel does need to go to Rome. It's a good plan."

I started, "Cass—"

"Hear me out," she interrupted. "I was involved in every part of restoring the office. If there is any anomaly, I'll spot it. I'll stay here, go to the office tomorrow, and return the tapestry to the client if Whatley can get it released. You go to Rome. You've seen the Amazon. Between you and the guard, the pair of you might be able to get an even closer version sketched of her appearance. Two heads and all that good stuff. Besides, if you don't, you'll continue worrying about the guys while they worry about you. This way you'll all have each other's backs."

"You'll be here by yourself," I objected. I could hear Jack's and Nico's voices over the speaker, adding to the protest.

Cassie talked over all of us. "I'll make sure I have the superintendent or another officer with me at all times. When I'm done with the office survey, I'll head to New York while you guys are tied up in Rome."

"I don't think—"

"It's the best alternative, Laurel," she argued. "I can do much more to help us get info in New York than I can being your shadow. We were already planning to send Nico in a few days. I'll go there a little earlier and work the book angle."

I stared at her, and she raised her eyebrows in a silent question, asking "Well?" There was no good answer as far as I could see. I wanted her safe, and I agreed the two of us sharing babysitting services wasn't necessarily practical—but sending her off on her own sounded frightening and foolish. Even if there would be an ocean between her and whatever danger was interested in us.

"What do you guys think?" I asked.

Muffled voices came through the speaker. One of them had covered the mic. After a beat, Jack answered, "Cassie's plan makes sense. She'll be safer in America, and can work under the aid and protection of Beacham's New York office while she's coordinating with the publisher's personnel."

I had to agree, but voiced a few provisos. "Three conditions. One, you book a ticket as if you're returning to your parents to continue your holiday break. But you depart the plane at New York so anyone watching you leave London will be fooled in your true purpose."

"Good idea," she said.

"Next, you keep Nico apprised of your itinerary *at all times*." I raised an eyebrow to signal there would be no argument. "If we feel we need to call in the cavalry for any reason, we need to know where to send them."

"Done."

"Finally," I placed a hand on her shoulder as I spoke, "if anything starts feeling off in any way, you bail immediately. Make your excuses and actually go to your parents' place as quickly as you can."

"No argument," she said.

I shot a question to the phone, "Jack and Nico, do either of you have anything to add?"

"Have an officer go with you to your flat to pack tomorrow," Jack said. "For tonight, stay in Laurel's room. Don't return to your flat until morning."

"I'll send a charm bracelet like Laurel's to the New York office, Cassie," Nico added. "Watch for it and wear the jewelry for the same reason she is supposed to."

I caught the dig, but I knew Nico was teasing and didn't respond. But I did when Jack added, "I'll see who I can get to travel with you to Rome, Laurel."

"A bodyguard would draw attention. Use those magic MI-6 powers you won't tell me about to get me seated near the plane's air marshal. Nico can book my flight and email the ticket."

"Brilliant suggestion. We'll try to get you out of London tonight. Start packing whatever you think you'll need."

NINE

In less than ten minutes I had an email from Nico with my e-ticket for an eight p.m. flight. He said Jack was setting up a fix on the air marshal issue. I changed into a tweed pantsuit and white blouse. My knee-length red wool coat came out to cover for the favorite leather one I left hanging on the office hook before the break-in. After so many hours on my feet, the heels had to go. I chose my short-heeled travel boots. My high heels would go into my checked bag.

I packed and called Whatley to brief him on why I needed to go to Rome rather than stay in London. He offered no lecture or warning, promising he'd be outside my hotel within a quarter hour with a car to transport me to Heathrow. As I left the room, Cassie called down to room service, and I was kicking myself for not having ordered earlier.

Whatley's car waited at the curb, and he stowed my luggage in the boot. I slid into the seat to ride shotgun.

"I spoke to Hawkes a few moments ago," he said as we pulled away. "Seems we're in a bit of a hurry for you to make your flight."

As we flew across the flyover, he asked for an update. I talked as fast as he drove, though a little concerned I didn't know how much Jack had told him. We had enough trouble on our hands, and I didn't want to risk more by letting something slip.

Whatley asked a couple of questions, but remained intent on driving to get to Heathrow in the fastest possible time. I was grateful for my seatbelt, as I think I'd have been flung around the vehicle otherwise.

A siren may have been employed.

Whatley and his shield got me through airport security in record time as well. My luggage didn't make the cut though, and had to be checked. One of the security crew notified the gate I was on my way, and in a very short time I was boarded and taking my first deep breath in what felt like years.

For security reasons, I couldn't know who the air marshal was, but Jack called right before takeoff to assure me the man with the gun had my picture and my back.

Per instructions, I was one of the last passengers to disembark from our plane at Leonardo da Vinci-Fiumicino airport a couple of hours later, and Jack was pacing at the gate. I wasn't sure how he was there. I expected him at baggage claim, but I'd quit asking how the man accomplished half the things I didn't understand. Just filed everything under "he had his ways."

January temps in Rome are chilly. I slung my wool coat over an arm as I deplaned. "You must be starved," he said, relieving me of my carry-on and helping me on with the coat, before ushering me down the long terminal. "Cassie said you didn't eat dinner before you left."

"Famished. We have to get my bag first. I had to check—"

"No, we can't. The baggage handlers went on strike an hour ago."

I stopped. "What?"

Jack had walked on. He turned back and answered, "There was a nine o'clock deadline on getting a contract signed. It didn't happen."

"Unbelievable." I shook my head and resumed walking. "Do you know until I started working with you I never had to go without luggage? Now it happens every time."

"This is Italy," Jack replied, shrugging. "Somebody is always on strike for something. Tonight it's baggage handlers, tomorrow it will be waiters or taxi drivers. To be fair, however, the first time your luggage left on the plane to Nevada without you was due to Max's interference."

"He might not have picked me for the job if you hadn't caught everyone's interest asking about the sword and Simon."

"I thought you decided to take the job once Max told you Moran was involved."

Why did the man always remember whatever it took to win an argument? He was right though. The first time was my boss's fault. "Nevertheless, I blame you for getting our luggage stolen when Tony B's guys towed away the Mercedes in Miami. We never did get any of the stuff back."

"And we never will, so let it go."

I stopped again and looked back toward the gate, making people drift around us as they moved out of the terminal. "You don't think they'd let me get my own bag off the plane, do you?"

"Is crossing a picket line really how you want to spend your first night in Rome?"

"You're right." Time to buck up and change focus. I put my hand in the crook of his elbow and we resumed our journey. "Where are you taking me to dinner?"

"I thought room service would be nice. Got it all worked out with the concierge before I left."

"If we were in Spain, it would be the beginning of dinner time," I said. A yawn nearly split my jaw. "Oh, I'm sorry."

"It's contagious," Jack said, yawning himself. "Proving I was right about dinner in the room."

"Do I have a room down the hall?"

"It's a suite. I want to keep everyone together."

Rome is an amazing city—ancient, alive, and exhausting. I'd never choose a visit there in the scorching summer, but the tourists can be nearly as thick on a winter's evening. If we'd arrived on tourist visas, as opposed to a whirlwind recon, I'd have divided the city into halves and hit favorite places like the Forum, Pantheon, Piazza

Navonna, Trevi Fountain, and the Spanish Steps first. The next day charge to the Vatican museums, St. Peter's Basilica, and Campo di Fiori.

As it was, we were too focused on work to play, but our hotel was within sight of the Trevi Fountain. I hadn't seen it since the restoration funded by the Fendi fashion house, and I wanted to discover what a difference a couple of years scrubbing could make.

"Okay, a quick look," Jack agreed. "Then it's food and bed for both of us."

"Yes, sir," I said.

The January air was brisk, our breaths coming out as fog, but the area was still choked with people enjoying the famous sight and favorite Travertine-stone fountain. Initially begun by Nicola Salvi in 1732 and completed by Giuseppi Pannini thirty years later, the commission didn't have a smooth path politically when it was first awarded to a Florentine, Alessandro Galilei.

In the end, the outcome was spectacular with its papal coat of arms, plethora of angels, and even the shell chariot of Triton's guide Oceanus as the hippocamps are tamed. The addition of the more than one hundred LED lights to update the illumination made an already glorious public art object take on almost supernatural aesthetics. Amazing what a 2.2-million-euro restoration budget accomplished.

My Fendi bag slipped from my shoulder as I stopped to rummage for a coin. Jack handed me one instead.

"On three. We'll throw together," he said, winking.

I smiled and pivoted with him, leaving our backs to the fountain.

"One, two..."

We tossed simultaneously with our right hands. The coins flew over our left shoulders, per tradition.

He put an arm around my shoulders and steered me again toward our hotel's entrance.

"You know, of course, this means we'll both return to Rome," I said. "Think it will be together?"

"Would it be such a bad thing?"

I looked up at him. "Not if you always pick up the tab for dinner." Movement in my peripheral vision from around the side of the fountain suddenly turned everything serious. I leaned into Jack and whispered, "Let's move. The Amazon is on the east side of the fountain."

He stood straighter, but like a pro, didn't whip his head around to look. "You're sure?"

"Positive."

He tried to get me to stay back, but I followed closely, and we kept the crowd blocking us from her view. As we dodged around loiterers and evening strollers, her height was a disadvantage. All the lights in the area easily let us follow her movements as it highlighted her auburn hair. But her height helped her spot us getting closer too. Her gaze locked with ours. She ran.

Jack passed me my carry-on so he could cut and run. I rummaged for something sharp in my Fendi in case he needed backup.

The Amazon zipped completely around the fountain like it was a roundabout, shoving people aside with her long arms. She disappeared into the dimness of a side street with Jack several strides behind. No point attempting to help him with a direct run. I angled down another street, hoping to catch her in a cross-connect. I heard a fast motor rev up and race away. Another second and Jack's number appeared on my cell's screen.

"You okay?"

"Yes," I responded. "I assume the engine I heard was her escape vehicle."

"Correct."

"I'll meet you back at the square."

When Jack saw me approaching Trevi Fountain again, he slid a gun back into the pocket of his leather bomber jacket. I'd never even realized he had a firearm.

"Where did you get that?"

"From the car before we left. Come on, let's go to the hotel."

"We might want to avoid the main entrance."

"My thought exactly. Rear door it is." Jack pulled me close again, steering our path toward another of the less illuminated side streets, all the while his gaze registering what was going on in every direction.

I admit, I did a little three-sixty reconnoitering myself.

Ten minutes later, after a particularly circuitous route, we entered the hotel through a service entrance, went up a freight elevator, and were safely ensconced in the room. I ate until I got sleepy, which wasn't very long. It was past time for the conversation we needed to explore.

"What do we know?" I asked, once we could safely talk behind a closed door. I hid another yawn with my hand.

"She had to be following me when I picked you up at the airport. Otherwise, it would be too coincidental for her to be at the fountain the same time as us."

"Except we were at one of the most famous tourist sites in Rome. My fault, I know. Unless she has a tracker on you, or had you under surveillance somehow, it sounds more likely she had the most popular sites staked out and we happened on the one she manned herself. The one nearest this hotel."

"There is that," Jack agreed. "The fountain and the Spanish Steps are probably the city's two most visited night attractions."

"At least we know she didn't come with me from London. She was too busy killing a man here in Rome earlier today."

"Small favors."

I held up my glass and Jack added more wine.

"I read about a University of Alberta study recently saying a glass of red wine may have the same effects as an hour at the gym," I said.

Jack snorted. "I think we got enough of a workout tonight chasing our perp. You don't have to justify another glass of wine."

"It's what we women do." I ignored the pasta to pick at some of the fruit and cheese. Despite feeling close to starvation earlier, the adrenalin rush I'd pushed through the past hour was a dieter's dream. I popped another grape into my mouth. "Or the Amazon already knew you were staying here and was on a simple stakeout."

"Yeah." Jack sighed. "We probably need to move."

"Not tonight. I'm exhausted." My brain started working again. "How did you book this hotel?"

"Walked in once Nico and I left the hospital. I've quit doing anything in advance. Nico's ability to get into anything digital makes me look over my virtual shoulder all the time. You had the right idea in Florence."

"Welcome to the dark side," I teased, then yawned so deeply I thought I was going to pass out. "I want eggs Benedict in the morning. What little strength I had left is zapped. I'm too tired to try to eat."

"Never thought I'd hear you say those words, but I completely understand," Jack said, pushing aside his own plate of pasta. He rose and extended a hand to pull me from my chair. "Bloody hell." He yawned. "I think I'm too tired even to sleep. Or maybe I'm asleep already. I can't tell anymore."

I pulled a couple of alarm gizmos from my purse and walked to the door. "These should alert us if anyone comes in during the night. They have a tendency to wail. Is Nico sleeping here?"

"Who knows? His luggage is. He said he's going to bring in some computers to set up a command center, and there was someone he wanted to see tonight. Thought he might get some intel on the missing forgers."

I laughed. "Yeah, intel. I lay you odds it's a girl instead."

"You know I'm not one to take a sucker bet."

He called the front desk. "We need a laundry pickup, and we'd like to have it returned with our breakfast in the morning." After listening a few seconds, he hung up and turned to me. "There should be a plastic sack in the closet for your clothes. They can be laundered by morning, no problem."

"Thank you."

"You want to borrow one of my shirts?"

"I'll use one of the fluffy white robes in the bathroom."

He entered the room on the left. I stumbled into the room on the right after wrapping up in a robe and setting my bag of traveling clothes outside the door. I remember seeing the bed. I think I disrobed myself. Even that was up for debate.

TEN

My clothes did indeed arrive the next morning with breakfast. While I dressed, Jack set the table. I came back into the suite's lounge to see him stirring our coffee cups with a clear plastic wand. He pulled out the stirrer and stared hard at it.

"What are you doing?" I asked.

"Checking to see if the coffee is spiked." He held up a bottle resembling fingernail polish. "This was developed by a couple of guys to help women keep from being drugged in bars. You can paint it on fingernails, dip the end of a nail in a drink, and if any date rape drugs have been added the polish will change color." He held up the clear stick. "We're safe."

I took the bottle from him. "Does this work with poison?"

"No, just popular knock-out drugs. I'm counting on the premise if the Amazon got our coffee spiked, it would simply be something sleep-inducing ra ther than lethal."

"Can I keep this? To use on my nails for my own drug-checking purposes?"

"I was already going to suggest it."

"Nice." I grinned and set the bottle back on the table. "Cassie and I can function as walking drug tests."

When I suggested eggs Benedict the previous evening, my stomach had been overly ambitious. Toast and coffee with some spectacular fruit spread were hitting the spot adequately to help us wake up. The lock on the door thunked as we finished eating, and Nico rolled in with computer gear on a two-wheeled collapsible dolly. Fortunately, we disarmed my make-do alarm system when breakfast arrived. My gorgeous geek wore a particularly sour look on his face, and I was sure the dark look would have gone nuclear if he'd had a high-pitched squeal pealing in his ears.

"Morning, Nico," I said. His response came in the form of a grunt. I raised my eyebrows questioningly at Jack, and he gave a serious look and shook his head. Okay. This should be a fun trip.

Nico started stretching cords and plugging in power strips.

"Need some help?" I asked.

"No."

We finished our coffee as he positioned a third monitor. Jack headed back into his room for a jacket. I filled a cup with coffee and offered it to my techno wingman. "Here, Nico, have some caffeine."

"*Grazie.*"

"Get lucky last night?"

He gave me a grin finally. "I could ask the same of you."

"You know everything was all business here."

"Um-hmm." He finished the coffee and set it aside, opening his laptop as he spoke. "I'll wait for Jack. I don't want to tell my story twice."

"Jack is here," he said, reentering the space as he straightened his collar.

Nico flopped into a nearby chair. "Gaia connected me with her informant last night at dinner. As I told you earlier—Oh, did you tell Laurel? I don't want to repeat—"

"No, Laurel knows nothing," I said and crossed my arms. "Feel free to repeat."

"It's not like we didn't have other things to think about, or run from," Jack said, setting his hands on his hips. "I didn't keep you out of the loop on purpose."

"*Mio Dio.*" Nico walked to the table to pour another cup of coffee. The pot was empty. "I already have a headache and none of this is helping."

He obviously didn't get lucky last night.

"Fill Laurel in and I'll order another pot," Jack said, crossing to the room phone.

I joined Nico at the table.

"Over Christmas, I heard about a forger here in Rome who disappeared from regular circles. He's known as *il Carver*. Through some research and a little hacking, I learned we had a friend in common, Gaia. I contacted her when we arrived yesterday, and she agreed to talk to me. Said she might be able to get me an interview with the forger. He'd been in hiding after another of his brother forgers was killed. He'd started putting different puzzle pieces together and didn't like the picture coming through."

"What kind of forger is he?"

"As his nickname implies, carvings. Especially religious carvings. Icons."

"Oh, good. I feared his name had a more ominous tone to it. Maybe it was the *il* that did it."

Jack came over to stand beside me. "Coffee will be up in a mo'."

"Good." Nico sat down at the table and sighed. "Seriously, I'm getting too old for this."

"You're not even thirty." I laughed.

"I'd like to actually turn thirty too," he said. He pulled back the curtain and looked down at the sidewalk.

"Were you followed?" Jack asked.

Nico shrugged. "We were chased last night. We had almost finished our meal when *il Carver* looked up and almost choked. Two men in dark coats entered the restaurant and looked around. Before they saw us, I pushed *il Carver* so he fell off his chair to the side, and told him to get under the table. Gaia and I shifted the plates around to make it appear there wasn't a third person. The men stayed, finally taking a table near the front of the restaurant."

"Did they spot your forger?" Jack asked.

"Only as we left. I'd planned ahead. When I paid the bill I asked if we could go out the back way for convenience. The waiter was suspicious, of course, but I'd paid the bill and gave him a good tip. He told us to follow him. Gaia and I did, and I carried away the forger's coat with mine. As we got to the kitchen door, *il Carver* broke from the cover of the table and zigzagged through the diners. The two men spotted him and gave chase."

"They were after him."

"Yes, his wariness was justified."

My turn for a question. "The research you and Cassie found helped you spot the pattern of forgers who'd recently met untimely deaths. Is this something the whole forger community is buzzing about, or simply *il Carver's* personal epiphany?"

"From what he said, he hasn't talked to anyone about it. He confirmed what he'd heard was true, and went into hiding until he learned more."

"What had he learned?" Jack asked.

Conversation stopped with the sound of a knock on the door announcing room service. I asked about Gaia's background and Nico said it had nothing to do with art or forgeries. Jack crossed the room and checked the peephole before turning the lock. Minutes later, with his cup refilled, Nico launched into what was discussed the previous evening, picking up where he'd left off at the coffee's arrival.

"The forger community isn't necessarily close. Everyone has his own area of expertise and is afraid of competition for the better paying clients. This forger wasn't the most personable fellow either. Not one to meet others for drinks and chatting." Nico blew across the top of his cup. "He noticed too many of his ilk meeting untimely deaths. The career choice is risky, but he felt the risks were rising unnaturally."

"Lucky for him, he sounds a little paranoid," I said. "From what happened last night I guess the paranoia kept him alive."

I walked over to grab my coat from where I'd left it on a chair the previous evening. Nico continued with his story, "We got away fast enough to find a cab. But the bad guys had a car and rammed us. They tried to grab *il Carver* but he fought. Gaia and I helped. One guy hit *il Carver* over the head and crammed him into their car. We tried to get away from the other guy to help, but the driver found the motor wouldn't work. He got out again to pull the forger from the back, precisely when two police cars arrived with lights and sirens. The men got away before police could stop them."

"What was the cab driver doing all this time?" Jack asked.

"Do you know *il Carver's* real name?" I asked at the same time.

"The taxi driver was the one who called the police," Nico said. "He shot a video of the entire thing with his cell phone. And, no, *il Carver* wouldn't tell me his real name and neither will Gaia."

"Did you get the video?" Jack and I spoke together.

"Of course." He took a tentative sip of the hot coffee, then returned the cup to the saucer. "After that, the police called an ambulance, and Gaia argued with the taxi driver about who was paying for the damage. I stepped in and offered to give him Max's contact to try to get the foundation to pay the cab repairs if he would email me the video."

"Max will explode," I said.

"I know." He grinned. "I only offered help. No guarantees."

"Anything else?" Jack asked.

"I spent the rest of the night at either the police station or waiting outside the trauma unit. We finally left the hospital when the forger was assigned a bed and moved from trauma. I will check on him periodically through the day. After I get some sleep."

"What are the computers for?" I asked.

Nico swung his cup around to point. "Something I did learn last night is there are a couple of new names to research. One sounds Russian, the other Chinese. I don't figure either of them are important in what we're looking at, but I'm going to hack into some servers to find out. See if they lead anywhere. However, *il Carver* did admit he's done freelance work tying back to a relatively new client he's heard connects to an organization with a Greek name."

"Ermo Colle?" Jack asked.

"The very one."

There it was again. No direct tie, but the hint of one to the organization with an uncanny ability to seemingly hide in plain sight.

"No name recognition when I asked him any of the names we know associated with Moran," Nico said. "Nor when I mentioned Tony B. I must assume *il Carver* is a more low-level contact since he'd only done freelance work recently. He may only know middle men."

"And he's running away," Jack mused.

"Smart man," I said.

"Indeed," said Nico.

"Can you email me the video?" Jack asked.

"Meant to already." Nico sighed and pulled out his cell. He tapped his screen a couple of times. "Done."

"What about theories?" I asked. "Does he remember anything about the job he was on to suggest people would come later to kill him?"

"No. At first he thought it might be some kind of professional jealousy, and each forger was killed by a different competitor. According to *il Carver,* the money really is good. However, at dinner he said he'd turned down a second job from them. They acted okay with it, but he knew from talk with a friend a few days earlier the same job had already been given to another forger who killed himself the week before."

"The forger committed suicide *after* being hired for the job?"

Nico nodded. "When *il Carver* asked about it the answer was the dead man was depressed, drank too much and probably used drugs. But *il Carver* knew the whole story wasn't being told. The men trying to hire him, who said the forger was depressed, acted like they were hiding something. All body language, but *il Carver* got concerned."

"How did the other forger die?"

"Slit his wrists in the bathtub. When they came to *il Carver* and he realized it was the same work and they weren't completely telling the truth about the death, he decided to be suddenly very busy. He admitted to me he had no evidence about anything, but he was superstitious enough to trust his instincts and say no."

"They could be killing anyone they fear might make their

secret commissions public," Jack said. "It's an angle we'd already thought of, but this is the first bit of evidence to back up any of our suspicions."

I put on my coat, pulled my hair free, and told Jack, "I'm going to check my makeup one more time and freshen my lipstick. While you're waiting on me, why don't you brief Nico on our evening adventure?"

Even through the closed door, I could hear the murmur of their voices. A quick check of my makeup and I was confident the light discoloration on my chin was masked. The hot coffee had done a number on my gloss, as I expected. I finished up by running a quick brush through my hair and pulled gloves from my coat pocket as I reentered the room. The guys had moved over to the computers. One of the laptops was booted up. The coffee cup had become an extension of Nico's hand.

"I'm ready whenever you are," I called.

"Great. Everyone's up to speed on everything. We'll compare notes this evening on what transpires today," Jack said. He turned to Nico and added, "We're heading for the police station to talk to the detective in charge of Tony B's murder. I assume you'll be sleeping this afternoon."

Nico couldn't respond until he finished a huge yawn. "Yes. I'll get a few things started here, then nap."

"I'm leaving my gun in the safe," Jack said, walking across the room to match action to words. "Don't be afraid to use it."

"If you don't mind, I just got released for using a gun in Florence. I don't think my grandmother would survive my getting jailed again."

"Better than killed," Jack said. "The guys last night proved they play for keeps, and the Amazon showed her hand as well."

Nico frowned. "Maybe I'll get us new accommodations before I sleep."

"If you do, leave a message at the front desk," Jack replied, checking the peephole again before opening the door.

"In case we get tied up somehow, can you try to touch base

with Cassie this afternoon?" I asked. "She's supposed to meet with Scotland Yard at the office before catching a flight to New York."

He nodded. "I need to talk to her anyway. On my way here I overnighted a charm bracelet to her." He set his cup on the floor and half-rose, checking his pockets. "I have your charm. The envelope is—"

"It's okay, Nico," I said. "I'll get it later. Jack and I will be at a police station. What could be safer?"

I heard him chuckling as the door closed behind us.

ELEVEN

We were in Rome. The Eternal City. A place to visit Renaissance masterpieces like the Sistine Chapel and ancient wonders like the beautifully columned Pantheon designed to shout a tribute to every god. Or wander off to discover a lovely little café with the greatest pasta primavera and maybe discover an off-the-beaten-path fresco. Possibly even run across a shop with a wicked little dress to distract an adversary and let me use my legs to the most advantage. An endless variety of unique venues calling constantly to visitors. I loved Rome. Loved the Vatican. Loved the pickpockets. Loved everything that made this ancient city as relevant today as it was two millennia ago.

I could whine about the expectation of spending the day at a Roma police station, or vent frustration over the baggage handlers who held my luggage hostage in their collateral bargaining. These were small irritations, and bigger issues had to hold our attention. We had to keep one step ahead. To do so, we needed to use every resource available. Our best hope of finding the next clue had died with Tony B, those answers safely hidden in his memory. The forgery factory in Florence and all we'd subsequently found proved we needed to keep moving forward. The pieces of intel pointed to something bigger than a simple museum theft.

If the police investigating the thug's murder could help, it was in our best interests to do what we could to aid in their mission.

Tony B also made *The Portrait of Three* disappear exactly as he'd threatened he would. I wasn't sure if he'd given the grouping away like he said in Florence, or if it was somewhere he'd controlled—like my gut told me. He'd threatened to destroy the paintings if I reported them, and he was probably enough of a bully to try something that despicable, but I had to believe he sold them instead. Thieves simply did not purposefully destroy masterpieces. It was like building a bonfire with thousand-dollar bills. Regardless, this was one more secret out of my reach as well, and something else Jack and I needed to discuss when every moment of our time and attention wasn't tied up thwarting this illusive heist plan.

Jack took a jagged curve and brought me out of my reverie. Our car was the rental he used to pick me up the previous evening. A speedy little blue Fiat. It had to be fast to keep from being hit by the other vehicles on the road. While he drove, I gave him details about the mysterious jewelry box and photo I received the evening before. Part of the telling was to get his take on things, but a big part was to keep my mind off the fact every other driver in Italy seemed intent on killing us. Jack, of course, acted unconcerned, but I thought it was false bravado—each time I scrambled to find something to hang on to.

"Do you have pictures?" he asked, when another gasp made me stop speaking.

"On my phone."

"Why do you think it was sent to you now? After thinking about what you said on our call last night, I agree it was Rollie. Though I still question your grand plan to break into the Mayfair address."

I ignored the dig and answered his question, "Yes, Rollie's my first pick, but I'm not sure why I received the package or the timing of the gift. Unless it wasn't him...Maybe someone sent it to warn me."

"How do you mean?"

"Each picture has shown my mother with the same man. A man I recognized as looking like Rollie." I felt a lump forming in my throat, but I pressed on. "It's someone who knows about my mother's link with Moran's family. Someone who had the case...and..."

I couldn't say it. Being fairly certain my beautiful mother had too-close ties to someone related to Moran was overwhelming enough. A tear made its way down my cheek, and I hurriedly brushed it away before he noticed.

"I need to know, Jack. I need to know what kind of connection she had with Moran and his family. The photo looks damning, but I can't—"

He took a hand from the steering wheel to clasp mine. "Are you afraid your mother's fatal car accident was really murder?"

The lump in my throat doubled in size, and I nodded. I was glad I didn't have to meet his gaze.

"Do you have anyone to ask?" he said softly.

I had no idea if he asked to make me angry enough to talk, but if he did the words worked. Another car nearly sideswiping us added to my fury. I pulled my hand loose and pushed his toward the wheel again. "No, and you already know that, Mr. Dossier Man. My mother and father are dead, two paternal grandparents deceased, two maternal grandparents lost in Alzheimer's. Both my parents only children—like me."

Jack chuckled. "Mr. Dossier Man?"

"I was being nice. You don't want to hear what I was actually thinking."

"I'm sure you're right."

Honestly, the man was a genius. The short exchange was enough to shatter all the tension locking down my brain and tongue. "The only relations I have are distant ones, and if I asked anyone about this I'd have to explain why I wanted to know. Until I have more information, I could unavoidably stain my mother's memory. I can't get additional info without telling people my suspicions."

"Or they could assume you're thinking your father killed her."

I stared out the windshield, ignoring the frantic lane changes in front of us. His words stopped my thoughts. Why hadn't I considered it already? "You're exactly right. I'm obviously blocking on this. I was thinking she may have been killed by the man in the photo. She apparently had ties to the family, after all. Though that brings up another puzzling issue. When Simon escaped, he told us Moran gave orders to protect me. Is Moran keeping me from being killed based on a connection to my mother, or does he want to question me on what I know?"

His hand rested on the stick shift. I placed a hand over his and turned to say, "I need to know if my mother's fatal car crash was truly an accident, or if my father was responsible for her death as a result of her relationship with this other man. Or if something else about her ties to Moran's family created a reason for her to die. Jack, I need your help. I know we're busy at the moment, but I believe this might be important."

We stopped for a traffic light. He turned his hand to clasp my fingers. "I believe that's an understatement. As you've already surmised, it begins to answer the question we've been asking for months about why Moran never had you killed when he had the chance."

"Yeah, I figured my father had the underground connections. I never figured on it being my mother."

"We don't know anything for sure, but it makes for a very intriguing twist," he said, squinting at the traffic before us. I wondered exactly what he was thinking.

"So you'll do some digging?"

The light turned. He kept his gaze straight ahead, but I could see him make the same half-smile he always did when he apologized for pissing me off. "At this point I would have regardless, but it makes it much easier when you're onboard with the idea."

"Something new and different."

He laughed at my quip, but sobered when I added, "You'll be careful. Right? This is my mother, after all."

"Absolutely. Trust me on this, Laurel. I'll do everything I can to guard your mother's reputation. However—"

He cursed as another car zipped in ahead of us and nearly sheared off our front end. After both our pulse rates returned to something closer to normal, he continued, "My bigger purpose is to protect you, and stop the art heist. I'll move as carefully as I can, but if it comes to a choice, I'm going to take whatever route I determine necessary to get us the information we need to stop a crime and keep you safe. I won't do anything to shine a bad light on your mother without reason, but you have to understand the priorities. Email me any pictures you have of the items, and I probably need to see everything when we get back to London."

As I nodded, the lump returned in my throat. But I knew I had to speak.

"Okay, I will." I took a deep breath. "I trust you, Jack. I trust you."

TWELVE

Rome police headquarters was as noisy and busy as any I'd seen in countless major cities in the world. While precinct houses aren't my favorite hangout, I admit to touring my fair share for business reasons. But I worked hard to make sure none of my pro bono "reclamation" work placed me behind bars in any of them.

The man charged with finding Tony B's killer was a compact dark-haired detective named Micelli. I was happy to learn he spoke excellent English. My Italian remained better suited to restaurants and parties than police stations. Micelli led us back to a small conference room.

"This seemed best to talk," Detective Micelli said, holding open the door and motioning for us to enter. It could have easily been an interrogation room except for the large smiling man sitting at the table.

"Roberto Nichetti is an artist," Micelli said, waving a hand toward the big man. "Roberto, *Signorina* Laurel Beacham...and Jack Hawkes you know."

Of course.

"Jack makes friends everywhere." I smiled to soften the jab, but I wondered what else he hadn't told me.

"Roberto and I go way back." Jack cocked a dark eyebrow at me, then grinned at Roberto. There was definitely a story there.

Micelli held out a chair for me before sitting on the other side of the wooden table with Roberto. Jack partnered up on my side.

Roberto opened a file and flipped out two sketches. They were colored pencil drawings. One of the drawings showed the Amazon full-faced. The other was in profile. Most police renderings I saw were variations on the Identikit-produced type. Both of Roberto's were excellent.

"These are very good," I said, pulling the sketches closer.

The Amazon's chin and jawline looked sharper than I remembered. "Her lower face wasn't this chiseled when I saw her. She may have been working out, to change her facial appearance." I wiggled a finger around the chin on both drawings. "This might be softened somewhat."

"Hawkes brought Roberto in," Micelli said, smiling. "He said this result would be better. Getting a drawing with color by his artist."

I looked to the side and nodded to Jack. "Good call. These look much more like her than I expected."

They truly did. The guard at the hospital apparently took pains to memorize characteristics when he checked her fake ID. There was more life to these pictures and a tinge of her hard edge which hadn't come through in the Scotland Yard image produced months ago.

"The security camera catching her leave showed she never removed her gloves," Jack said. "No chance anywhere of fingerprints."

"We have men watching all earlier videos," Micelli said. "We are to see if we can learn how she arrived and when."

I didn't hold out much hope this practice would lead to anything. From the frown on the detective's face, he likely agreed with me.

"Anything look different to you besides the jawline?" Jack asked. "Or is there anything to change?"

Roberto had given her hair an almost flat auburn. "The hair wasn't one solid color when I saw her. It was streaked with salon highlights to make it almost a fiery red. Not a cheap dye job either, I might add."

The artist went into a canvas bag at his feet and pulled out a big handful of pencils. He picked out several warm and gold tones and held them out to me. I chose a couple of orange shades, a jonquil yellow and a shimmery golden. With a nod, he quickly updated the hair and flipped the pictures back around for my opinion.

"Much better. You do need to check with the guard from yesterday. She may have changed her hair color after I saw her."

Micelli waved a hand. "*Non, non.* This is why you must come to see. Women spot these kinds of things. Little thing, but can help."

In a final touch, the artist had added the eyeglasses she'd tried to hide behind when I saw her in September. To the side was a note I knew said something about glasses in Italian, but I wasn't sure what. "This note." I pointed to it. "What does it say?"

"Officers are going to businesses selling this frame, hoping to locate information on the woman through her..." Micelli searched for his words. "Her eyesight script...prescription. The guard recognized the frames. His sister wears the designer."

I shook my head. "It's probably a waste of time. She wore these same frames when I saw her several months ago but the glass was clear. No need for a prescription."

Micelli let off a quiet string of curses, excusing himself to make a phone call. As soon as the door closed, Jack asked Roberto if he knew *il Carver.*

"He is...how you say? *Poof.*" Roberto's hands mimicked the kind of surprise gesture a magician used in a disappearing act.

"You mean gone?" I asked.

"*Sì.* Gone."

Roberto's supply of English seemed to be exhausted at this point, and he began speaking quickly in Italian. Jack switched languages, and their exchange became fast and quite animated.

I didn't know if Micelli knew about Jack's fluency, and I doubted either of the men wanted the detective to know about their current conversation. It had a kind of "let's keep this between us" air to it. To avoid being simply a decorative fixture in the room, I tuned out the talking and kept an eye on the narrow window in the door. I tapped Jack's arm when I saw Micelli returning.

"He's coming."

Jack said something quickly and Roberto nodded. I didn't know exactly what was said, but picked up enough to know they planned to meet later.

Everything wrapped up pretty quickly from there. Micelli thanked us for coming and offered to show us out, but asked the artist to stay behind. Jack and Roberto exchanged a look, and the detective interpreted it as concern.

"Is nothing. Don't worry," Micelli said. "We want to give time for changes. For when scans are made, make sure all come out dark enough."

"It's fine," Jack said quickly. "We had talked about lunch. We'll get together some other time before Laurel and I leave Rome."

Roberto followed Jack's cue and said, "*Sì, is buono.*"

"Call me when you're free," Jack told him.

"Oh, here." Micelli passed each of us a business card. "If you think of anything later, call my cellphone."

I keyed the number into my phone. We said goodbye, then retraced our steps back through the building.

On the street I glanced around, as was becoming my new habit. Rome has a lot of people on its sidewalks in a typical day, but I didn't see an Amazon anywhere. I wondered how many people were in her contingent. At least her and one other. Someone else was driving the getaway car at the hospital and the second vehicle last night.

"Did the Amazon escape last night in the same car as you saw on the hospital security footage?" I asked Jack.

He shook his head. "Last night was a sports car. Probably stolen."

We neared our Fiat, and I brought up the other video. "Are you not going to share the attempted kidnapping video and Nico's information with Micelli? What happened last night to Nico could tangibly be related to Tony B's murder."

"I agree, but at the moment I can't conclusively prove it. Tony B wasn't a forger. *Il Carver* was. Last night's skirmish could be the result of professional jealousies. We only know what *il Carver* told Nico, and we could be swayed by the fact that what he said ties closely to the information we already believe."

"You aren't going to suppress the video, though, right? We could work the angle ourselves, but we're getting stretched pretty thin."

He gave a tired chuckle. "Yeah, pretty thin. No, I'm considering contacting a friend in MI-6. The suspicious deaths cover more than Italy, and the only way they tie with Tony B's death is if we assume so."

"Pretty coincidental." Though bright sunlight felt good, I was grateful I hadn't packed my coat in my checked bag.

"True. We have to keep all of this in a manageable sequence if we can. I do need to contact my friend in the Italian military police."

"The one who was with you and Nico at the hospital?"

"Right." The car was in sight, and Jack clicked the fob to unlock the doors. "We have some time to kill until Roberto is able to call me."

"I didn't really follow your conversation," I said. "Did he have any information?"

"Maybe. We needed a little more time to talk, to correlate what names I have with which ones he knows. By the way, thanks for speaking up when you saw Micelli."

I climbed in. He shut my door and walked around to the driver's side.

"From your reaction, I take it Micelli doesn't know how well you speak Italian," I said as Jack settled into his seat.

He grinned at me and started the car.

"What's the scoop on Roberto?" I asked.

"He's an artist I met years ago. Nice guy." Jack looked away as he spoke, busy gauging an opportunity to merge into traffic.

"And..."

The mostly back view of his shoulders shrugged. He zipped out ahead of a white delivery truck. We heard a crescendo of horns, but our car remained unscathed. When we were comfortably in traffic, he said, "Roberto may have done a little counterfeiting work I may have kept silent about once all the money was confiscated."

It might sound unethical, but one of the ways to get people to help in work like ours is to look the other way sometimes when a crime is committed by someone who isn't a hardened criminal. Second chances often help develop great sources for future information.

He looked at his watch. "It's early for lunch. I'd go back to the hotel, but—"

"If Nico is working he won't want us around. If he isn't, he'll be asleep, which I don't want to do anything to disrupt either. Cranky tech guys aren't one of my favorite things."

"Does he know?"

"Yes, and he couldn't care less."

He laughed. "Nico really does call whatever shots he wants, doesn't he?"

"As long as he uses his superpowers to help me, I'll let him keep his attitude," I said. "He never fails to come through in the clutch."

"Do you think it's due to loyalty or egotism?"

"I absolutely know it's a combination of the two. As long as I keep Nico challenged, I'll be able to keep him. If he does anything slightly non-kosher, he does it to accomplish a necessary goal. He expects not to have to defend his actions, and I won't argue with him. If he wants to be cranky, I won't argue on that front either." I didn't know if this was for conversation or he wanted confirmation, but I was glad when my cellphone rang and I could change the subject.

I expected Micelli calling us with another question, but Caller ID showed a U.K. number I didn't recognize. I gasped. "Hello?" Adrenalin shot through my veins, terror that something happened to Cassie.

A male voice with a clipped British accent asked, "Is this Laurel Beacham?"

"Yes, who is this?" I almost screamed out "How's Cassie?" but thankfully he answered first and saved me embarrassment and worry.

"I'm Lincoln Ferguson. I report for the BBC and wanted to interview you about the recent recovery of the National Gallery masterpiece. Megan Jenkins said you need to reschedule and I want to follow-up."

He sounded sincere, maybe too much so. My radar hit high-alert. "How did you get my number?"

"Oh, right. I went by the foundation office first and saw the door sealed."

In my mind, I could imagine the crime scene tape stretched across the nailed-shut black door. If he'd called the foundation number, Cassie would have answered, and she wouldn't have given out my number to a reporter. He obviously had a good police source. Aloud, I said, "A bit of misadventure on someone's part and we're closed now for renovation. I'll be sure to contact you when I get back to London."

"You're out of the country the day after the break-in?" he asked,

He already knew too much, as I'd suspected. "I have an extremely packed schedule at the moment, Mr. Ferguson. I'm away more than I'm home. And I apologize, but I need to end this call now to attend a meeting."

"I understand. I appreciate your time, Ms. Beacham."

"Goodbye, Mr. Ferguson." I hung up on the call and groaned. "Great, now the press has wind of Simon's escapade."

Jack shot me a sympathetic look. "Did you really think something like that could stay away from the press? They'd jump on it out of concern for a terrorist angle if nothing else."

"Gee thanks, nothing like upping the ante," I said, shoving the phone into the Fendi. "I was hoping for a big news week after the holiday, so everything about me and the foundation got hidden. It'd be nice to actually get back to London before I have to put out publicity fires." I blew out a long breath. "I should never have told Megan Jenkins I would do that interview. Now I have a reporter on my tail who's looking at stories in two different directions."

"At least one of the directions is positive. You should be applauded for your success at recovering the painting."

I shook my head. "You know as well as I do that kind of public praise causes new headaches."

"Yeah." He patted my thigh. "Trying to make you feel better." He changed lanes and asked, "Did he tell you who gave out your number?"

"No, but he segued into having seen the office break-in, so I imagine through police contacts."

"Could it have been Megan?"

I laughed. "No way. She knows me too well. She would have called on his behalf first."

"Be sure to tell Whatley."

"No need. I don't want to tattle. It isn't hard to find anyone if a reporter is conscientious enough, and Lincoln Ferguson probably is."

Jack snorted. "Lincoln Ferguson? I'd say so."

"You know him?"

He nodded. "Up-and-comer trying to make his mark. Since you're American, think Anderson Cooper on his rise up, but without the famous mother. I'd lay you odds he wasn't the scheduled interviewer on the masterpiece's return, and got on this when he learned about the frontal attack on the foundation office."

"This does not sound good."

"No, it doesn't. Stay on your toes around the guy."

Our little car glided up to a stoplight and Jack said, "Back to the original conversation. Have any errands to run, or want to see something while we're waiting?"

I checked my cell to see if there was a message from the airlines saying I could pick up my bag. Nothing. "I could buy some clothes. But between this outfit and the backup in my carry-on, I'm probably good as long as I use hotel laundry services each night."

"How about deciding on another hotel?"

I shook my head. "We kind of left the job with Nico. If we switch things up now, and he does too, it's counterproductive and will likely tick him off."

"True."

The light changed and we resumed forward movement.

"We're close to the Santa Maria della Pace," I said. "I'd love to see Raphael's *Sibyls* in the chapel there. It isn't real touristy, especially in January."

"Will it be open?"

"If it isn't, the custodian is at the cloister next door. Easy to find him and ask to be let inside."

"Sounds good."

Minutes later we were at the church complex. The doors to the chapel were locked, and we headed to the cloister, or Chiostro del Bramante, which was a second treat. The cloister was the inner central design element in what was originally a complex comprised of a monastery and the adjacent church. The design reflected Renaissance ideas and the period's proportioned concepts of harmony and equilibrium. The space even inspired Michelangelo.

I was ready for a caffeine fix, and suggested going by the café on the second floor before we looked for the custodian. Minutes later, coffee in hand, I said, "Come on. We'll go stand by the window in the lounge. We can get a first glimpse of the *Sibyls* from there."

The lounge was a short distance past the café, and my favorite window in the world was exactly as I recalled. The view looked into the chapel and perfectly framed Raphael's fresco. Five hundred years old and it continued to wow me, even from a distance.

Original in its time due to Raphael's use of the church wall's full height to create a two-story representation of the prophets and sibyls, the work elevated already great architecture and delivered iconic status. Raphael complemented the supporting arch of the chapel with the grouped forms of the four seated sibyls as they received angelic instruction. He complemented the vertical windows by using the standing prophets to mirror the architectural effect.

"No matter how many times I see this work, I'm always amazed at his talent to give an illusion of space to the characters through his pier structure method."

"You're—"

My cell rang, cutting off Jack's response. He held my coffee as I dug in the Fendi for my phone.

"It's Cassie," I said, then answered. "Hi. Did you find anything in the office?"

"No, it was as I thought," she said. "The police nailed the front shut yesterday, and we went in through the back door."

"Yeah, I knew about the door. Had a phone call today from a reporter who went by and saw it."

"A new problem?"

"We'll see," I said. "Tell me about anything you found inside during the search."

"Simon and his crew pulled a bunch of files from the cabinets and your desk, but I looked pretty carefully and didn't notice anything missing."

"Was the carpet pulled up anywhere? The walls—"

"Nothing," she said. "Pretty counterproductive overall."

"When's your flight?"

Jack handed back my cup.

"Not until five. The New York office booked me a hotel room."

"Max is going to love having you on hand," I said, turning back to the window and the lovely view. "Make sure he doesn't get used to it."

She laughed. "No worries. Look, I called because I need to talk to Nico."

"He was going to call you. He overnighted your charm bracelet. I figured to New York, but I didn't actually ask."

"Yeah, I would assume the same thing. I've tried to call him off and on for the last twenty minutes and it keeps going to voicemail."

"He probably crashed. Last night started out with a meeting for him, but ended up with two goons chasing him and the people he'd been with. One ended up in the hospital. Nico is okay, just tired."

"Oh, good. I kept calling and calling. He's always woken up before after multiple calls. Must have really been wiped out."

"Exactly, I—" I stopped breathing and stared at Jack. He grabbed my coffee from me again, and I saw my hand was shaking. I clutched his arm and squeezed as I worked to keep my voice steady. "Cassie, I'll go check on him and have him call you. Don't worry."

"Okay. It would help if I could talk to him before I leave. I need to know how to do something computer-wise, and I think he can save me some steps."

"I'll call you—or he'll call you soon. Bye." I hung up and said, "Nico isn't waking up for calls. We didn't check his pot of coffee like you did ours. We need to get back to the hotel."

I snatched both cups from Jack, tossed them into a trashcan, and fast walked down the cloister.

"Laurel, wait."

"Come on, Jack. He could be drugged, or worse." My words caught on a sob, and I felt my cheeks wet with tears. I wiped them away with my gloves and changed to a slow jog.

"Wait!" Jack put a hand on my shoulder to slow me down. "I checked the pot at the door. Before I brought it to the table. I had another stir stick. You and Nico were talking and didn't notice me testing it."

I sagged against the wall in relief. "Thank goodness. The awful fears I had."

"Maybe it's a phone glitch because she's not in Italy."

"Could be," I said, hitting his number with my auto-dialer. The call went to voicemail. "No luck."

"We've had more than our share of monsters popping out at us lately." Jack pulled the keys from his pocket. "Do you want to go and check to be sure?"

"I know I sound silly, but I really do," I said. "If he's asleep we can go ahead and pack up and pick where we're going to stay tonight."

My cell rang.

"I didn't realize I had my ringer turned off," Nico said. "What did you need? Then I should call Cassie."

"Call Cassie," I said, relief making me almost woozy. "She's been trying to reach you."

"Okay, but if you're done with the police, come on back. I've found something and I want to show you before I go to sleep."

"Will do."

A short time later, we were stepping off the elevator and doing a quick detour around two men in cleaning uniforms with a big laundry cart filled with sheets.

Jack got the green light with the keycard and opened our hotel room door. I entered the suite and stopped in my tracks. The room was complete chaos. Nico's computers were gone.

I raced to one bedroom. Jack headed for another.

Nico was nowhere to be found.

THIRTEEN

"Jack, those guys—"

He dashed out the door.

The elevator closed before Jack reached the men, and he disappeared down the stairwell. Thinking we needed to take it from every angle, I rushed to the elevator and hit the call button, grabbing my cell from the Fendi as the elevator signal dinged for the opposite car. I squeezed through as the doors opened. There were already six people and luggage in the car, but I ignored everything and repeatedly pounded the close button on the panel. I prayed the two guys would have to stop at a couple of floors and get stalled in the other lift. When I hit the main floor I ran to the front door, knowing Jack would cover the service area. A black van pulled out of the alley. I raced toward it. The driver saw me. It was one of the cart guys. He peeled out, leaving behind an inch of rubber.

I hurriedly snapped a picture of the license plate.

"Did you get it?" Jack asked as he appeared beside me.

"Yeah." It was clear enough to see the numbers. "Let's get the car."

Seconds later we were back on the road, but the van had vanished.

"Track his mobile," Jack said, shifting quickly around a lumbering sedan.

Nico's GPS location showed up back at the hotel location. "It's not with him. It must be in the room."

"Bloody hell—"

I had the brainstorm. "My charm!"

"He had it in his pocket," Jack responded.

"Check the app!"

He tossed me his phone. "It's the one at the top. God, I hope he didn't change the frequency."

"If he did, he would have sent you a new app. Nico can do this kind of stuff in his sleep." I felt a lump form in my throat and forced a deep breath to calm me down. We didn't have time for anxiety.

"Here, I've got it," I said. "Looks like we need to turn at the next block. Should I call Micelli?"

Jack blew out his cheeks, then cursed when another car cut him off from the turn he needed to take. He muscled his way back into the lane, and we were speeding away again.

"Yeah, call Micelli. I'd like to handle this ourselves, in case we need to get in under the radar, but we can't take the chance. Send him your shot of the vehicle's plates."

I kept an eye on the screen app while I used my cell to connect with the detective. Jack couldn't help himself from trying to watch the van's progress and kept glancing over. "Keep your eyes on the road. I'll tell you if they turn again."

The car rocked through traffic like a dingy in the high seas. If I wasn't already scared to death we were going to lose Nico, the ride would have likely pushed me over the edge. As it was, I held on to my phone with one hand and kept a tight grip on Jack's cell with the other, to keep an eye on the blinking dot that taunted us.

After a short time on hold, Micelli answered. I told the detective what had transpired in the last few minutes and explained I'd sent the picture to the email address on his business card. Jack kept us running in the direction the silver charm headed.

"Do you know where they're going?" Micelli asked.

"No. Can you see if the registration from the plate tells you anything? In case the van isn't stolen."

"I'll try, but probably it is stolen and the plate's worthless," he said. "I will get someone on this and call you back. Where are you?"

"Jack, he wants to know where we are."

I held up the phone. Jack shouted out the cross streets in Italian and added in English, "Get someone to track this mobile, Micelli. Send units the direction we're headed."

Times like this were why I knew Hawkes wasn't your average art recovery expert.

"I'll leave this line open," I said to the detective. "Let me know when you have anything we can use. We'll listen for sirens."

"Very good," Micelli said. "Wait for the *polizia*. Do not go in alone."

"I hear you." I didn't necessarily agree with him. It would all depend on how fast they got their uniformed asses in place. I didn't want to lie, but I sure didn't want to tell him the truth.

"Good," Micelli responded.

Jack obviously caught what my message truly meant, however, because he turned and shot me a wink.

What was this winking business all of a sudden? I let it go. It was better than talking and letting Micelli in on what he was missing.

A patchwork-colored teeny car—well, smaller than ours—cut us off, and Jack hit the brakes and wheeled wildly to grab some new space somewhere. I reached over and laid on the horn.

"You know no one in this country even hears a horn anymore," Jack said, shimmying into place and hitting the gas again.

"Someone must or we wouldn't hear them going off all the time." My gaze stayed fixed on the blinking dot. "Besides, it made me feel better."

Jack laughed. "Well, there's reason enough then."

"Damn straight."

The dot turned. "Take a right in..." I looked up and tried to calculate distance. "Probably three streets."

We moved back behind the jerk who cut us off a moment before and I checked each side street as we passed. The area was changing over to light industrial, and the buildings were seguing from retail shops and tourist draws to less flashy storefronts and small warehouses. The dot kept moving on the screen, but slower.

"Turn here?" he asked.

"Yeah, I think so."

Ahead of us the street gave way to a larger industrial park. It wasn't one like in the U.S., all carefully designed and built to one plan. This space incorporated older bricked buildings with newer warehouse construction, but everything was within a tall fence. I wondered if we were driving into a trap. But we had no choice.

"Do you see the van?" he asked, then he shouted, "Micelli, are you there? We're in some kind of industrial trade zone."

There was no response from the detective, but I could tell we weren't cut off. I answered Jack, "No, there are too many trucks." I looked at the screen. The dot made a left turn. "They went left up here. Maybe if I get out and run ahead—"

"Hell no. You stay with me."

I didn't like the way this conversation was going, given the fact we might have official ears listening in. I pretended to drop my phone under the seat to keep Micelli from hearing and whispered. "What are we going to do? You left your gun in the safe, right?"

He nodded, eyes still firmly forward. "Don't look right now— keep helping me spot the van—but do you have anything in your bag of tricks to use as a weapon? Can you feel around for something?"

"I have some sharp things—" The dot turned again. "They took another left. A block or so. We would be able to see them if we weren't surrounded by large vehicles and warehouses."

"If this car wasn't so bloody small."

Yes, the Fiat definitely had height issues.

Jack turned again, and we found we were leaving through a back exit. Ahead we saw the van. Both of us shrieked. I fished under the seat to retrieve my phone.

"Micelli! Micelli! Are you there?"

A second later: "*Sì*. I am here."

"We found the van. We're following it. Are you tracking us?"

"*Sì*. You should see cars and hear sirens."

"Nothing. No lights, no sirens."

Our Fiat got closer. We were only one car away from the dark van. The street was filled with working vehicles, and our mini-wheeled vehicle was overshadowed by the heavy trucks.

"They are coming," Micelli said. "Don't do anything dangerous."

Jack's face looked like he was about to blow. My phone sailed back under the seat. I hoped any conversation Micelli heard wasn't clear enough to understand. Or could be held against us.

The oncoming lane emptied for a moment, and we swung in, accelerating and shifting quickly enough to make the car roar in protest. I didn't need to watch the dot on the screen anymore and dove into the Fendi looking for potential weapons while I had the chance.

I pulled out a heavy silver cuff bracelet. "Can you use this like brass knuckles?"

He took a quick glance and nodded. "See if you can flatten it a little."

I put it in the floorboard and stomped it a couple of times with my foot. Holding it up again, I said, "A little better. I have my travel-sized hairspray too."

Through the speaker, I heard Micelli sputtering. I started to ask where our backup was, but in the same instant I finally heard sirens. As did the occupants of the van. The vehicle accelerated again. Jack followed suit.

Out of nowhere, a truck came at us. We were going to get T-boned.

Jack slammed on the brakes and twisted the wheel hard to the right. The truck turned left. The metal on the sides of both vehicles met and screamed in protest through the skid. The impact propelled us into the side of a flatbed truck parked for loading. Our Fiat slid under the bed. A split second later, we finally stopped. Our windshield sat a mere inch away from the steel frame of the flatbed. We were alive. With luck, Nico was too.

I scrambled out my side and dragged the Fendi behind me.

Jack's cell was in my hand, but mine remained somewhere on the floorboard of the car. It didn't matter.

Jack sent out a few choice curse words as he wiggled out of my side of the car.

"Are you okay?" I asked.

"Yes." He grunted. "I feel like a square peg trying to work through a round hole."

"I think the opening is more a warped pentagon," I rambled. Then I saw the blood. "Your hand—"

He gripped the frame with the injured hand and pulled free of the Fiat. "It's nothing," he said, wiping the blood onto his jeans. "It's my neck and shoulder we need to worry about."

"I can call—"

The truck suddenly roared to life and raced away. The vehicle fishtailed for a second, belched out a dark plume of smoke from the tailpipe, and disappeared in traffic. We didn't even get a license number or a good look at the driver.

"Well, he's obviously not waiting for the police to make a report," Jack said.

"Neither should we." I ran in the direction the van headed. "I don't know if the truck driver is part of this whole crazy thing or not. Maybe he's had a few with lunch and didn't want to risk a DUI. Come on, let's find the van."

Jack hurried alongside me, holding his injured left hand and arm rigid across his chest.

"You're sure you don't need a doctor?" I said.

"The police will be here momentarily and will have questions. Let's move."

Watching the dot, we traced their route, west for a moment, followed by north again. The flashing light kept us company. Sirens blared from every direction, but we stayed focused on the dot as it slowed to a stop.

"They've stopped," I said. "They could be changing vehicles."

"Bloody hell."

Trucks rumbled by, blocking our views. We split up to try

triangulating to catch the van between us, but as we rounded our respective corners the dark vehicle zoomed away, moving too fast for us to catch or follow on foot.

"Looks like Nico's rescue is up to the *polizia* now," Jack said.

I showed him the screen. "Maybe not." The blinking dot remained fixed in place.

Breaks in traffic revealed Nico wasn't on the other side of the street.

We ran across, hopeful he was hiding somewhere nearby. Until we saw the package abutting the curb. It was a small brown envelope, sealed, with Nico's name printed on the outside. Behind it on the curb were several dark drops looking suspiciously like blood. The sidewalk sported a number of recent scuffmarks, like a struggle had occurred.

"Damn." I seriously wanted to cry or break something. Preferably break someone.

"Wait a minute." Jack picked up the package and held it as he rotated in a full circle. The lot in front of us sported partial construction. Beside it was a building already tagged for demolition. A storefront business took the block across the street. Another sat beside the construction site.

"What are you thinking?"

We could hear the sirens screaming closer and stop back in the area of our accident.

"Oh no," I said. "They aren't chasing the van. They're homed in on my cell in the wrecked car." I felt the pit of my stomach drop even further. No one knew where Nico was.

Jack, however, didn't seem phased at all. Rather, he was on alert. "Look at the scuffs."

"By the blood?"

He nodded. With a few long strides he crossed the construction. He turned and looked again in each direction.

"What are you thinking?" I asked.

"I'm thinking there's no way they would have known to toss out this package."

"Unless they had a transmission detector, and the charm set it off."

"True." Jack kept turning, staring hard in every direction. "But if that was the case, why did they wait to test for a transmitter?"

"They finally realized they were being followed electronically?"

"Or they never checked, and they didn't know this package even existed." He put the envelope into a front pocket of his jeans. "Come on." He jogged toward the boarded-up building and the door sporting a hefty-looking padlock.

"You think he's in there?" I whispered.

"I think he's somewhere nearby." Jack kept his voice low. "I think they dropped him off around here, and if they didn't leave someone to guard him, we may be able to get to him before they return."

"What if Nico is here but being watched?"

"We may be able to overpower the guard. Help me look for something to break this lock."

"You do remember I'm carrying a set of picklocks?"

His laughter was the silent kind, showing how stressed he was.

I started working on the lock, and Jack blocked me from the view of anyone passing. He explained his reasoning. "I think he was dragged out of the van, maybe fighting with them and the charm fell out onto the ground. I think they didn't want to be caught with a kidnap victim when they heard the police sirens approaching and there's a good chance we'll find him inside."

"I hope you're right."

"Me too."

Less than half a minute later the lock snapped open. I handed Jack the cuff I'd flattened in the car and a mini-flashlight I kept in the Fendi. He put the cuff over the knuckles on his right hand. I slipped my purse strap over my head to make it lay cross-body, leaving my hands free to carry hairspray in my left and the sharp pick in my right.

A cat yowled as it streaked out of the darkness and disappeared around the corner. I jumped in fright. Jack paused a moment. I didn't know if it was to get his pulse rate back down to normal or to let his eyes adjust to the near darkness.

The odor of mold and rotting wood permeated the space. Also the nasally irritating smell of urine and some kind of chemical odor. I wondered about squatters and if there were more cats. Or worse.

When Jack moved again, his steps were careful. The wooden floor was broken in places and trash and construction debris littered the room, making us pick our steps. He turned to check all directions with the flashlight before he let me enter further into the space. I stayed with my back angled to his, to keep an eye on the door as we moved deeper inside. Closing the door again would have been safer, but I wanted our exit kept accessible for a fast break. Conversely, I had no desire for someone to slip in behind and catch us unawares.

A few feet in and we heard a kind of rustling scramble sound behind a half wall. I wondered about rats after seeing the cat. Jack used his flashlight hand to warn me to stop. He moved way out and around to see what was there without being close enough to be taken by surprise.

When he rushed behind the wall, I knew he'd found Nico.

"Are you okay?" Jack and I chorused when we finally got the gag from his mouth.

Nico started to nod, then groaned. "I ache all over."

"Did they knock you unconscious?" Jack asked.

"No. They hit me on the head, but it was mostly to overpower me. Tied me up and carried me away in a laundry cart. I could barely move, and they gagged me until we were in the van."

"We saw you leaving, but didn't realize at the time what was going on," I said, working on the knotted ropes at his wrists while Jack fought the ones at his ankles.

"They came into the room with a master key?" Jack asked.

"Yes. One second I was working on the laptop, and the next they were in the door, one restraining me while the other seized the equipment. I had my phone in my hand, and I tossed it under the side chair, so they would not have my contacts and data."

"They stole the computers," I said.

"*Pfft,* I have it..." He tapped his forehead, "...all here. They were hired muscle, and the one grabbing my gear said not to hurt me."

"To ransom you or to get information out of you?" Jack asked.

"I don't know, but it gave me the idea to pretend to have a concussion in the vehicle. They removed the gag when I moaned and let my eyes roll back. I forced myself to vomit. Between my being sick and the *polizia,* they changed plans."

"Good thinking."

Jack and I supported Nico between us.

"We must hurry," Nico said. "They dropped me here and are coming back as soon as they're able to lose the *polizia* and get another vehicle. Where's your car?"

"We don't have a car," Jack said, sliding his head through the opening to check outside.

"Why? You were behind—"

"A truck hit us," I said. "The police should be close by. They were tracking my phone, and it's still in the car. We can report everything and get a ride to the hotel. Or do you need to go to the hospital?"

"No hospital," Nico said. "Twice in twenty-four hours is too much."

Well, he obviously wasn't okay. He was dragging his left leg for one thing. I planned to take a closer look when we hit sunlight.

Jack gave the all-clear, and we moved out in tandem. I stopped to close the door and relock it.

"Come on," Nico said.

"Go, I'll catch up." I finished pushing the heavy plywood door and held it with my body while I worked the latch and the lock. Seconds later, I was back supporting Nico's other side. "If we'd left it wide open, they would have known to look for you without checking there first. This will buy us a few minutes."

"A few minutes may not matter," Jack muttered. "With all of this traffic, they could be on us any time and we'd never know."

Nonetheless, to be safe we took a second to get our bearings before hurrying in the direction of where we'd last seen our car. Nico hobbled as fast as he could, and his ankle seemed to loosen up a little as we moved. He said, "I found something before the guys came in. Another forger in Cologne, Germany. He died a few weeks ago, but his cousin is someone we've used before."

My mind ran quickly through names. "Do you mean Ralf?"

"Yes, their fathers were brothers," Nico said. "When we get back to the hotel I will pull up the details about his relative with my cell and send it to you. I sent a text to Ralf already. The GPS on his phone confirms he's in Cologne at his old neighborhood, but there was no reply before I was kidnapped."

Ralf Burkhard and I shared a skill set, but his was much more highly developed than mine. And used more often. A trained acrobat and adrenalin junkie, he'd performed across Europe and Asia in his teens. Until he learned about five years ago he could gain a significant raise in annual income by working as an upper stories man—yes, a cat burglar—with a team of thieves. I'd learned a lot from studying his techniques to use in my own "reclamation" projects, though he was unaware of my interest. He only knew me as someone he could trust when he wanted to pass information into the hands of law enforcement without his name being associated. I assumed I'd been used for his gang's purposes before, to get competition behind bars and out of the way. But the projected outcome always matched my own objective, and I justified leaving him free to work another day.

Besides, he stayed away from art. He simply reported on others who stole it.

"If we don't hear from Ralf before we separate, I'll try to contact him myself," I said. "What's his cousin's name?"

"Jürgen. Same surname."

"I've heard the name Burkhard before," Jack said. "Isn't Ralf connected to the group run by Charlie Wallz?"

"If we're keeping this off the record, yes," I said. "Otherwise, no comment."

"Will he talk about his relative?"

"Good question." Ralf had never discussed his family members with me, though I already knew he had several cousins in shady lines of work. He may have not replied to the text because of an innate suspicion about talking outside his circle, despite the fact it was impossible for anyone to arrest this relative. "I may need to brainstorm ways to persuade Ralf to meet us if he proves resistant to the idea."

We stopped to let several vehicles pass before the street was clear enough to cross. I felt exposed, wondering if the dastardly duo had hijacked another car already and would be by at any second. "We need to get off the main thoroughfare."

"Not much choice until we get out of this industrial park."

There was that.

"I suppose the next thing is for us to catch a flight to Cologne," I said.

"Night train through France or Switzerland would be better," Jack replied. "Less chance of us being noticed. Not a perfect plan, but better."

Nico shook his head. "Go whichever way you want, but I agree with Jack. You're supposed to pre-book a couple of days ahead, but I can probably take care of it."

"Are you staying here in Rome?" I asked him.

"No, I'm going to New York," Nico replied. "This is getting too dangerous. Cassie doesn't need to be alone, whatever the safeguards she's promised to take."

"Good point," Jack said. "Are you sure you should fly alone?"

"Give me a cellphone."

I handed over Jack's, and we moved into the shadows between two buildings. Nico leaned against the brick wall and his fingers flew over the screen. He gave the device back to me after a couple of minutes. His voice sounded weaker when he said, "Call Cassie. Tell her I got both of us on a later flight. I emailed her an e-ticket to use instead of the one she was originally scheduled to fly. I got both of us in first class."

Max was going to have another fit. Aloud I said, "First, I'm calling Micelli and getting us picked up here. You're not walking another step."

Before I could do so, however, a dark sedan barreled around the corner and headed toward the empty building.

"This way," Jack said, moving us into the alley.

"Should we hide behind some of these dumpsters and crates?" I asked.

"Be the first place they look. We need to keep moving. They'll be looking for Nico traveling alone. They have no idea we found him."

"Thank goodness for the charm," I said.

"Yes," Nico said. "My little idea seems to be tracking everyone but you."

On the other side of the alley, we crossed the street. A closed shop front used a lock on its door I knew I could easily open. Jack looked for alarm wires, but the place seemed to be deserted. Apparently the owner assumed no need for security expenses on an empty building. I went to work. Minutes later, we huddled inside, hidden in the side shadows, watching for any sign of the dark sedan.

Within minutes, the sedan returned and parked almost out of sight. The two enormous bruisers we'd seen earlier in the hotel hallway entered the alley we had just left.

Jack cocked an eyebrow and tilted his head for his "I told you so" look.

I dialed the number for Micelli and tossed the phone to Nico. "Stay hidden, but keep a lookout and report their movements. Tell Micelli our current location as close as you can. Tell him to track Jack's phone by GPS if necessary."

The number on caller ID was Jack's, and I knew Micelli would pick up for that reason alone. The detective barked in English. The conversation switched to Italian when Nico responded.

The place was practically bare to the walls. We moved to the back and foraged for anything to use as a weapon. I spotted a couple of two by fours behind a half wall and motioned for Jack to help me.

As far as defensive measures went, we didn't have much. It never stopped us before. When we returned to the front and slipped in next to Nico, he finished with the call. I caught myself holding my breath.

The two hoods exited the alley and stopped on the sidewalk, directly across from our hideout. They looked up and down the street. One talked a lot with his hands. The other stood quietly and glared at our window, pointing.

Jack pushed me back against the sidewall and Nico dived for the floor.

"Get ready," Jack said, moving away from me and hefting his two by four. "I'll get to the door and try to hit them when they come in. You two stay together, and bash them if they head your way."

In other words, if they take out Jack.

"Call Micelli back," I told Nico. "Tell him to get his ass here now!"

Nico had already hit redial.

As Micelli answered, we heard sirens again. The thugs stopped dead center in the road and stared at one another. A truck zipped by. The arm-waver started talking after it passed, but the quiet one punched his shoulder and pointed to the car. Their trajectory shifted and they raced back to the sedan. We could see flashing lights down the street when the pair roared away.

Three police cars tore down the street and blocked traffic in front of our hideout. Jack was the first to move, pitching the timber back near where we'd found it and twisting the lock to get out. I helped Nico hobble out. Jack was in a heated discussion with one of the officers, but another got the message, jumped in his patrol car, hit lights and siren, and tore off in pursuit of the sedan.

I stepped forward and broke up the argument between Jack and the remaining officer. "We would appreciate a ride back to our wrecked vehicle." Turning to Nico, I added, "Feel free to translate if necessary."

FOURTEEN

Rome *polizia* are pretty good cabbies. Two officers stayed to search the alley and the abandoned building while the third herded us into a patrol car and returned us to the wrecked Fiat. Of course, the truck driver who caused the accident was gone, but several eyewitnesses offered a description to the frustrated police. Of both the guilty driver and of us. When we finally showed up, the law enforcement team's frustration was colored over with anger. Eventually all the questions were answered and reports completed, and I got my phone from the Fiat—immediately ahead of the tow truck driver set on hauling the vehicle away. We called a cab to get back to the hotel. We might have caught another ride in a patrol car, but Micelli wasn't particularly happy with us anymore, and neither Jack nor I wanted to risk ending up at the police station again.

When we hit the hotel lobby I sent the guys up to the room and sidetracked to the concierge.

"We had a small traffic accident," I explained to the kind-eyed man behind the desk. "Does the hotel have a doctor on call who could be sent to our room?"

There wasn't one on the premises, but the concierge assured me a Dr. Cordova would arrive soon to look at both guys. When I got upstairs, Nico was crashed on the couch, his injured foot propped on the arm. Jack pulled the side chair away from the wall to more easily retrieve my power geek's amazing cell phone. With no computer paraphernalia scattered across their surfaces, and the left-behind power cords littering the floor, the tables looked bare and forlorn.

I knew the screens were only taken while they scooped up everything in their path, but the kidnappers having the laptop worried me. "You don't think they can follow up on what you were doing with your computer?" I asked Nico.

"No. Once they closed the cover it went to standby. From this point, they need my thumbprint to access data on it. Any attempt at a hack will trigger a self-destruct program for the hard drive."

"I'm glad you're on our side," Jack said, tossing the device to him.

I gave Jack back his own cell, before pulling out mine and heading for my bedroom to call Cassie. "There should be a doctor here shortly. His name's Cordova. I don't suppose I need to tell you to ask for ID before you let him in."

The next half hour went quickly. My conversation with Cassie was short but informative.

"Do you think the truck was sent to kill you?" she asked after hearing the latest news.

"I honestly don't know. Everyone here drives so crazy I'm amazed anytime we go anywhere and aren't killed. At the time, we'd completely kept our attention on the van. Someone could have shadowed our car without us even noticing. However, my money is on a coincidence as far as the car accident goes."

"Any ideas about who's behind Nico's kidnapping?"

"Not sure. The fact Nico was simply tied up and taken with his equipment implies they may not know exactly what they're looking for. Or it may all be related to his adventure last night."

One handed, I shifted my carry-on from the luggage stand to the bed. The bulk of my luggage in baggage-handler jail meant I had little to pack, but I needed to get moving. The room received maid service while we were gone. Real maid service. I wondered what she'd thought when she saw the state of the suite's front room.

"Speaking of which," I said. "Anything you forgot to mention earlier about the office search, and did you learn anything from

Scotland Yard about Nelly?" Hard to believe only twenty-four hours had passed since we'd found the restorer attacked in her flat.

"Whatley said they're continuing to gather information, but what little he did tell me points to concern she was a smuggler who slipped master works in and out of different countries," Cassie said. "You have to admit, she had the knowledge to disguise an object as something essentially worthless until it got through customs. Later, reverse the process and deliver it to whomever she worked for. I hate to admit it, but it wouldn't be hard for someone well-versed in art history and restoration. It would simply take nerve."

With Cassie's own background in this level of expertise, I couldn't resist a poke. "You're talking pretty confidently. I shouldn't be worried, should I?"

She laughed. "Remember, I said it would take nerve. I'd be stuttering and begging forgiveness before anyone even caught me."

"Good. I'd hate to have to be a character witness at your trial," I said, then mused, "I just find it hard to believe it of Nelly. I wonder if money was the lure or if she was blackmailed. Has she talked to anyone yet?"

"Her condition remains critical. They say it's touch and go for the next few days."

"I hope Whatley has a guard posted at the door of her room. Despite the fact it didn't help Tony B."

"He does," she said. "He said Jack already called and briefed him on what happened in Rome."

Interesting. Jack hadn't mentioned he'd spoken to Whatley or been given an update on Nelly. For that matter, I wasn't sure when we'd been separated long enough for him to make contact without my noticing. Maybe before he went to bed last night, or this morning when I was in the bathroom refreshing my makeup ahead of leaving to meet Micelli at police headquarters.

She continued, "Nothing else to report about the break in. No anomalies showed up on the X-rays of the floors or walls. Whatley emailed the images for me to review on my own. No hidden caches."

Another round of dead ends. "Did they at least identify the dead guy who tried to kill Nelly?"

"Not yet. He has no record. They're working with Interpol to see if his description matches any recent crimes in other parts of Europe."

Leaving nothing but more questions. Was the hit on Nelly the result of Simon seeing the address on Cassie's note? Or a hit on Nelly as either a smuggler or forger, as well as an expert restorer? If the answer was the former, it meant someone used valuable time to find the note and assign the injured guy to go to Nelly's flat. Which implied the break-in was more time intensive than a smash and grab. Time was something they did not have in abundance due to the Metropolitan Police's response to the office alarm.

"There is more news," she said. "It's worrisome. I got a call from the Chelsea warehouse where we have stuff stored. They had a break-in last night."

"Simon?"

"Probably. The thieves got away, and their faces were covered. Videos can't help."

"What did they take?"

"Nothing, luckily. Whatley drove me by to look. The lock was cut off our unit and a couple more around it. The video showed they got the door open about the same time the guard arrived, and the thieves ran off. The guard remained nearby through the night in case they returned."

"You saw inside?" I asked. "Anything looked disturbed or searched?"

"It looked like the way we left it. The guard spotted the break-in quickly and sounded the alarm for reinforcements before he confronted them. The company had me sign paperwork saying everything looked okay, and they replaced the broken lock with a new one for us. We need to double check those furnishings. Anything unused but salvageable from the office was placed inside. There may be something we didn't recognize as important."

I sighed. "I'll get Max to post a guard until—"

"I put a couple of your loud screamer alarms on the door and several more inside. I'm not sure a guard is the best option. After all, if it was Simon, he found the warehouse rental on his own. Beacham Foundation hadn't been using the space when he was in charge. If he bribed to get the info, I'm sure he would bribe or blackmail a new guard to get inside again."

I dropped my head into my hand. "Yeah, you're right. Any suggestions?"

"The storage company is aware, as is Whatley," she said. "I can ask for Scotland Yard to assign officers to periodically check until we either all get back to London or Simon is caught."

"Works short term. Thanks."

I asked if she'd received her new ticket assignment from Nico and filled her in on the change in plan. A knock on the outer door signaled the arrival of the doctor, and I needed to end the conversation and find out the medical expert's opinion on the rest of my team. Both guys said they were okay to continue on to whichever next phase we were all headed, but I wanted to hear from the professional to back up their statements.

"We'll make sure Nico is safely on the plane here in Rome before we leave him," I said. "You be careful getting to Heathrow tonight, Cass. Call Whatley for an escort if you think you need one."

"He already offered this morning, and I accepted," she said. "I'll call and notify him of the change in flight time."

"I hate to give you one more thing to do, but if you have the time to pick up the package with the credit card from Max—"

"Already taken care of," she said. "I called your contact at the Embassy and asked her to notify me when a package addressed to you arrived. She called about an hour ago. I didn't think it was a good idea to leave it there and run the risk of Max canceling the card and making you have to work him over again to get a new credit line. I put the card in the safe deposit box at the bank. Whichever of us gets back to London first will have the credit handy to use for hiring workmen and material."

"I knew I was brilliant for hiring you."

She laughed.

"What's the limit on the card?" I asked.

The figure she mentioned made me lose my voice for a second. Obviously I'd put some fear into my penny-pinching boss. I needed to remember what I'd said so I could use the technique again in the future.

"And the tapestry?"

"Whatley brought it this morning, and a very happy client is presently rejoicing in its return."

"Good work," I said.

"One more thing," she said.

"What?"

"Dylan called me."

I couldn't help grinning. "Did he ask you out?"

"No, but I told him you were out of town and I was flying out tomorrow."

"Effectively shutting him down before he had the chance to ask."

"Yes. Probably. Maybe."

"You want me to go along and chaperone you on a date?" I teased.

"I don't even know if he planned to ask me out. He said he was calling to say hello because we'd all been busy heading in opposite directions yesterday."

Yeah, right. "Look, when we get back to London, take Jack somewhere for coffee and pick his brain about Dylan. He knows him and can probably give you enough info to make you feel more confident about what you should say when he calls back."

"If he does."

I laughed. "He'll call, Cassie."

The mood was lighter as we signed off, but each of us warned the other to stay safe. I returned to the main room, where Nico was re-buttoning his shirt and Jack sat stoically, only wincing slightly while the doctor cleaned his hand.

The conversation between all the men stayed in Italian. I

picked up the odd word or phrase as I retrieved items we needed to pack. The gist was both men would be sore in the morning, but were fine to go as long as they took it easy. The doctor seemed to accept the accident story to encompass everything. Before he left, he asked if I needed any medical attention.

"I'm good," I patted my breast bone. "*Buena.*" The doctor nodded and repacked his bag.

Jack walked Cordova to the door and paid for his services. "*Mille grazie.*"

Nico emailed all the data he'd discovered to Jack and me while we packed.

"I'm going to do a workaround to get you seats on the train leaving for Cologne about seven tonight. I'm sending another text to Ralf saying you're on your way there." Nico called out to us. His fingers flew over the screen. "I can't get you berths on the train, but the seats recline."

"Staying away from berths is probably better," I said.

"Why?" Jack asked.

"We need to keep our phones on in case Cassie and Nico want to reach us, or if Roberto calls you. This way we can keep each other apprised and rest about as comfortably in reclining chairs in one of the club cars."

"Okay," he said. "One stays on watch while the other sleeps."

"Also you won't have to worry about someone breaking into your berth, kidnapping you, and shoving you into a laundry cart," Nico muttered, finishing his keying as he spoke. "There. You're both set. Check in at one of the ticket booths before seven p.m. I've emailed you both ticket information and itinerary."

There was one more headache ahead of us. I turned to Jack. "Are you going to deal with the rental car company by phone? Or stop by the counter when we go to the airport with Nico?"

"I'm thinking it will be faster by mobile," Jack said. "If I show up at the airport counter we may never make a train tonight."

I couldn't help wondering if they were right about us going by rail. So many more hours and opportunities to be caught en route.

There would be more opportunities to get away, and it was safer to jump from a train than a passenger jet. Driving offered the safest option if Jack wasn't already persona non grata with the rental company, and we weren't both exhausted. I had a feeling I would be renting our cars as principal driver for a while.

"You're getting a lot of experience telling rental car companies they aren't getting their vehicles back," I said. "You may have a whole new career ahead of you in diplomatic work."

Jack grimaced. "Don't remind me. I continue receiving the odd call from the Miami company every few weeks about that damn Mercedes."

"Another time or two for you to lose a car and you're going to be on the worldwide 'do not rent to this driver' list," Nico ribbed him, grinning for the first time since we'd found him. "You may already be in the top ten."

As Jack started on his cell with the car rental place, I called downstairs on the room phone to get our bill prepared and schedule a taxi to the airport. The doctor had bandaged up Nico's ankle, and he moved much better with the added support. He helped me get the bags to the door. Jack got louder and more impatient, but at least it was all in Italian. I pretended it was white noise.

When we were ready to leave, Jack said something to end the call, and we all headed for the lobby.

"I think the person at the other end was still talking when you hung up," I said, slipping my purse strap onto my shoulder and grabbing my carry-on bag.

"Undoubtedly. Whenever one person got tired I was passed along to someone else," he said. "We are staying far away from the car rental counter when we get to the airport in case they're tracking my mobile."

"You don't really think—"

"I was joking, Laurel." The glare he sent my way told me to keep my questions to a minimum.

"You can drop me at arrivals and take the cab on to the train,"

Nico said, thankfully changing the subject. "I'll ask for a ride from one of the skycaps if the walk is too long with me carrying my bag."

"I'd feel better if we—" My phone pinged, and I hauled it out of the Fendi. It was a text message from the airline. "Well, we have another reason to go to the airport. The strike is over and my bag is no longer a hostage."

The elevator arrived and one elderly lady was onboard.

"Perfect," Jack said to Nico. "With the strike over you can check your bag."

Our fellow passenger looked at us quizzically, but didn't say anything. I smiled at her, and at the lobby she got off the elevator ahead of us.

I wanted to tell her to count herself lucky. The conversation she overheard was the most normal one the three of us had shared all day.

FIFTEEN

In due time we arrived at the airport. Jack stayed with Nico through check-in, partly to help with the bags but mostly to be sure no one followed our limping geek. Then he met me at the office in baggage claim where I collected my recovered wardrobe. I knew it was silly with the hotel professionally cleaning my tweed outfit the night before, but I was almost giddy with the idea of putting on different clothes in the morning.

As we walked back to the taxi stand, he said, "I don't understand why Roberto hasn't called."

"Maybe Micelli kept him busy all afternoon. A lot has happened today, but it's only five o'clock. Not yet a Roman dinnertime," I said, looking at my watch for confirmation. "Why don't I notify Micelli we're heading out and you try to call Roberto?"

"Let's get a cab first. Less chance of being overheard."

Minutes later, we were in a taxi and heading for the train station. Micelli stuck to English as we talked. He wasn't thrilled with the idea of us leaving, but I think he was a little relieved just the same. Jack wasn't able to connect with Roberto, and he asked to talk to the detective before I signed off. He asked if Roberto was at police headquarters.

"Thank you, yes, keep me informed," he said after Micelli had controlled the conversation for a few minutes. "You can reach me at my number, or call Laurel at this one if necessary."

He ended the call and handed back my phone. "Micelli has no idea where he is. Roberto left about an hour after we did."

"Do you want me to give you reasons not to worry?"

"No," he said. "I'll tell myself all the things I would be saying to you. Which you wouldn't believe either if our roles were reversed."

"Not everyone can disappear in this case."

"Keep repeating that to yourself," he said. He pulled something from his pocket. "Give me your bracelet. I want to add this charm to it before I forget."

I handed him the silver chain bracelet and he worked the charm's small ring into one of the links. He closed the loop tight with his teeth. "There. May not pass muster with a jewelry designer, but it should hold tight until we can get it done better."

"It's lovely," I said, holding it up for inspection. "Has the unique craftsman look to it."

"As long as it tells me where you are."

The cab pulled to the curb outside the train station. We were soon on our way inside with our bags.

The train for Cologne left in an hour and would get us to our destination before sunrise. We checked in without a problem and had time to grab a quick meal before boarding. Without comparing notes, we both looked for a table hidden from the main thoroughfare, choosing one surrounded by several groups of laughing travelers.

We pretty much ate our ham sandwiches in silence, but I couldn't keep from watching the people around us. I was surprised when I looked down and saw my food nearly gone. Jack had already finished and was watching me watch everyone else. He smiled when I noticed I'd been caught.

"Sorry," I said, setting down the last bite of my food and wiping my hands on a napkin. "I'm probably being a little hyper-sensitive, but—"

"There's no such thing. I'm beginning to think our instincts are all we have to bank on, and yours have been golden most of the time. Even when you were slipping away from me," Jack said. "Never apologize for being careful."

I shrugged. "We make a good team."

He laughed, tipped back his beer and drank the rest.

"What?" I asked.

"Words I never believed I'd hear you say."

I felt a blush rising and exited quickly, citing a visit to the ladies' room while I had the chance.

When I came out, Jack was waiting at the door with our bags. His face showed me he wasn't there simply as a precaution.

"Is something wrong?"

"A call from Micelli," he said. "Roberto was found behind his favorite bar. His throat was cut."

We were a subdued pair boarding our long silver and orange-trimmed night train about seven in the evening. Because he brought the artist into the case, Jack blamed himself for Roberto's death. I gave all my arguments about how there was no way the Amazon or anyone else connected knew Roberto was the artist of record. We both knew, however, there were leaks in every avenue of law enforcement, and criminals weren't the only informants who worked for the other side.

"The third innocent person killed, and a third killer," I whispered once we'd chosen seats. "What's the deal with that M.O.?"

Jack put an arm around my shoulders and pulled me close, speaking softly into my ear, "If you can overpower your victim, it's a good way to do the job. The throat is cut, they can't cry out, and the end comes pretty quickly. Of course, you're likely to walk away with blood all over you."

"Not a good fashion statement, but effective."

"Right. But I'm not sure it was a third killer using the same M.O."

The conductor entered the car and did a head count. I smiled at him and he nodded back, walking past us to the back door.

Jack quietly continued, "The first killer could have done this one as well. We know the person who confessed to killing the Greek over the snuffbox was a ringer. As far as the next murder goes, the DNA results proved for sure Tina killed her mother in Miami. She's in jail, which puts her out of contention for Roberto's hit."

The second murder was the one in Miami where Tina worked things to make it look like she was the victim. It was several hours later, and after Tina fled the country, that the true identity of the dead body was determined.

"We know the Amazon was in Rome within the last twenty-four hours," I said. "Are you theorizing she could have been killing the Greek the night before I first met her in London?"

"Definite possibility."

"I wish we knew who she works for."

"Another conundrum."

More people moved in and filled some of the seats around us. No one sat close enough for concern, and I didn't think anyone was particularly interested in Jack and me.

"Leaving us to infer a slit throat is the current assigned murder method for whatever group is behind all of this. Or what? It's the most convenient option?"

Jack said, "I've been thinking about this, and why Tina would have killed her mother in such a ghastly manner. She could have shot her with a silencer and not left incriminating DNA. She didn't seem the type to get a power trip from bloodstained clothing."

"No, definitely not."

"Which is why I'm wondering if Tony B told her to kill in that manner. Kind of sadistic, but fits his personality. It allowed for the death in Miami to look more like a mugging in the alley, but a shooting would have worked equally as well."

"He could have hired the Amazon to kill the Greek and search the Beacham office after Simon disappeared?" I asked. "On the other hand, it doesn't fly when we know she killed Tony B in the hospital yesterday."

"Change of loyalties?"

The final train whistle sounded.

After learning Simon gave Tina the snuffbox, we'd pretty much operated on the theory he'd been responsible for the Greek's murder in September. "If we assume Tony B had the Greek killed, how did Simon get the snuffbox later?"

"You're right, it doesn't fit with the facts," Jack said. He twisted in his seat and stretched out his long legs. "To be truthful, I'm kind of falling into the trap of thinking Tony B was evil incarnate."

"You're convinced he and Simon weren't both working with Moran?"

The train slowly pulled out of the station.

He shook his head. "No. Tony B showed up at the Ermo Colle event in Florence. I'm not sure of his connection or why he was there, but I can't tie him to Moran."

The train started a rhythmic shushing sound below us, and our seats rocked gently side to side.

"We saw Scarface with Rollie soon after the event, and you said Scarface has a connection to Tony B," I reminded.

In October, when we left the event in Florence, we had dinner then walked to a palazzo I'd had a suspicion about. The negative feelings escalated when we were seconds from being discovered on the way there by an angry Rollie as he strode down the sidewalk chewing out a hired mercenary Jack recognized. It was only through Jack's quick reflexes we weren't discovered. Less than an hour later, we broke into the palazzo and things got worse.

"Scarface, as you refer to him, is hired talent," Jack said. "While I've never known him to work for Moran, it doesn't mean he couldn't have taken on a new commission. I've tried to check in the last few months for more current detail on him, but he's gone deep underground as well."

The train was clear of the station and railyards and headed into the darkened city environs.

"You've decided Rollie doesn't have any connection to Tony B?" I asked.

He blew out a long breath. "I don't know. They were together briefly in Miami on the video, sure, but it could have been a contrived thing by Tony B or his wife. If I knew why Tony B went to the Florence event the next day, it might be different. He hadn't seemed to know you were going to be there, so—"

"I know why he said he was there," I said. "He implied he was giving up *The Portrait of Three* at Ermo Colle's request—"

He whirled in his seat and gripped my shoulders.

"What did you say?" he asked, his eyes wide in surprise. These were the paintings I'd seen in Tony B's Miami office during my kidnapping. All were masterpieces alone, but together, especially with the *Juliana* centerpiece by the reclusive artist Sebastian, their value was unparalleled. Beyond the monetary loss, their subsequent disappearance, and my fear they would be lost again for another dozen years or more, or had been destroyed as Tony B threatened if I did anything to hinder his plans, fed my guilt over escaping without them. Despite the fact I hadn't had time to liberate them and barely made it safely away myself.

"I didn't believe he gave up the originals," I explained. "I didn't say anything before because I hoped to go after them later myself. But when the Miami detective said none of the paintings were in Tony B's office when it was searched, I assumed I was either mistaken by his comment in Florence, or he'd hidden or destroyed the masterpieces."

"You saw them? You saw the *Juliana*?" he shook my shoulders a little as he spoke.

The chief reason I didn't tell Jack was they didn't have anything to do with the mission we were supposed to stay focused on, and I didn't want to sidetrack anyone. Regardless, my plan remained to keep their recovery a future project on my mental itinerary.

I never anticipated this reaction.

"Yes, I saw them. As well as a second, unrelated painting by Sebastian. A large Tuscany scene I hadn't known existed." I said. "Tony B had all of them in carefully controlled rooms. *The Portrait of Three* were further protected by being housed in another interior room. He said he'd purchased them. Hadn't been the thief, but knew they were stolen. He showed the paintings to me after he read an op-ed piece I wrote about their loss to the world. He said he did it to set my mind at ease, but it was really to gloat. I never thought I'd see them again."

"You saw them?" he repeated, a dazed look on his face.

"This was the second time," I said. "The first was on the night the paintings were stolen. At the same museum in Florence fifteen years ago. I was there with Grandfather when they were to be revealed, but all three were stolen before the crowd saw them. My memory of the theft is what unnerved me so at the event last October. The new owners redecorated the building to look exactly as it was the night of the disappearance."

"Oh my god. You were that mouthy little girl." He shook his head.

I pulled back in shock. I'd had no idea we'd met before. "You were the bossy teenager who yelled at me and caught the guard's attention so we had to leave. I was so angry at you."

"I just said you had to go back—"

"And I wasn't a little girl," I interrupted. "I was twelve. I only wanted to look at the most beautiful painting I'd ever seen. *Juliana* was—" I stopped when a sob caught in my throat.

"Juliana was my mother," Jack said softly.

My right hand flew to cover my mouth. His eyes shined for a moment, then he blinked rapidly and rose from his seat. His voice was thick as he said, "Stay here. I'll be back."

He disappeared into the next car.

SIXTEEN

"My mother was Sebastian's student before I was born," Jack explained.

He'd been gone for a good half-hour before he returned. I'd wanted to give him the space he needed. Who could have known the shock of my innocent comment? I was worried and had decided to track him down exactly when he walked back through the door of our car and returned to his seat. He had yet to look me in the eye.

"Sebastian was already famous," he continued. "He liked to give young artists a leg up in the business. My mother was one of his favorites."

"Was he your father?" I asked.

He laughed silently, shook his head, leaned back into his seat and closed his eyes. "No, but you clearly read the dossier I sent to you."

"What little there was of it," I said.

My words made him smile. "You'd like the rest of my story."

"As much as you're willing to tell me," I said and waited.

The file he sent to me in December showed he was raised by a single mother, Juliette—no father's name mentioned—but I naturally didn't put her name with my knowledge of the painting at the time. No reason to believe there was a connection. The expense for his schooling came from several wealthy sources. Nothing in the file had mentioned anything about the artist known as simply Sebastian.

Finally, Jack sat up and turned his head to look at me. He said, "After a few years of Sebastian's tutelage, my mother realized she was an excellent copyist but didn't have the imagination to create great works. She'd fallen in love with him. But his wife was ill, and my mum felt conflicted about the situation. She left, briefly fell for another married man, which is how I came to be."

He returned his head to the seatback and stared straight ahead, continuing his story in a quiet tone, "I was shipped off to boarding school as soon as I was old enough, leaving Mother free for other interests. By this time, Sebastian's wife had died, and my mum felt guiltless about resuming life as his paramour."

"Did they marry?"

He shook his head. "She never married. She stayed with Sebastian until she passed away from breast cancer."

I knew from Jack's dossier his mother died several months before he graduated from Oxford, and he joined the Royal Navy a week after. I'd wondered when I read the file if his decision to enter the military was due to her death, but this didn't seem the time to ask.

"She kept busy by copying works she loved and giving them to people she adored. You saw one of those on the yacht."

"*Woman Dressing Her Hair.*" My words came out as a whisper.

He nodded.

I finally grasped why the painting made such an impact on me. "The brushstrokes reminded me of Sebastian's—but not quite."

"Yes. However, she never copied one of his works. She couldn't get the light and color correct."

"The same problem everyone else has."

"She'd worked with him long enough to where the technique she used was really more his than her own," Jack said. "*Woman Dressing Her Hair* was copied a few months before she first left him. She painted the copy for herself, had always liked the work, but gave it away to Margarite when the original went missing."

Margarite was the woman in charge of the yacht we stayed on in Miami. One reason I'd wanted to see her again was because she knew my mother. She was also the other person in the first mysterious photograph. The picture I'd received in Florence.

But there hadn't been time lately for any travels not related to stopping the heist. Funny how she was twining together both my life and Jack's through friendships to our mothers before either of us was born.

"Margarite was the painting's owner?" Why hadn't I seen her name anywhere in the meager documentation we'd found about the work?

"No, the owner was her lover," Jack explained. "It was her favorite of his paintings and had been lent out in an exhibit. Then disappeared. My mother sent the copy and Margarite has treasured it ever since. She's asked me several times if I would like to have it. Maybe someday."

There was something I had to ask. "Why did Sebastian sell *Juliana* originally? It's obvious from the painting he adored your mother. The work is flawless. Incomparable. Why did he let it go? And why didn't he paint another after it was stolen in the exhibit as *The Portrait of Three*? Or did he?"

Jack looked at me and smiled. I could see his teal eyes shining again from the hint of tears, but he didn't flee this time. "He sold the painting in grief over my mother leaving him. She was much younger than he, and Sebastian thought he'd never see her again. He said looking at the painting made him feel like his heart was being ripped out of his chest. Besides, while others have made a fortune off Sebastian's work, he has given away more than he's sold for himself. After she returned, it was years later, and she was a mature beauty in his eyes. He painted her several more times, but he never tried to duplicate the original work. He had the real thing. All he ever wanted."

"So...the loss of the *Juliana*...All of this..." I stammered. "Is it why you do what you do?"

He gave a low chuckle and took my hand. "Yes, it sounds like my mother's painting affected your career choices as much as it did mine. I always hoped I'd find it again. Stumble onto it like you did, or discover it when I was working to recover another work. I can't tell you how many people I've asked for information on any of *The Portrait of Three* paintings. I thought if I'd even found one of the other works I might find the portrait of my mother eventually. No one ever had any information to help, but I've never quit looking. Though with the original owner deceased I imagine I'd be dealing with the insurance company if I ever did get my hands on the painting again. You say all three were together?"

"Yes. They were perfect. Exactly as they'd been the night they disappeared. Tony B didn't tell me who stole them, but it wasn't him. I wish I'd said something when you and Nico picked me up after I escaped—"

"No." He rubbed the top of my hand with his thumb. "If you had I would have likely barreled back inside and gotten us killed. We would have never gotten to Florence or learned everything we've subsequently pieced together. You are probably the one person in the world who understands my feelings on this, and can appreciate why I'm disappointed, but glad I didn't know at the time."

I nodded, but I didn't speak. I was afraid I might say too much. My grandfather loved art almost as much as he did his family, and I grew up understanding how important every medium was to mankind. When he died and my father spit on everything my family built and protected the previous couple of generations, art was the way I could escape from the hell my life had become. I'd lost my home, people I'd thought were friends, and everything I'd identified with my life. Except art.

At twelve, I'd seen *Juliana*, and knew it was the most perfect work I could ever witness. Like Jack, I'd hoped to be able to find and recover *The Portrait of Three* and return the work to the world.

"One more reason to figure out this Ermo Colle conundrum," Jack said. "You say you think Tony B gave copies instead of originals?"

"He was playing mind games, don't forget," I said. "It was a feeling I had, but could have been exactly what he wanted me to think."

Jack's expression turned moody, and I thought it was a good time to change the subject somewhat.

"There are many legends and myths about Sebastian," I said. "Is he really living in Italy?"

"I'm sorry. I'm sworn to secrecy," he said, offering me an apologetic half-smile. "He's been taken advantage of to such a degree through the years, his self-imposed exile is both protection from those who wish to exploit him and the people who love him too much. I haven't seen him in several years, though I need to make the time to do so. He hasn't been strong in a while. He still paints, but his mind is more in the past than the present. What little money he has left goes to those who take care of him. After he lost my mother, he didn't handle life well for a while. Now he needs someone with him all the time."

Such a sad story. I couldn't help but hope I'd someday be able to convince Jack to take me to meet the great man.

He pulled out his phone, and I read the action as a message he didn't want to talk anymore. The lights in the car dimmed, and the hum of conversation around us quieted a little. It was late and the car was winding down.

"Look," I said. "We have about nine hours before we hit Cologne. Do you want to sleep first, or—"

"I'm not sleepy," he interrupted, holding up his cell. "I need to send some texts, and I'm going to try to get a chat going with Micelli to find out what he knows about Roberto. Why don't you sleep first shift, and I'll wake you when I'm ready?"

"You promise to wake me, right?"

"I'm sure my brain will need an escape from all of this in a few hours."

It wasn't exactly a promise. I didn't think I was going to get anything better though and accepted it. I handed him my phone. "In case Cassie calls," I said. I pulled my coat from my lap and draped the warm wool over me and the Fendi wedged into the seat with me. He may not have been ready to sleep, but between the warmth and the movement of the car I was out in minutes.

* * *

Jack woke me a little after three. My cell was buzzing softly in his hand. The screen showed Ralf's name in Caller ID.

"Hi, Ralf, thanks for calling," I said, trying to get my tongue to sound a little less thick. I turned toward my seatback to keep my voice quieter and reduce any risk of eavesdroppers.

"I apologize for the lateness, or rather earliness, of the hour," he said with a chuckle, his German accent heavily coloring his perfect English. "My time was already committed." He didn't elaborate, and I assumed someone had lost something precious overnight.

"No problem." A yawn followed by a deep breath helped shake out some of the cobwebs in my brain. "You got Nico's text, right?"

"Of course. It is why I called you."

Duh. Wake up, Beacham.

"Right. Sorry. Look, the train will be in Cologne in a few hours. Can we meet and talk later today?"

"About my cousin..." Ralf's words hung in the silence.

"I promise. Nothing to get you or your family in trouble. This is important, Ralf."

"You're coming alone?"

I looked at Jack and bit my lip, trying to decide what to do. I chose the truth. There was no way Jack would let me meet Ralf without him. "No. I've been warned to be more cautious. The guy who's with me though, he's only working toward the same outcome I am. Nothing to worry about. You can trust him as much as you trust me."

"Good." I could hear relief in the one word. He continued, "When Nico said in the text he was heading for America, I was afraid you were on your own. Things are too dangerous for this."

There was dead air again, and I held my breath, afraid to talk and risk losing his cooperation. Finally, he said, "Send me a selfie of the two of you when you arrive in Cologne. Make it touristy. Say you'll be here for the week and want to get together for drinks."

"Okay...Is there a time we can—"

"We'll meet today," he said quickly. "I'm just being careful. Be in the cathedral at noon. Hang around the Saint Christopher statue. You'll see it without difficulty."

"I know it. I've been there before. Big guy with Jesus on his shoulder. Can't miss him. I'll rub his pilgrim's staff for luck or something."

He laughed. "Yes, do that. If I'm not there at noon, hang around. I'll be coming, or I'll send someone with a message."

"Ralf, I'm sensing you weren't really surprised when Nico contacted you about Jürgen and the information we're seeking," I said.

"I'm only surprised it took this long," he replied. The line went dead.

I filled Jack in on anything he hadn't heard. He whispered back Cassie and Nico were safe, and Micelli's department chalked up Roberto's death as a robbery.

"Maybe he's right," I said.

Jack frowned and raised his left eyebrow.

My jaw was again possessed by a powerful yawn, which triggered a similar one from him.

"Wow, I need coffee, and you need sleep. You should have woken me earlier," I said.

"No need. I'm only yawning because you did," he said.

"You're yawning because you're tired. No more arguments," I said. "I'm going to go and find a cup of coffee, and when I get back I want to hear you snoring."

"I don't snore."

"Yeah, keep telling yourself that. Remember, I had the room next to yours in the suite."

Actually, I had no idea if he snored. I'd passed out so fast when I hit the bed in Rome a herd of rhinos could have slept in the next room and I wouldn't have known.

All I needed was to find a helpful train employee, and I was on my way to the heavenly coffee car. I got two cups. One for me, and one for Jack in case he chose to be stubborn. When I got back to my seat, however, I found he'd taken my orders seriously. No matter. Two cups would wake me up even faster.

Most of the car was asleep, but a few people were talking. One twenty-something woman was knitting. A couple of teens and a guy in a suit were absorbed in whatever was on their phones. Jack hadn't seemed concerned when he filled me in on what had happened while I slept, and I tried to relax and not think about bad guys coming through one of the doors at any moment. It didn't work. I sipped from the first cup of coffee. It wasn't midnight yet in New York. I could have called Max, but I chickened out and sent texts. I sent Cassie a text telling her to not worry any more about *Woman Dressing Her Hair*, but to note any data on *The Portrait of Three* she or Nico ran across. I didn't tell her yet what Jack revealed about his mother and the paintings. It seemed too personal to share. If I felt my team needed to know I'd ask if he wanted to tell them, or get permission before I divulged anything. I reread all my latest messages, trying to keep my mind off bogeymen as I caught up on the related texts Jack had read and synopsized for me after I finished talking to Ralf.

There was nothing he hadn't revealed. They were in New York and safely ensconced in a hotel near the foundation office. I went back over the email attachments Nico sent earlier, and wished I had a bigger screen. Zoom options are terrific, but full detail on a whole image at a time would have been stellar. Nevertheless, my wonder geek had come through superbly. I flipped through his notes in the digital file on my phone, and followed up with the attachments of official documents he'd likely gained via his hacking talents, marveling again at what was available to techno-wizards.

Ralf's cousin, Jürgen Burkhard, known in underground circles as an up-and-coming forger of the kind of high-priced abstract artwork popular at the moment with Chinese and Russian millionaires, was killed behind his favorite watering hole after closing the place down with friends. Everyone parted company at the door, and one of the friends walked with Jürgen to the corner, where the friend turned east and the victim continued north. Yet, when the trash from the bar was removed at final cleanup an hour later, the forger's body was discovered propped against the dumpster. Coincidentally enough, his throat was cut—like Roberto's and practically everyone else who'd lately been pseudo-associated with this potential art heist.

Well, not everyone. From our past research we knew several European forgers had met rather unusual deaths, from peculiar electrocutions to creative suffocations and hair-raising car accidents. Many cases were quickly closed for the first two types, as situations strongly suggested accident or suicide. Only one of the last could be absolutely proven murder due to tampered brakes. The cases might be coincidental—or seem so to anyone investigating. After all, these victims worked in the riskiest of high-risk fields.

Coincidences happened, sure. Get a big enough pool of victims and any number of patterns could occur.

I didn't believe coincidence was the answer for anything here. For as long ago as fourteen months, a higher than average percentage of forgers helped build the European fatality stats. Late summer through fall and early winter, the preferred method for killing forgers was a knife blade across the throat—and all of these murders couldn't be muggings.

The Greek I'd found on our September pickup near Milan was not the first such death, I discovered, though he would always start the timeline in my mind. Before he was killed, there was a similar slashing in Dublin over the summer solstice, and a month earlier at Cannes during the international film festival. Spain gained the gory prize with five more over fall and winter—shared between Barcelona and Madrid—and all marked as closed cases due to muggings. I knew Simon was at Cannes near the end of spring, and he loved the weather in Barcelona year round. We hadn't been able to place him at Milan, however. He was supposed to be busy during that time window retrieving an art object he ultimately absconded with—if the sword even existed.

A copy was left behind. We'd never tried to match that faked sword with its creator, but I put it on my mental to-do list. To see if the swordsmith was still breathing. The forgery was one of the pieces that hooked me into this puzzle originally. I had yet to learn if there was even an original Simon stole to begin with. My gut said yes, which meant its forger was at risk as well. If not already dead.

Flipping through the digital police files, to my mind the best evidence at the crime scene of Ralf's cousin was a toss-off remark noted in the crime scene file about a strand of red hair discovered on the body. Unfortunately, no usable DNA could tag the hair to an individual, but it didn't keep me from believing the Amazon had skipped away free.

I thought seriously about trying to pick Jack's pocket for his cell, to see if he'd made any notes or had more info. I'd given him my phone, after all. But he needed the sleep, and I needed to learn to trust him. He'd been pretty good lately about sharing.

I opened the websites for the *Guardian* and the *New York Times* to check what news had hit in the last couple of hours and what was trending. Nothing particularly interesting to our mission.

Finally, I pulled up some travel sites to re-familiarize myself with Cologne. Or Köln, as the natives call Germany's fourth largest city. It was one of my favorite places for its inclusive nature and broad range of events. Nearly two decades ago, Grandfather had taken my grandmother and me on a luxury Rhine cruise, and Cologne was our starting point. In the years since, I found the city's calendar packed with spectacular events and activities, over twenty-two thousand each year. There was always something to do when I met friends, from art and cultural opportunities to dynamic rock concerts. A day's shopping was always an option with their amazing pedestrian mall—known for being the first in Germany.

Nico and I even attended a gaming convention there a few years ago. I went as his arm candy. Once we got into the huge hall I quickly realized my role was to distract his competition. A few of those sweet nerdy guys still sent me emails several times a year.

Shortly before we crossed the bridge over the Rhine, I left our car to grab a coffee for Jack. It was a couple of hours before sunrise and only the growing wash of city lights foretold we were nearing our destination. I had a feeling my traveling companion was going to need help waking up. When I returned to our car, however, he was already awake and looking a little wild-eyed.

"Here." I shoved the coffee into his hand and regained my seat. "Sorry if I woke you as I left."

"No, a guy bumped my shoulder on his way to the WC," he said, then took a long sip and closed his eyes. "This is wonderful."

"I thought it might be appreciated."

"We're almost there?" he asked.

"Yeah, a few minutes."

There was plenty of time before the appointment with Ralf. We stayed back and let most of our fellow passengers disembark ahead of us. Getting off the train was as uneventful as the journey, and no one caught our attention in the crowded station either. I was beginning to think the guys really had known what they were talking about when they suggested skipping the plane. Also much easier and more incognito than if we'd had to book a flight and find a hotel late last night. Of course, I'd actually slept a decent amount of time during the ride. Jack, on the other hand, immediately found the nearest coffee kiosk in the station and continued mainlining caffeine.

I pointed toward the sign for the lockers. "Let's leave our bags here until we meet Ralf."

"Okay."

A toilette sign was on the wall nearby. "On second thought," I said, "I'd like to change clothes first. Can you wait for me by the restroom?"

"Think I'll do the same," he said.

The stalls were mostly empty, with a couple of women at the sinks. Within minutes, I'd removed the sturdy travel tweeds and white blouse I'd worn every waking hour in the last forty-eight, to slip happily into black lined wool slacks and a royal blue high-necked blouse I'd worried I would never see again. I silently thanked whatever airport gods made the baggage handlers go back to the table when it counted. The dirties went into a plastic bag placed into a side pocket of my luggage.

I used the opportunity to slip out a couple of the handy gizmos I always had to put into my checked baggage to get through airport security. My personal favorite could open most electronic doors as easily as a household garage door opener. The little lovely went into one of the less obvious pockets of my Fendi. These were the things I didn't bother telling Jack about. He'd seen some of my goodies, but not all. As much as he did things his own way, whether his methods were completely above-board or not, he'd squawked a little in the past about a few of my habits. I didn't want to hear any lectures today. I did want to have my gadgets as backup, however, if we found later any were particularly necessary.

Be prepared, I always say. My Fendi alone was proof of the philosophy.

When I left the stall two women finished at the sinks. We traded smiley hellos before they left. There were a couple of stalls filled, but I had my pick of sinks and mirrors. I refreshed my lipstick and ran a comb through my hair. Things were feeling promising again as I rubbed a few dabs of lotion onto my hands. Slinging my coat over one arm, my Fendi went onto the other shoulder. My carry-on was anchored atop my rolling bag and I was ready to go.

I was almost to the exit when a woman charged out of one of the stalls and plowed into me.

SEVENTEEN

The woman was between me and the door. She held tight to the strap on my Fendi and yanked hard at the huge purse, trying to flee.

At least I assumed it was a woman. The dark glasses, knitted hat, and bulky coat effectively eliminated any ability I had to determine gender or description. We were about the same height, and likely the same build, as our tug of war was a dead heat. Her sneakers, however, had better traction than my leather-soled boots.

There were only two other women in the restroom. One shrieked, and the other stood stock still. I wasn't getting any help out of that quarter.

My boots were worse than barefoot at the moment. She got us almost to the door, and I had an idea she had help on the other side. I was running out of options.

She pulled with both hands. Apparently she didn't have a weapon for intimidation. I counted my blessings. There was only one option. I maintained control of the Fendi with one hand and risked letting go with my right to dig into the side of the purse by the strap end I was holding. She took advantage of my one-handed grip to give a mighty tug. Just before the strap broke free from my grip, my hand came out of the purse with the item I kept in the side pocket.

I hit her square in the face with a blast of travel-sized hairspray.

Her hands flew to her face. I gave her another shot of spray. She shrieked in pain. Definitely a woman. There was also something...

My Fendi dangled from one of her arms. I pulled the purse free and pushed out of the restroom, dragging my rolling bag behind.

"Jack! Help!"

She came roaring through the door and pulled at my left arm. I hit her hard with my right fist. As I feared, she did have an accomplice. A tall guy with a heavy dark beard moved close and clamped an arm around me. I saw Jack appear from one side.

"Jack, over here!"

The accomplice turned and noticed I had reinforcements coming. He shoved me and I fell to the ground. Big Beard tugged my assailant's arm and pulled her quickly down the terminal with him, going deeper into the crowd.

"Are you okay?" Jack hurried over and helped me up, but stretched to try to keep them in view.

"Yeah," I said, checking both my purse and luggage to make sure nothing had spilled.

He stepped away. "Stay here, I'm going after them."

I hurried and put a hand on his arm to stop him. "Don't. Nothing was taken, and if it's more serious than a purse snatching they may be hoping to separate us."

"You're right, I wasn't thinking." He ran frustrated fingers through his dark hair. "We do need to report it to security."

The next half-hour we spent giving vague descriptions and pointing out the scramble outside the restroom door when the security video was reviewed and stopped at the relevant point. Security filled out forms, recording our names and contact info, and tried to find out how long we'd be in the country—like we had any idea—before sending us on our way with their thanks and a caution to be careful.

We found lockers for our gear, and as Jack lifted my large bag I teased, "You were longer in the bathroom than I was, Hawkes. I even touched up my makeup."

He gave the bag a good shove and closed the door. "The problem with men's restrooms versus women's is there are less stalls to accommodate more urinals." He leaned close and whispered, "When you're changing clothes and concealing a weapon, it's always a good thing to wait for a little privacy."

"I'm glad it didn't take any longer. I am doubly glad you have a gun."

"Makes two of us."

The train station, otherwise known as the Hauptbahnhof, sat right on the plaza called the city center. Everything outside was in the shadow of the great cathedral, and through the station's huge front windows it was easy to see the historic church and nearby signature shops for retailers like Lacoste and Swarovski, even if the dark store signs showed they were closed.

It was a quick walk out of the terminal without carrying anything heavier than my Fendi. Which wasn't a lightweight, by the way, but it usually contained everything I needed. The well-designed outdoor space was well lit for early morning commuters and tourists like ourselves.

"What do you think?" Jack asked when we finally got a little distance from other people. "Purse snatcher or Laurel snatcher?"

"I would stick with purse snatcher. Except for one thing." I stopped and turned to him. "You're going to laugh."

He stared off into the horizon, then looked back at me. "I can't imagine anything about that experience or this day to make me laugh. Not at you anyway."

"She squealed when she screamed. Like Melanie."

His expression was one of disbelief. He squinted at me and asked, "Are you saying you think Melanie from The Browning was your purse snatcher?"

"You asked."

The executive director of The Browning in Miami was not my fan, despite the fact the foundation I worked for could do a lot of good for her gallery and artists' studio. Her hatred of me stemmed from a mean girls incident while we were college students and interning at the same museum. The fact she had a thing for Jack, and he seemed to have a thing for me, didn't help either.

With a chuckle, he turned me around and we continued our walk across the plaza.

"I said you'd laugh."

"You certainly did." He was quiet for a moment, then said, "Tell me, do you really think Melanie would go to all this trouble? My thought is she would readily hire someone to kill you, but wouldn't actually do anything herself and risk breaking a nail."

"I think I preferred you laughing," I said. "If it had been Melanie, and she or her accomplice had a gun, we'd be dead."

Jack shook his head. "You'd be dead. She would have only wounded me. She likes me."

I closed my eyes momentarily. "Ohmigod, I'm partnered with an idiot."

"A sexy idiot with a British accent," he whispered in my ear. "Women love that."

"Most women do," I said. My retort kind of lost its effectiveness when I couldn't keep from chuckling at our lapse into dark humor.

The ass just grinned at me.

Suddenly, I had a thought. "Almost forgot. We need to send a touristy shot—"

"Oh, the selfie. Right." Jack scanned the area. "The stone arch would work. Leftover from the Roman years. Can't get much more touristy."

What was left of the stone arch on the city center was originally the north gate of the Roman city that had first graced the location nearly two thousand years ago. We posed where the most light shined on us and our historic backdrop, and used Jack's longer arms to get the best possible selfie.

"Think it's good enough for him to recognize us?" Jack asked.

"Yes. The arch gets short shrift, but this is all for show," I attached it to a text message and sent the shot to Ralf's phone. A few minutes later, we found an open *caffe* on one of the corners and went inside for breakfast.

"It's too early in the States to connect with anyone," Jack said.

"Until I can talk with someone in New York, I'm going to work my mobile on European contacts to get some intel started about your guy in the jewelry box photo. One more thing before I forget. Where exactly was your mother's accident?"

The orange cinnamon Danish that had sat on my tongue so lovely a moment before suddenly tasted like ashes. I answered mechanically, "About a mile outside of the Scarsdale city limits."

I appreciated him pursuing my mother's accident when we had extra time. After all, I'd asked him to do so. It was the realization I would have to hear about her death again which disconcerted me, this time in a new and frightening way. Leaving me a little...well...I guess frightened was enough of a word at this point. I'd faced down diabolical criminals and outsmarted seasoned art thieves, but it took nothing more than the thought of reopening family history to shake me to my core.

Time to shove the inner child back into the mental playroom, Beacham, and pretend you're an adult again.

I should have never kept this secret from him and Nico after the first "gift." The original photograph hadn't even actually implicated my mother to the extent this new one did. Yet while I didn't have answers, I was terrified of asking more questions.

Past time to start.

"I need you to email me what you have," he said. "Are the pictures on your mobile?"

"Oh, sorry." I came back to the present, grabbed my phone from the cream-colored tabletop and woke the screen—wishing I could wake myself as easily. "I meant to send everything to you already. Keep getting sidetracked."

"It's not like you've been twiddling your thumbs," Jack said, smiling. "They've been too busy most of the time to dance over the little keyboard."

"You could have—" I started to ask why he hadn't gone into my pictures and emailed them while I was asleep and he had my phone, but stopped.

The old Jack would have done exactly that, and I wasn't sure how the current Laurel felt with the realization of another change. Equally perplexing, I wasn't sure why I'd handed my "life in one device" over last night without another thought.

I'd blame it on exhaustion.

"What?" he asked when I didn't finish.

I shook my head and hit Send to forward the shots. "Never mind. My thoughts are wandering. Let me know if you need pictures with more detail. Or you can see the pieces yourself the next time you're in London. They're in the safe in my hotel room."

At about eight thirty, sunlight started teasing through the windows. Soon after, we'd completely exhausted our personal information resources.

"Nothing to do until we meet your friend," Jack said. "Let's walk for a bit and discuss things we don't want overheard."

"Agreed." I stacked our trash to bus the table. We put on coats and I slipped my Fendi onto my shoulder. Our trash went into the bin as we left the shop.

In my experience, waiting was not something Jack did well. Information gathering can be addicting, but even after the brouhaha in the bathroom he'd quietly sat down to breakfast and worked. Not once had he given any sign of a breakthrough moment or restless attention. The fact he stuck it out in the *caffe* with coffee and pastries for a couple of hours told me this walk likely had more to do with him finally needing to break free than anything else. To keep himself awake.

At about ten degrees above freezing, even with the clear sky and sunshine, the walk was the definition of brisk. Jack suggested we start down the pedestrian zone called the *Schildergasse*. Cologne boasts miles of walkable shopping zones, and any other time I would have gone store to store, probably ending up in the Belgian Quarter to decide between unique accessories and offbeat clothing in the small boutiques.

My walking buddy, on the other hand, truly wanted to talk.

"How is the best way to approach your friend?" he asked.

I stared straight ahead, thinking for a second before replying,

"I should be the one who actually talks to him. At least in the beginning—until we see how things go. He was glad I had someone with me for the protection angle, but Ralf is as wary about all of this as we are, and is going to use up his trust stores pretty quickly. We have to remember he's only meeting with us because his cousin was..."

A couple of talkative women walkers drew up alongside of us, and by tacit agreement Jack and I stayed silent until they finally quickstepped away.

"Did you get a chance to review all of Nico's email attachments?" he asked.

"Yes. It would be nice if we could get one of the coroners to compare the wounds," I said. "To see if it was possible to determine whether the same knife was used in any of the deaths."

"Good luck. I chatted with Micelli last night. They've already turned Roberto's body over to the family."

"They don't waste time."

"It was ruled an anonymous mugging. No one thinks it will be solved."

"Of course none of the murders will be solved if they keep burying the evidence with the bodies," I said. More than a little sarcastically, I'll admit. "It's great Nico got us a look at a lot of the official info. And don't forget you work with us now. If you try to turn him in, I'll call you a liar."

"Down, Mama Bear." Jack laughed. "I am dazzled and amazed daily over what can be retrieved through unorthodox channels. As long as everyone's ethics are in the right place, I have no qualms about forgetting where I got necessary intel."

"Of course, that's if you were MI-6," I said, since he still hadn't admitted anything.

He cocked an eyebrow and gave me his damned cheeky grin. "Right. If I was."

I shoved my hands in my pockets and stomped a little as I walked away. "Would it really kill you to admit anything?"

"It might." A couple of his long strides and he caught up to me.

He said, "You realize, however, you wouldn't be so bloody interested in who I am if you weren't...*interested*."

"What?" I stopped short, turning to stare at his grinning face. "I'm not interested, Mr. Conceited. I'm curious."

His gaze locked on mine. "You're interested."

Suddenly, I was feeling warm. "I think we've talked about this long enough."

"I don't think we've even begun."

Calm, Beacham, keep calm.

"Look," I said. "You work with my team. I'm responsible for them. I need to know things—"

"It isn't anything more?"

I caught my lower lip with my teeth. He grinned at my "worry tell," and my tongue took over with brutal honesty. "Even if it was *anything more*. It will never *be anything more* until I learn the rest of your history—preferably from you, rather than your damned dossier. You know all twenty-eight years of my life, but you left out the last decade in yours. Those last ten years' experience is pretty much what I have to work with every day. If you were MI-6, of course."

For several beats, his face stayed a rock and his gaze remained steady. Neither of us blinked.

"When we return to London, I'll see what I can do to satisfy your curiosity," he said finally, putting additional emphasis on the last word. "If we make it out of this alive."

"Always the optimist, Hawkes."

"Absolutely."

A steady wind wound down the *Schildergasse*. My lovely red wool coat and black gloves were adequate for running from door to cab or Tube, but I was getting downright frozen after my emotional heatwave passed. "Why don't we head back to the city center? See if we can find someplace around the plaza to get out of the cold."

"I didn't know you were a wimp."

"From a long line of wimps, thank you very much."

With the moment passed, we grinned at one another and

changed direction. I looked at my watch and saw it was opening time for the Museum Ludwig. I'm not a huge fan of expressionist sculpture and pop art, but this museum was a favorite of mine anyway. Plus, if I needed to talk to Ralf about his cousin's work in forging abstract art, I probably needed to get my mind into twentieth-century works.

As we neared the building, I said, "How about if we duck into the museum? We should be able to talk quietly in there, and I could use a refresher on contemporary art."

"Fine," he replied. "This is the collection the husband and wife gave to the city, right?"

"Exactly." Irene and Peter Ludwig lived a modest lifestyle, but chose brilliantly when they purchased modern art. By the time of their deaths, they had amassed a treasure trove of art spanning the last century and all contemporary mediums. The museum had always felt like "fun art" to me, with the largest collection of pop art outside of the U.S. The 1960s may have been the heyday of the movement, but all the icons were represented in the Museum Ludwig.

We entered through the glass doors. The white walls would have appeared sterile if not for the bright hanging pieces and bohemian sculptures scattered around the rooms. An artist I remembered from The Browning event in October had a monotype exhibit up, and a crew was straightening the chrome frames displaying his provocative work. A photographer shot pictures of the pieces and directed a young man, presumably the artist, to stand in various locations and poses.

My phone vibrated in my pocket. I motioned to Jack I was moving into a corner to talk.

"Superintendent, hello," I said quietly, after reading Whatley's name on Caller ID. "What kind of news do you have for us?"

"I'm afraid your restorer didn't make it," he replied. "She never regained consciousness and passed away early this morning. She simply lost too much blood at the time to recover."

"Her information died with her," I said. This was awful. My

mind couldn't reconcile the Nelly I knew with the extra passports and her agitated state the last time I spoke to her. What could have made her get involved in something like this? Was she working with Simon, or did he send his man to kill me and she got him first?

"Yes, well, we'll continue pursuing leads," Whatley said. "If you have any ideas, or get any new information—"

"We will definitely let you know," I said.

"Delivered your assistant safely to Heathrow," he continued. "Her traveling partner was waiting for her at the departure area."

"That was Nico, yes," I said. "Thanks again for your help."

"No trouble at all. They said you were leaving Rome for Germany last night."

It wasn't really a question, but I answered, "We're in Cologne at the moment."

"Hawkes is with you?"

"Yes, do you need to speak to him?" I caught Jack's eye.

"No, no. Simply making sure I know where everyone is."

"I understand, Superintendent. If we cross borders again I will let you know."

"Very good. All I can tell you at the moment. Unless you have something to pass my way?"

"Sorry, but I'll let you know if we turn up anything useful," I said. "Thanks again for letting me know about Nelly. Do you know if she has family coming in to handle funeral arrangements?"

"Not yet. We're making inquiries," he said. "She kept pretty much to herself, and the neighbors didn't know anything about family to notify. It will be in the papers, and people hopefully will come forward. However, we like to connect with them first whenever possible."

The two of us signed off, and I spent a minute filling Jack in on anything he hadn't overheard. We were standing by a glass cube holding a sculpture resembling brains and intestines. Two crewmembers came by, lifted the top of the cube and withdrew one of the pieces. Everything about the exhibit seemed to be a work in progress.

We moved out of the gallery room and headed for the more well-known pieces of the collection. In particular, I always enjoy Warhol, and knew there were several of his works on display. Before we reached the escalator, however, Jack turned and strode toward a man in a suit and trench coat. Something about him looked familiar, but I couldn't place him. When he saw Jack coming closer, he turned around and fast-walked his way toward the exit. Jack sped up. The strange man broke into a jog. I crossed Warhol off my mental list for the day and raced after them.

When I reached the museum entrance, Jack stood there alone. I crossed my arms and frowned as I stared out the glass. We were off to the side to keep from hindering people as they entered the doors. The other man was nowhere to be seen.

"Guy on a motorcycle picked him up a second ago," Jack said.

"Who was he?" I asked.

"The man from the train who woke me up when he left his seat."

"I knew he looked familiar after you left to intercept him, but I couldn't figure out who or why I recognized him," I said. Jack had a talent for spotting people who didn't want to be noticed. I'd even found myself at the receiving end of his superpowers.

"He added the hat and glasses," Jack said. "I was relatively certain it was him and positive when he started running away."

"Am I to suppose he isn't the only person following us?"

"I would say it's a foregone conclusion."

EIGHTEEN

"I'm thinking I need to call Ralf and cancel the appointment," I said, pulling my phone from the Fendi. We walked out the huge glass doors. Back on the wide plaza again, I could feel eyes everywhere.

"Call and warn him we may have a tail, but don't cancel," Jack said, taking my free arm by the elbow and steering me toward the train station. "Before we go any farther, we need to see if we have any electronic devices anywhere on our bodies. Besides your lucky charm bracelet, of course."

I wiggled my wrist and made the charms jangle, just as my phone call went to Ralf's voicemail. "He's not picking up," I said.

"Tell him the situation. Ask him to watch for a while before approaching, to see if he spots any shadows on us."

The voicemail recording ended, and I began my message. Jack kept talking, "Tell him to drop a message near one of us or send a text if he sees a shadow and thinks we need to reschedule."

He stopped talking, and I was able to finish up what I hoped was a coherent message. Except Jack's comments had me obsessing on the idea of possibly being re-assaulted in the train station bathroom. "I'm not sure a public restroom is the right place—"

"We're not using the loo," he said. "We're going to do everything out in the open."

"Excuse me?"

"If a bug has been planted on either of us it's likely in our coats or your purse. I have a handy device in my luggage to do the checking for us."

"Sounds much better."

"I thought it might."

Ten minutes later, we felt confident about staying in our clothes. Nothing gave off a warning squeal.

"So, James Bond, any ideas?" I asked.

Jack's gaze bore into mine, but I knew it was nothing personal. I could see the wheels of his brain turning behind his teal eyes. After a few seconds the personable Hawkes came back and he said, "He could have some type of directional mic. Or another kind of device to allow him to listen to everything we said to each other on the train and afterward from yards away. Between a directional mic and simple visual techniques, it would be enough to stay on our trail."

"This is feeling creepy," I said. "Do you think he had any partners?"

"If he's smart and doing his job right, he does."

"You make me feel so much better."

He laughed. "Let's go on over to the cathedral. If we can't get lost in the twenty thousand who visit this cathedral every day, at least we can make finding us less easy."

"Okay," I said, pulling my Fendi more solidly on my shoulder. "Do we need to stick to texting and cut down on the talking?"

"Something to think about, but first, take off your coat," he said, bending to dig farther into the bag he'd left half unzipped on the station floor.

"Why? Your gadget said there was no transmitter."

"It did." He pulled a dark wool jacket from the bag and laid it across the top of the locker door as he removed the bomber jacket he'd been wearing. "While your red coat looks great, it doesn't blend in well. No matter how large the crowd is."

He traded me his leather jacket for my long warm coat, and folded the heavy red wool to fit into the locker after he added his bag. "We'll figure out what to do about all of this once we get more information and can make a better assessment."

The bomber jacket was warm and big and smelled like Jack,

the earthy and pleasant sandalwood-based scent I hadn't yet been able to find in any retail cologne. I loved the roomy pockets, and slipped in the travel-sized hairspray I'd used on my bathroom assailant. Much easier to grab it from a pocket than have to pull it from my purse.

We were about an hour away from the meeting time and heading to the cathedral made sense. As we left the station, Jack pulled me close. "Play along," he whispered in my ear. "If we need to talk, let's go the couple route. It will be less conspicuous than the two of us seeming to ignore each other and texting all the time."

I could have argued. I saw too many couples doing exactly that every day. My thumbs weren't crazy about nonstop texting though, so I agreed.

He kept his arm around me, and his head bent close to mine as we walked slower than we had been doing earlier. I was a little grateful to be back in the cold air.

"When we meet Ralf, you need to get him to deliver any information he might have from his sources that can expand on the official law enforcement files," Jack said. "The police might have learned part of what he knows from other criminal informants, but I'll bet your source knows things no one ever told when they were questioned."

"You're probably right. Do we show him the file attachments?"

Jack steered us toward a raised planter. We sat along the rim. "Let's see if we need to," he said, sitting close and keeping his voice barely audible. "Asking him questions about data we pulled from the files is one thing. Ethically, we're way beyond shaky if we actually show him the official files."

"Especially since we don't have official authority to have them ourselves." I almost breathed the words.

His chuckle was low and rich in my ear.

"If I miss anything during the meeting, you'll be close to jump in. Right?"

"As close as I am now," he said. "You and Nico may thoroughly trust this guy, but I don't have the luxury."

I was getting uncomfortably comfortable sitting with his arm tight around my shoulders and his breath warm on my neck. It was time to move. "Okay, let's go and head for the cathedral. Unless you have an idea of anything else we need to talk about or do before—"

"We could snog here for a while. Get our cover solid for anyone watching us."

I seriously wondered if the guy was reading my mind and stopped myself an instant before I bit my lower lip and gave myself away again. I covered with a shaky kind of laugh and patted his thigh. "Down, tiger. I'm sure your queen wouldn't ask you to do anything above and beyond."

"Who said it was my queen's idea?" His gaze bore into mine.

Okay, I was officially out of rebuttal words. I covered temporary laryngitis with another laugh and rose from the side of the planter, grabbing Jack's hand to pull him toward the cathedral. So it wouldn't appear to him like I was running away.

But I did want to run away—and I didn't. When my gaze met his I could tell he knew exactly how off-balance my emotions were at the moment, because he wore the self-satisfied smile that told me he knew everything I didn't want him to know.

The realization made me irritated enough for my confidence to return full force. "Quit trying to push my buttons, Hawkes, and come on. We have work to do."

"Pushing your buttons was the furthest thing from my mind," he said, walking beside me.

I wanted to say "pull the other one," but he'd laugh and make me angry again, and I didn't have the energy reserves to spare.

The Gothic cathedral filled one whole side of the city center. The thing about the Cologne Cathedral is it is huge. I mean, too-big-for-you-to-get-the-whole-thing-in-your-camera-phone-no-matter-how-far-away-you-back-up huge.

"Amazing they could make the towers so tall," Jack said. "What are they? Five hundred feet?"

I delved into my memory of European Cathedrals and Associated Religious Art from coursework my junior year and said,

"They used squirrel cages to lift the blocks." Nothing like an art history professor who loved the great cathedrals to provide every interesting element of their construction. "A worker would walk a wooden wheel, much like a giant hamster wheel, and the movement raised a pallet of those incredibly heavy blocks. Each block weighed about a hundred pounds. One man walking the wheel could raise pallets of material more than six times his weight, and raise the load as high as the ropes extended."

Admission was free, and we joined the rest of the pilgrims and tourists heading inside.

"One big piece of real estate," Jack murmured, looking around.

"We're to wait by St. Christopher."

"Naturally. Who better to guide us than the patron saint of pilgrims and travelers?"

St. Christopher was easy enough to spot. Ralf wasn't there yet, of course, but we took a minute to check out the space—and escape routes—in case things turned dicey.

The reconnaissance complete, I said, "Come on. Let's play pilgrim."

I'd been to the cathedral several times before, and knew from the way Jack was more focused on the crowds than the awe-inspiring heights he'd visited in the past as well. In the Middle Ages, Cologne became part of the European pilgrimage route in dramatic fashion. The bones of the Magi had been housed in Milan until the twelfth century. This grand new Gothic cathedral offered enough space for every pilgrim to stop in and pay their respects to the three kings who made their own journey to see the Christ child, so the bones and golden reliquary were given to Cologne. A pilgrimage stop for some, a holy spot for all.

The crowds hadn't diminished with time either.

"At least the masses give us the ability to hide in the mix," I said.

"And allow our followers to do the same." The look he gave me was grim.

We paid our respects to the altarpiece by fifteenth-century

international Gothic painter, Stefan Lochner, a giant in Europe's northern art renaissance movement. At the Milan Madonna, we stayed and pretended to talk, pointing up at the highlights of the masterpiece while we actually watched to see who in the crowd left before us—and who stayed as long as we did.

As we passed by the candles, I lit one in hopes of gaining a blessing on this mission. I'm not overly devout, but in this case I felt we needed every advantage. I moved away and Jack stepped forward and lit one as well.

"You want to head down to the vaults?" Jack whispered in my ear. "To see the evidence of how rich and powerful the city's archbishops were."

"Think I'll pass," I replied. "I prefer my pilgrim experiences not to be in subterranean locales where I only know one exit."

"I concur."

I looked at my watch and saw it was time to meander back to the rendezvous point. As we backtracked, my brain roamed over the big picture around us, keying in on the way this cathedral was designed in the shape of a cross, like a legion of others across medieval Europe. Divine dimensions, mimicking John the Baptist's words in Revelation about measuring God's heavenly city.

St. Christopher was right where we'd left him. After joining the procession around him and spending a quarter hour oohing and ahhing with the other tourists checking out the statue, Jack sent me a message. *Let's go by the wall. Compare notes by text.* I waited a beat before walking casually toward an empty spot at the outer wall. He followed. There were already a number of teens and twenty-somethings doing the same thing, and we fit right into the décor.

I take it you haven't seen Ralf, Jack texted.

No, but I've noticed a repeat guest to our party, I answered.

The man who looks like a farmer or the brunette trying to look like a schoolgirl?

I wanted to laugh, but responded, *The school girl. She's my age if she's a day.*

Don't be catty. She's younger than Cassie, but definitely past 6th form.

That's high school in America, right?

Close enough.

I raised my gaze a moment, as if resting my eyes from the screen or thinking. No one jumped out fitting the nickname. I typed, *What does the farmer look like?*

Fifties, half grey hair, half brown, rough skin on his hands and face, sturdy canvas duffle coat in blue with a bleach stain on the back of the arm. Probably doesn't realize about the stain, but made him easy to spot. A second later, Jack sent, *Hate to ask the obvious, but you haven't missed a text?*

No, checked before we started this. Held the phone while touristing so I could feel it vibrating. Nothing.

He added, *There's a kid. About 12. Went around the corner when we came over here. Looked away whenever our eyes met the last 10 mins or so.*

Watching?

Yeah, but may be looking for marks.

Pickpocket?

That's my thought, Jack said.

I had nothing more to add, and he stared off in the distance like he was out of texting material as well. A look at the clock said we were nearly thirty minutes over the meeting time. I typed, *Let's wander like we're taking a last look at the stained glass. It will get us logically around the church and give Ralf a chance to see us if he's late for some reason.*

Jack read his screen, nodded, and added, *Besides lighting a candle, hope we don't have to send up a prayer to St. Jude too.* He shot me a grave look and pocketed his phone.

I started to tell him not to start thinking lost causes, until I remembered Roberto and realized to what purpose Jack likely lit his candle. I pushed a worry about Ralf to the back of my mind and told it to stay put. Caught myself chewing my lower lip as we walked away.

Even with my short heels, my legs were starting to ache from standing and walking on hard surfaces all morning. This wasn't a time for whining, however. As we neared the "schoolgirl" I said brightly, "This place was definitely designed to make us feel small, and show us our place in the whole scheme of life. Come on, darling, we'll let it swallow us up for a while and tour the stained glass. The walls almost glow."

My *darling*'s face showed he was struggling not to laugh. He held out his arm, and I slipped a hand into the crook of his elbow.

An amazing fact about Gothic cathedrals was the many purposes of the windows. From a structural standpoint they actually provided a means of light and doubled as engineering tools. But the stained glass served another purpose. The colored glass above us reflected the passing of the centuries, and the compositions depicted the biblical stories people could "read" in the glass in an age when most were illiterate. In difficult times, the cathedral bathed churchgoers in light, and the towering beauty allowed them to vicariously experience heaven on earth. Heavenly art.

The range of artists contributing to the work included Gerhard Richter's modern play of colors. Almost an abstract in sunlight. The artistry bathed the church with jewel-toned divine light. I whispered, "Enough stained glass to cover two football fields."

"Your football fields or mine?" Jack asked.

"Ours probably. I first heard the comparison at Cornell."

Jack stood behind me. Then crashed into me. I was knocked down for the second time in as many days.

"*Scusi, scusi.*"

The words of Italian were what caught my attention.

"It was the kid," Jack said, searching his pockets to see what was missing. "His accent was fake."

The pickpocket was gone before I could barely be sure he was male. Young, dark, and gone.

"Are you okay?" Jack held my arm. We should have both fallen, but didn't.

"I'm fine. Did he get your wallet?"

"I've never had one apologize before," he said, checking his pockets. "Everything is here, including..."

A burner phone. A burner phone turned on and showing a text message.

Yes, you are being followed. Waited to be sure. Go to Baden-Baden. Check into a hotel and go to the casino tonight. Will make contact on Laurel's phone by 20:00 to tell where to meet.

Attached files displayed pictures of the schoolgirl and the farmer, as well as a man both of us remembered seeing after we'd arrived in Germany.

"I'm feeling a little creeped out," I whispered.

"They rotate to try to keep from being spotted." His frown deepened.

We tried to walk sedately from the cathedral, but all we could think about was getting to the train station and trying to slip our tails.

NINETEEN

Baden-Baden is in the Black Forest, though the locale isn't as dark as it sounds. The town is a place of rejuvenation and entertainment, with the bases covered by a world-class spa and one of the most beautiful casinos in the world. Monaco will always be my favorite for both, but Baden-Baden is an extremely close second and much more relaxing. I wished we were there for different circumstances, as I definitely could have used a battery recharge.

As it was, I got a quick nap on the fast train taking us from Cologne to the Black Forest destination. The train had six-passenger compartments. We couldn't get one of our own, but there had only been one other person in ours, leaving us room to stretch out and relax. Our travel companion, a man, was already reading when we got on the train and continued to read in the car when we got off at the station.

Buses ran from the Baden-Baden train station to the town center several times an hour, so we didn't have to wait long. Jack manhandled both our large bags and I grabbed the carry-ons. As he settled in the seat next to me I could see he was exhausted.

"Did you sleep at all on the train? The compartment seemed quiet enough." I said. I'd taken the opportunity to catch another cat nap and felt mildly refreshed.

He shook his head. "Too many things running through my brain. I sent some messages around. Received a text back from a detective in Scarsdale. He's going to see if he can get the lead detective on your mother's case to talk to me, maybe send copies of his notes."

"I need to call Cassie and Nico," I said, looking at my watch and subtracting five hours. "Except it's too early for them to have met with anyone." I laughed quietly. "Who am I kidding? I want to hear their voices to know they're okay. Tell them we have a never-ending army following us, and to be sure no one is stalking them. I feel like a mother hen. Which is usually Cassie's job."

"I already texted Nico with a brief rundown of events."

"You haven't heard from them?"

He looked at his watch. "If either is even up, they probably aren't functional yet. I said in my text not to worry about contacting us unless they had something to report, as we're in the middle of a dilemma ourselves."

"A stagnant one at the moment."

"Yes, waiting is always the hardest part."

We were soon in the lobby of a charming hotel sitting right on the cobblestoned old center. Jack got us connecting rooms. Now that Nico wasn't with me I wondered who was footing the bill. Something we needed to discuss.

Our bags were deposited in the rooms, and we received a brief tour of the accommodations. When we were alone once more, I opened the door between the rooms and pointed at Jack's bed. "Nap. No arguments."

"If you stay in your room."

"I'll stay in the hotel," I said. "But I might actually want to go down to the lobby to find something to read or drink."

He sat down on the bed and fell back. "God, you're right. I about fell asleep on the bus. If you promise—"

"I promise. I'll wake you in a couple of hours and we'll go to dinner."

"I should be hungry. You're probably hungry."

"You're too tired to be hungry, and I can take care of myself..."

There was no point in saying anything else. He was out. I grabbed him by the back of the ankles and rotated him until most of him was on the bed. I removed his shoes and pulled the drapes, making everything a little more comfortable for sleeping. I contemplated raising his head to actually get a pillow underneath, but he looked so peaceful I decided to let him find it himself as he slept. I walked back into my room and closed the door until it almost latched.

Ralf's instructions said we were going to the casino, which meant I needed to unpack enough to determine if I had something suitable to wear. First, though, I pulled out the burner phone and sent him a text giving the name of our hotel. I hoped he remembered the number of the cell and would accept the message. I could have sent the information via my phone, but I figured he sent us the burner phone for a reason. The boy could have slipped a note in Jack's pocket instead.

"Well, no, he couldn't. The phone allowed him to send the pictures too," I mused. It didn't matter. I'd already sent the text.

I decided on my wardrobe choice. The little black dress I always traveled with made the cut. My outerwear options were limited, and it looked like my red coat again, despite Jack's reservations. "It's not like I can keep wearing his bomber jacket all the time."

The en suite bathroom was very small, but sufficient. I thought about a shower but would have to deal with my hair, and if this evening ended like most of our adventures I'd need another shower later anyway. I soon had my makeup off and reapplied.

Killing time was killing me. To rescue my patience, I walked to the nightstand and picked up my room key. I jumped when the room phone gave a ringing burst. "Hello," I said quietly. One ear listened to the desk clerk, the other was at the wall to determine if Jack had been disturbed by the sound.

Apparently Ralf did want to know where we were. The front desk informed me a guest waited downstairs to see me.

"I'll be right down," I said and hung up.

Opening the shared door a little wider, I could see Jack breathing steadily and deeply. It wasn't exactly a snore but...

I scooped up the room key and my wallet, thinking I'd get the drink I mentioned before I returned. When I got to the lobby, I was pointed in the direction of a small lounge. It wasn't Ralf. An older gentleman stood alone in the room, dressed in a heavy coat and boots, with enough snow on his dark slacks to indicate he might have hiked there. He walked closer, extending a hand to shake—

It was Moran. I turned to flee, but he caught my arm.

"Please, *Mademoiselle* Beacham. Laurel, if I may. You have nothing to fear from me at this time. I have come to warn you."

"How did you know I was here?" He could make all the assurances he wanted. I was not going to believe him.

"I've had people looking out for your wellbeing." He hadn't yet let go, but used his free hand to wave it in the direction of two high-backed reading chairs. "Please, sit with me for a moment. We need to talk."

"Okay. But I'm not leaving this hotel." It wasn't merely from my promise to Jack—I knew better than to trust this man.

I chose the chair nearer the door, and he finally released my arm. We each leaned over the small table between the chairs to speak without being overheard. I was prepared to scream long and loud if I thought it necessary—but I felt more curious than threatened. "Why the cat and mouse with all the people following us? If you're trying to kill me—"

"*Non, non,*" he said, shaking his silver head. I saw a felt hat at his feet and wondered if it was his. "I am not the one trying to harm you."

"Who is?"

"The name used is Ermo Colle, but it is not really anyone's name. It is a clean name and suits his purposes. Even the face is different from the original, I am told. The man acts powerful, but he is afraid." Moran looked up and trained his gaze on me. I saw faded blue eyes under bushy brows and wondered exactly how old he was. "He is afraid of you."

I shook my head. "I don't know Ermo Colle. Tell me what he looks like."

"He would just change his appearance again." Moran reached over and gently clasped my hand. "You are a threat to him."

I gambled and said, "You're working with him. Why don't you stop him from doing whatever you don't like?"

His face reddened. Frightened, I wanted to move away, but he gripped my hand tighter. I pulled, but he hung on and spoke, his tone soft, but his words intense, "Listen to me. My organization is mine alone. Ermo Colle is dangerous to you."

"Why?" I successfully jerked back my hand. "Why should I trust you? To help you take out your competition? Help you take over? You sent goons after me in London—"

"*Non, non.*" He shook his head and the combed-back steel and silver hair didn't move a fraction. "Imbeciles. They did everything all wrong."

"Because I didn't let them catch me?"

He sighed. "Here, I will prove I've not come to harm you. I want you to have something."

He rose from the chair and started patting pockets until he found the right one. The item he withdrew was something I recognized immediately and had missed terribly.

I couldn't keep from smiling. "A telescoping baton," I said.

"You broke my assistant's wrist that time in America. You were very good with it," he said.

"My favorite defensive weapon, but illegal in the U.K. I left mine in America," I said. "Even there I have to be careful. Some states allow them. Others, like New York, consider them illegal offensive weapons."

"You need this while you're here. If you want to leave it behind when you depart Germany, so be it," he said, slipping the collapsed baton into my hand and closing my fingers around it. "Keep it handy as long as you can. Keep it with you always."

"Thank you," I said. "But we still aren't friends."

He gave a hearty belly laugh and retook his chair. "Oh, you have very much of your mother in you."

"Why did you send the compact and the jewelry box to me? Who is the man in the picture?" I put the baton in my lap, and had to clasp my hands together and rest them on top to keep from reaching for him. If I did, I was afraid I might start begging for information.

He shook his head. "The items belong to you. I've thought for years to send them to you, but we've gotten at cross purposes, and I didn't want to give you a shock."

"Why do it now, so many years later?"

"It was important." He looked at me and lowered his brows, looking very serious. "The pattern has changed. It is not a game anymore. Lives are being lost as the numbers shift. You needed to know what you didn't know. To put the facts together more correctly. Know who you can't trust. Not simply who is trustworthy."

"How does a jewelry case from my late mother tell me who to trust?"

"You've had a shock. You don't need more."

"You're wrong there, and you can't show up here and expect to be believed for purely altruistic reasons. Without me asking questions."

He sighed heavily. "My English, it is…"

"Don't try to snow me, Moran. Your English is as good as you want it to be. Do you know anything about why European forgers are being killed? Is it your doing?"

"Why would I kill the lifeblood of my industry?" He raised his brows and looked so innocent, even while admitting with his words he dealt in forgeries—and I couldn't touch him for it.

"Who is committing the murders?"

"I…I have my suspicions. With any luck, they should stop soon."

"How? What aren't you telling me? Give me a name, Moran. Help me stop this. Is Colle behind the murders?"

He put a finger to his lips and smiled. I hadn't been talking loudly and assumed it was his means of telling me he was keeping the knowledge secret. I knew for sure a moment later when he patted my hand and rose again from the chair.

"Be careful of Colle. I'll keep a person watching you. Someone better than the man you spotted this morning at the museum."

"He was your man? How many others were there? We know there are more." I stood up and we were nearly the same height.

He buttoned his coat, then retrieved the hat from the floor. "As my man left, someone else assumed his mission. He'd seen other people watching you. He came with you from Italy, but the others were already in Cologne."

He held his black gloves and rested his hand on my shoulder. "I am ready to retire to my vineyard. The game is more dangerous than before. Art is not the only thing people move. Masterpieces are not the fastest way to get rich today. Stay away from Ermo Colle."

With that, he shook my right hand and headed for the door.

"Wait!"

He turned. "Yes?"

"Was Tony B working for you?"

The word he uttered was pitched low, but I was fairly positive he said *connard*. "Okay, you didn't like him either. Can I assume a no?"

"Have you ever known me to do anything other than first class?" he asked. "I've always admired the way you did all your work—knew what you needed to know ahead of time."

I could feel a blush rising and squeezed the baton. This was not going the way I wanted. "If you admired the way I did my homework, help me. Please. Was Tony B working for Ermo Colle?"

An expression flickered across his face. Too quickly to read or even be sure it wasn't my imagination.

"You can find what you need elsewhere. You always have," he said.

When he set his hat on his head and turned again to leave, I blurted, "Will you tell me about my mother? About how you knew her?"

His face crumpled, and I was afraid he was going to cry. However, when he spoke, his voice was strong. "I let her down." He nodded his head and said, "I knew. I knew." He turned and hurried away. By the time I got to the lobby door he was climbing into a car waiting for him outside. I ran to get the tag number, but I was too late.

The hotel's small bar was open, but empty. I ordered a hearty sandwich on crusty bread and the house wine, a dry white the region was known for. There was a lot to process, and I had no idea where to start. At the same time, I wasn't sure I'd learned anything concrete. I felt in my pocket for the baton and felt safe for the first time in weeks. Was this what he came for? To give me the weapon?

My sandwich arrived and I ate and drank methodically. The more I thought, the more I recognized the visit was all about my safety, exactly like he said. Was he protecting me as I was supposed to believe? Or was this all a ploy to con me into trusting him? First the gifts of my mother's things, the photographs. How could I help but see she obviously trusted someone close to Moran—at least the implication was there. Then he gave me a weapon tonight. A weapon he knew I'd used successfully in the past. To pacify me or to up my guard?

Yet if he came to persuade me—to protect me—why did Simon break into my office? Was Simon trying to take me somewhere to keep me safe? Moran didn't act threatening tonight, but when this whole caper started he sent Weasel and Werewolf to try to chloroform me on the Tube train. How was that being protective? I'd only escaped by stomping on the foot of Dylan's friend and jumping into a cab with them. Obviously, I needed to make some notes on what to ask Moran the next time he materialized in my life.

Back to Simon's theatrical stunt. Why would he go in with a battering ram if Moran's orders were to keep me from being harmed by Ermo Colle? Was Simon working on his own? I wished I'd thought to ask before he left. However, self-recrimination wouldn't solve anything. No reason for me even to consider the question until I had time to think it all through.

I reconsidered the questions I had asked. The way Moran answered each one. The responses never actually matched their respective queries.

The barman gave me a pen, and I used a napkin to jot down what I remembered of the impromptu Q and A. This was going to take some ruminating over before I'd know what he was really telling me.

After I exhausted my memory, I gave back the pen, pocketed the napkin, and ordered a sandwich and a beer to take up to Jack. A glance at my watch said we had about an hour to get to the casino by eight p.m. I didn't know if Ralf planned to contact us by phone or at the casino, but the time was in his text with orders to go there, and we needed to get moving.

By the time I got upstairs, I could hear the shower running in the next room. Gambling starts in the afternoon at Baden-Baden and goes into the wee hours. I hoped the shower helped Jack wake up, as I had the feeling it would be a while before we'd see these rooms again.

I heard the water stop and slipped in quickly to leave the plate and bottle on his nightstand. Back in my own room, I pushed the door completely closed and headed for the closet. My dress was ready to go, but I wished for a pocket or two to keep the baton handy and out of sight. I pulled the lovely weapon from my slacks and held it out in front of me. One flick of my wrist and the darling extended from about half a foot to nearly two. The sound alone made me tingly. I struck the mattress a few times for practice.

Jack called through the wall, "Is this food mine?"

"Yes, we need to go soon. Should I call the desk and order a car?"

"I'll do it."

I smiled. He was so predictable.

My baton needed a holder of some kind, to keep it on my person until I needed it. In a few minutes, I'd taken a belt and fashioned a kind of garter-holster, returned the baton to its smallest size, and strapped it in the holder. I slipped the black dress over my head to determine if any sign of the weapon could be detected when I stared in the full-length mirror.

It looked okay, but not good enough. Digging around in my

luggage, I looked for any kind of clutch purse. Down deep, I found a royal blue silk-covered bag barely bigger than the baton. It would have to do. I prayed I would know the doorman for the night and could talk my way inside without being wanded.

TWENTY

Jack was ready to go when the desk called to say our car had arrived. We hadn't had any time to talk, but I figured telling about my late-afternoon chat would wind him up to give me a lecture anyway. Putting off a recap of the Moran interview was fine with me.

At the last minute, I removed my mother's bracelets from the clamshell case in the Fendi and added the glittery bangles to my right wrist. I hoped they brought me luck, and not just at the blackjack tables. I put on my coat in the elevator, then straightened Jack's tie.

"Is it okay?" he asked. "I did it without looking."

"Let me wrangle the knot a little," I said. "There." I patted the tie against his chest, looked up, and smiled. "Perfect."

"You clean up well too," he said, returning the smile. "Did you find something to read?"

I stopped myself a millisecond before I chewed my lower lip. "No, I made some lists. Trying to put everything in perspective."

"Good idea. We probably need to compare notes again."

In the car. I'd tell him in the car, I thought. Maybe I'd hold the baton while I told him.

Our driver pulled smoothly away from the curb. Well, as smoothly as one can on a cobblestone road. It was time to face the inquisition. "Jack, I—"

His phone rang and gave me a reprieve.

"It's the detective in New York."

"By all means, get it. We can talk later."

"Yeah, Shultz, thanks for calling me back," he launched the conversation. I felt the tension in my shoulders ease a little.

The conversation ended as the car pulled up to the casino portico. What I'd heard of the exchange revolved around cop shoptalk, and factoring in the wide time zone differences between here and New York to allow Jack to talk to the retired detective.

"Did you catch any of that?" he asked. He stepped from the car and reached back to help me out.

"Enough. It sounded promising."

"I'm almost wondering if it would be worth a field trip. If I can see all the files." He returned his phone to the inside pocket of his suit coat. The walk had been swept of snow and ice but remained slick in spots. Jack offered his arm, and I put one hand through the crook of his elbow and wrapped the other around his forearm. I used my upper right arm to clamp the shiny blue clutch tight by my side.

We walked along the portico, fairy lights shining in the gables. Friezes of Grecian gentry decorated the space above the entrance. I recognized Triesa at the door talking to one of the guards as we approached. She was dressed elegantly in winter white. "Triesa," I called and waved.

"Is it really you, Laurel Beacham?" She laughed and clapped and scampered our way. "You haven't been here in months. We've missed you!"

Triesa was a former blackjack dealer who worked her way up to a general manager position, or whatever they call the level in German. She was originally from Paris, but had settled into the resort area nicely. I'd always gone to the sultry brunette's table whenever I came to play. Nowadays, I made sure I went by her office to visit before I left each time.

"Work," I said in explanation. "I was supposed to get a vacation in September, and I couldn't even break away long enough."

"You should have come here. We would have hidden you away."

My hope for tonight. Aloud I said, "We wanted to break away for the evening. For some fun." I patted Jack's arm and smiled up at him to be sure he was playing along. I needn't have worried. Jack introduced himself in French, speaking in one of his amazing accents—this time full Parisian—and had Triesa charmed in no time.

"Come, it's cold here," she said. "We'll get inside quickly."

Things looked promising. She bypassed the line in and waved for us to follow, hugging the wall and avoiding any security procedure. We got our coats checked, and she introduced us to the "gatekeeper" who subtly checked names, faces, and apparel choices before visitors received permission to grace the gaming area. Jack's suit and tie easily passed muster, as did my dress, though my nearly bare arms did miss my coat.

"Bernard, make sure they are well taken care of," Triesa said.

"Always," he replied, stepping back to allow the three of us to enter.

Triesa put a hand on my arm. "I must go back to the door. I am waiting for someone else to arrive. You look cold. Can I send down a wrap from my office?"

"That would be fabulous."

She gazed at each of us in turn. "You'll be at blackjack."

Jack nodded, and I said, "You know my game."

Triesa walked away. Jack and I entered the opulence.

Built in the 1850s and designed along the lines of the palace of Versailles, the casino immediately gave the feeling of stepping back into the French courts of Louis XVI and Marie Antoinette. I just hoped our mission tonight wasn't as doomed as their reign. Ceilings in the gaming room were several stories high, with luxurious wallpaper covering the lower eight or ten feet, and the plaster and paint beyond showcasing the gilded trim work detail. Carved doorways and entry arches let a steady flow of gamblers choose their games and level of risk. The chandeliers always took my breath away. Crystal and brass, almost dripping light, and looking as if they could rain down diamonds. No wonder Marlene Dietrich called Baden-Baden the most beautiful casino in the world. It was also a favorite of Kaiser Wilhelm I and Russian author Dostoyevsky.

We strolled by black and red roulette wheels framed by highly polished wood, and watched players at tables alternately sit stoically by what was left of their winnings or fiddle nervously with the chips. Everywhere was the sound of clicking chips, spinning roulette wheels, and the swish of cards dealt for blackjack. The air felt electric. What I loved about Baden-Baden was the way the crowd was made up of more middle-class than at Monaco. People came to have fun with friends, dress up, and pretend to be a royal. Given the odds favored the house, this made the experience more palatable to me.

As we arrived at a blackjack table, a casino employee in a dark suit walked up with a cream-colored wrap in his hand. "From Triesa," he said.

"Thank you," I said, immediately settling it over my shoulders. He gave a respectful nod and left. I would have asked how he knew who I was, but Triesa was always good with description, and security cameras had our picture dozens of times over.

Jack carried my phone in a pocket so we could leave it on vibrate. Minutes after we had our chips and settled into chairs, he was handing the cell back to me. Ralf's name appeared on the screen. I pushed my chips Jack's way. "Stay here. I'll find out where he wants to meet and be right back."

I hurried away before he could argue.

"Hi, we're in the casino playing blackjack," I said in way of greeting. Actually, I was on the far wall trying to catch a little privacy, but the neighborhood was the same.

"Do you know the back meeting rooms?" Ralf asked.

"Yes."

"Meet me in the second one as soon as you can get away without being noticed."

Quite an optimistic statement when we were in a casino with top industry security and cameras covering every square inch.

Seconds later, I had Jack up to speed. He finished his current hand, then tipped the dealer a chip and scooped up the rest to follow me.

We chose a circuitous route, and I stopped to greet a couple of friends I noticed along the way. The meeting rooms weren't restricted, but I understood Ralf's concerns and wanted to move cagily but without creating suspicion.

We entered the paneled hallway to the meeting rooms just as another man was leaving. I knew Jack would memorize his features and didn't bother trying. I turned the doorknob of the second room and poked my head in to make sure I had the right one. Ralf pulled the door open when he saw me.

"Come in, come in."

He looked as rail-thin as ever, and his impish face made me automatically smile. I always wondered how many times his grin got him out of tight spots. He was not dressed in a suit and tie, but he was in basic black. There was no way he came in through the front entrance.

"Moonlighting in a second job?" I quipped after he'd closed the door behind Jack.

He grinned and held out a hand. "Ralf Burkhard. You must be Jack Hawkes."

Jack raised an eyebrow, but only said, "Pleasure to meet you."

"Someone has been doing his homework," I said.

"Like you wouldn't have done the same," he replied, directing his grin at me to take any sting out of the response.

We clustered around the table near the outer wall, our conversation pitched low to reduce the risk of being overheard by the adjacent rooms.

"We're so sorry about your cousin's death," I said.

"Tell me what I can do to help," Ralf started the conversation. "My cousin was young and stupid due to immaturity and probably greed. But he should not be dead."

"We need to know about any jobs he did that sounded a bit off," I explained. "Did Nico tell you—"

"Yes." He nodded. "I think I know. He was commissioned to do five abstracts for a new client. Ermo Colle."

"Five different paintings? Or—"

"No. The same one five times."

"Was he told to add a forger's mark?" I asked.

He nodded. "On four, yes. We talked about it—laughed at the client's request—and tried to figure out why four and not all. Or any."

"What did the forger's mark look like?" Jack asked.

Ralf flipped out a notecard resting under one of his hands. "Like this."

"Can we have this?" I asked.

"Absolutely."

It was a new brand we hadn't researched yet. I snapped a picture of it with my phone. "I'm sending this to Nico. He can check it out while they're working the other avenue."

"We have access to the official files on your cousin's death," Jack said, without elaborating further. "Is there anything you know unofficially to help us do what we need to do and possibly identify your cousin's killer?"

Ralf shook his head, making his hands into fists on the table. I could feel his frustration when he said, "My cousin was a brilliant artist, but too young to spot when he was being used. I've heard many stories about forgers who've met his same fate in the past couple of years. I cannot prove this Ermo Colle is behind all of them." He covered his heart with his right hand. "I know here."

"We agree with you unequivocally," Jack said. "The organization comes up clean at every turn, as does every person connected to it. We need something to use—"

"There are many layers," Ralf said, his hands fisted again.

"Yes, and the fact each layer is impenetrable simply heightens our suspicions. We have people who know people, but we don't have a primary source witness who has actually worked for Ermo Colle and can tell about it."

"Like my cousin."

"Exactly."

Ralf dropped his head down for a moment to rest on his fists, then he pushed off from the tabletop to stand and pace his side of the table. He was never a mellow person, but I couldn't remember seeing him wound so tightly. His belief, of course, was one we'd already suspected. After talking to Moran, however, I was more convinced. The old man didn't give me proof and a description, but if I knew anything after pursuing him all these years, I knew he had his finger on the pulse of the criminal underground. The murders may not have tagged back directly with anyone affiliated with Ermo Colle, but there was a connection.

"Can you give us a description of someone in the Colle organization you suspect?" Jack asked.

"Better. You can see the head man here, tonight. At least it is rumored he will be here. The casino has been preparing for his arrival. To them he is a big businessman with lots of money. They haven't yet seen past the mask."

I thought back to Triesa's attendance at the front door. "This is a good idea, Ralf. We should be able to spot him without giving away our interest."

He rose from his chair and motioned it was time to leave. "You can go first. I'll slip out afterward."

And no one will see you go. I wondered if he'd depart via a window or a more unconventional route.

The guys shook hands again. Ralf kissed my cheek, and I grasped his hands. They were much warmer than mine. "Be careful."

"Exactly what I was going to tell you."

We were soon down the hall and back in the gaming area.

As we walked, I spoke, "We need to find—"

"Triesa's whale," Jack finished.

"I wonder if he's here because of us or if it's a coincidence."

"Do you think the people watching us worked for him?"

Past time to tell about my meeting with Moran. I motioned Jack to follow me to a quiet corner and offered a quick but thorough rundown of what happened earlier in the hotel lounge. His face grew darker with every sentence.

"Why the bloody hell did you meet him alone?" Jack's rage was quiet, but his gaze felt lethal.

"I thought it was Ralf. I told you, I texted Ralf the name of our hotel."

"When you saw him, you should have—"

"I didn't know it was him until I was halfway into the room. He looked German. And nice."

Jack blew out a breath. "You said he looked French and nice the last time."

"He did. He looks different and the same every time."

For several seconds, all I got was a steady glare. Finally, he said, "You should have told me right away."

"You were in the shower when I got back."

"You could have told me while I was eating or dressing."

"We needed to hurry." Frustrated, I raised my hands halfway in the air, palms up. "I was going to tell you in the car, but you stopped me to take the detective's call. Then we were here and Triesa came up and got us inside so quickly, and we needed to play a little to build our cover, and Ralf called. This is the first opportunity, dammit."

"Not really, but—"

"At least I didn't go to Rome and call you," I finished.

We glared at one another for a minute, and I realized we each had hands on our hips and our faces were only about an inch apart. I relaxed and stepped back, hoping security would believe it was a domestic squabble and pay no more attention to us. Jack obviously assumed the same and offered his arm. We resumed playing congenial date night.

"He told you he only had one person at a time following us?" he asked.

"Yes. He implied the other watchers were from Ermo Colle, but he didn't say definitively. Are we good?"

"Yes, okay," he said. "But it's really not the same."

The man always had to try for the last word.

"It's exactly the same," I said. Emotion made me huff a little before I plastered on a fake smile to display to the room. "The only difference is I had the information this time. Not you."

"As long as we're clear—"

"Shut up, Jack."

TWENTY-ONE

Spotting Triesa's whale was easy enough. The crowd around the roulette wheel applauding over the high-stakes bets and wins steered us in the right direction. She was still with Colle but trying to leave. He was a distinguished-looking man in his early sixties with a marvelous head of blond hair that didn't look like it came from the salon, though it obviously had.

We snagged spots near one side of the wheel, and Triesa noticed me as she walked away. She sidetracked. "You look warmer," she said, laying a hand on my wrap-covered arm. "More comfortable."

"No one takes care of people better than you, Triesa. Thank you."

"If I don't see you again before you leave, please come back soon," she said. "We miss you."

We shared a quick hug and she disappeared in the crowd.

"Anything?" I asked Jack.

"Not yet."

He turned so his back was to the table and I could take over momentarily. I watched Colle, but stayed hidden by the bystanders who stood two-deep behind each of the players. Colle didn't look my way, and he seemed to have his own posse surrounding him. I wondered again about what Moran did and didn't say. If the old con man had actually been playing fox in the hen house.

Jack turned back around, set a few chips on the table, and placed a bet on black. I kept my place a little behind him to see the table and most of the participants. The ball landed on red. Colle won. Everyone cheered. Jack shoved another chip onto thirty-two.

Colle put a pile on three. Cheers rose up again when the single digit nailed the prize. I noticed the person standing next to our croupier and nearly swallowed my tongue. It was the schoolgirl all grown up.

I squeezed in beside Jack and gave him a sharp nudge, angling to give my back to her and hide both our faces. "See who's playing groupie to the croupier?"

He nodded, unconcerned.

"Any plans?"

"Best way to keep surveillance on a person watching you is to pretend you don't know you're being watched."

Probably some logic there somewhere, but I found myself chewing my bottom lip.

Excitement erupted at a table nearby, and things suddenly went quiet at ours. I used the moment to step back and adjust the wrap, raising my right arm to pull the material higher on my shoulder. My cascade of bangle bracelets cut through the silence.

Colle whipped around, displaying a look of near horror.

"I'm sorry," I said, cornered. "I didn't realize they'd make this much noise."

The crowd around him stared at me, then looked back at Colle. His expression changed. Not any more relaxed, but different. Yet, both responses reminded me of...No.

It had to be a trick of the light. A shared expression. Ten years...

I started to move away. I'd been made, after all. Jack put a hand at my waist and signaled for me to stay close. I sat beside him and looked elsewhere, but I kept an eye on Colle. A shiver ran down my spine when I noticed he was doing the same. I watched his hand and detected the tiniest shake. Nerves?

Moran's words haunted me. *He's afraid of you.*

The croupier spun the wheel again, and Colle lost this time. The odds remained against Jack.

The loss seemed to signal a timeout for Colle. He spoke quietly to his entourage, and the sea of bodies parted to let him pass through. I told Jack, "Stay here. I'll be right back," and hurried away. I could feel the air movement as he tried to catch me, but I was faster.

"Hello, I'm Laurel Beacham," I said. Colle waved away the two people beside him and shook the hand I offered. The handshake gave me the proof I needed. Age and plastic surgery changed his face, but the way he gripped my hand remained the same. Like the surprised expressions he'd exhibited at the table when he heard my mother's bracelets. Though it was confirmation, shock rushed through my veins.

"Daddy. It's really you." I felt tears on my cheeks. How? Why?

He sighed. "Hello, kitten."

A second later, he pulled me close, wrapping his arm tightly around my shoulders.

"Don't look back at your young man," he whispered into my ear. "Or he'll be dead. Walk with me, and we'll do a little talking."

He led me back into the direction of the meeting rooms, and I really wished I'd found out Ralf's escape method.

A ruckus coming from behind us told me Jack tried to play white knight. I wondered how many of the people at the table were truly gamblers and how many were paid stooges of...well, my father. My mind couldn't believe it.

"We thought you were dead all these years. Do you have any idea what I went through?"

"Hush. We'll talk in private or not at all."

If death was waiting for me, at least Jack or Nico could find my body with the charm bracelet. I moved the zipper on my clutch as quietly as I could.

The room wasn't the same one where we met with Ralf, but it was identical. One big difference, however, was the gun and silencer my father pointed in my direction.

"Sit down, we'll go to the car momentarily," Colle said.

"I'm not ready to leave."

"You weren't asked. There are things you need to understand."

"You'll answer my questions?"

The gun seemed to grow bigger by the second.

"I'll tell you what you need to know," he said. "Not here."

I'd already put my hand in my clutch, hidden under Triesa's wrap. My fingers tightened around the baton.

"I think I'm good, just the same."

"Sit—"

I whipped out the baton and flicked it. Ready for action. We were barely a foot apart. I slammed down on the wrist holding the gun. He gave a cry of pain, and the weapon slid across the table. Away from me. He reached to grab the gun with his other hand. I whapped him across the top of his head, near one of his temples.

His hand flew to the side and knocked the gun out of sight, to the floor. His head slammed onto the tabletop.

I didn't check his pulse. I didn't hunt for the gun. I ran like hell.

In the hallway I was immediately caught from behind. Two very muscled arms grabbed me in a hug when I tried to break free.

"Stop, and I'll get you out," his deep voice whispered in a French accent.

"Who are you?" I struggled against his grip.

"Rollie says *salut*."

I stopped moving, and he let me go. I didn't know if I was making a better choice, but my options were quickly narrowing.

"Can you get help for my friend at the roulette table?" I asked.

"Already being done."

His face was one Ralf sent on the phone. "I hope you're not lying to me," I said. "I've had a really long day, and it hasn't improved any after dark—"

"Come on."

He led me into an office, pushed one of the walls and created an exit. "Here." He handed me a silver ring with a fob and a key. "There is a black BMW parked nearby. Drive to your hotel. Park as close as you can on the street and leave the key with the front desk clerk."

"Where are you going?" I asked, suddenly feeling a little lost at the idea of being on my own.

"After I see if Colle has been discovered, I'm going to check on your friend."

I felt immediately better. "Thank you."

He disappeared out one door while I ran through the other.

I found the car. As I pulled away I saw a limo at the entrance. From the back, the woman exiting the vehicle looked like Melanie. She turned her head and I was certain. I forced myself to keep my foot on the accelerator instead of stamping on the brake.

What was she doing here? Seeing her made me positive she was the person who accosted me in the bathroom. She must have planned to snatch my bag in the train station toilette and let her backup goon stop me when I gave chase. She'd been chummy with Tony B. Was she with Colle?

I drove on autopilot to the hotel, deep in thought over this new twist. At the front desk, I gave the clerk the key and Triesa's wrap, asking they hold the one and return the other to the casino. I started to ask for my coat to be retrieved when the wrap was delivered, but decided to wait and see how things unfolded in the near future. Triesa catering to Colle—no way I could think of him as my father—didn't surprise me if he was only a wealthy businessman to her. But it was past time to be careful. The last risky chance I took got me a gun pointed in my face.

Opening my clutch for the room key, I gave the baton a loving pat. While I'd chased Moran for years, my mind had a new take on the man, and I was grateful for the gift of the weapon and his continuing protection. Though I didn't want to get used to it either. This couldn't lead to anything long-term. I didn't get answers from Colle, but I planned to take a shot at getting a few from Moran.

He had answers I really wanted, both professionally and personally. I'd never take anything for granted when it came from Moran's direction. I couldn't afford to. I would, however, try to get more information about my mother if Jack wasn't successful.

As he left the hotel, if Moran hadn't spoken about letting her down, I probably would have been more suspicious his cryptic answers meant he had something to do with her death. Yet in the meantime my own father rose from the dead and pulled a gun on me, after having assumed a persona I'd hunted for months. Hired people to stalk me. My suspicions shifted dramatically.

I entered the room, slipping off my heels. I pulled the baton from my clutch and tossed both items onto the bed. My clothes from earlier laid across the seatback of the chair. I was hungry and back to Jack's bomber jacket. I needed to wear something more in tune to the jacket's style than an LBD and heels. I quickly changed.

As far as I knew, my cell was in his jacket pocket. All of my numbers were in my phone. Nico might have some ideas, but it would likely only bring him and Cassie into my worry circle. Still, it was worth a try.

I sat down on the bed and lifted the receiver from the room phone on the nightstand.

"Hang up."

The bathroom door had been closed when I entered the room. When I looked up it framed Simon's body. A knife gleamed in his hand.

"Do you know you're the second person who's pulled a weapon on me in the last hour?" I said, feeling suddenly pissed off at the rapid change of events. Restoring the receiver to the phone, I shifted to hide the baton with my thigh. I covered the weapon with my left hand.

"You have a tendency to make people want to kill you," he said, taking a step closer.

"I could say the same for you." I smiled as my fingers wrapped around the steel baton. I pointed to the knife with my right hand. "Did you and Moran disagree on my care and safety? Or have you had a falling out?"

"Let's say I switched allegiances."

"Was it something I said? Or something my father gave you?"

"Ah, you know, do you?" His smile was pure evil. How in the world had I ever slept with this man? But my mother did marry my father. Possible genetic flaw for the women in my family.

"How long did you plan to wait here tonight?" I asked.

"Until you returned from your night of losing and I could finish the job."

"I only made one bet."

"And?"

"I lost." I gave him a slow smile. "Then I hit the daily double. I found out my father is alive, but I may have killed him for good. A girl can hope anyway."

He lunged, but I was ready. The baton whacked his hand seconds before the knife could reach my throat. The weapon flew over his other shoulder and clattered to the floor behind him.

The next instant, he was on top of me, using his forearm to crush my windpipe. I used my right thumb to gouge his eye, while my left hand continued beating him with the baton. When the pain grew too insistent, he moved off me to retrieve his knife. I swung my legs to roll backward and land with the bed standing between us. The window was behind me. He moved to cut me off, but I opened the window and stepped out onto the narrow ledge.

Climbing is one of my favorite pastimes, but I usually do it with a chalk pack, safety ropes, and preferably a partner who isn't trying to murder me. Though at no time do I climb anything remotely similar to narrow icy ledges with leather-soled street boots. Extraordinary conditions called for extraordinary measures, however, and I shut out any thoughts about the three-story fall, telling myself even if I did tumble I'd likely only break a leg. Not that it made me feel better.

I felt worse when Simon joined me on the ledge with the knife. He stopped for a moment, apparently getting his balance. His back was flat to the bricked building. Looking at his feet, I groaned. He wore athletic shoes.

Jumping started to have more appeal.

I sandwiched the baton with my left arm and body. The weapon was at full length for readiness, but this method left both hands free to grab any possible hold along the way. As I quickened my pace one foot slid from the ledge. I recovered a second later, but I was shaking.

"Give it up, Laurel. If I don't kill you here, I'll kill you on the ground when you fall."

I passed the window beyond Jack's and tried to raise the sash. Locked.

"Someone is going to see us and call the police," I said, hoping I was right. Below us stretched a back alley. Cartons and opened packing crates leaned against the opposite wall. Two dumpsters sat halfway down the block. It really bites when a girl can't even count on an open dumpster to break her fall.

Shuffling again, getting farther away, I told myself Simon's feet were larger than mine. Even with the advantage of athletic shoes he could fall as easily. I mentally repeated the thought several times to myself.

Nothing seemed to worry Simon. "No one will see me if I'm quick."

"I'll scream all the way down. Someone will hear me and see you. They'll arrest you for pushing me."

Chuckling, he said, "As usual, you underestimate my connections."

I seized the far end of the window frame. Having the extra couple of inches of space while I passed the glass felt almost a luxury. My frightened inner child said, *break the glass and escape.* The rational part of me cautioned, *and bounce off the glass to plunge to your death or slit your wrist when the glass shards penetrate your fist.*

Original plan it is, I thought. Slowly. Carefully. Moving with my feet turned as much as possible to be parallel with the building.

Simon picked up speed.

I slid to the other side of the window and was again face to face with the bricks. I contemplated trying to turn around while I could use the recessed space. If all my weight was against the building and my heels on the ledge, could I travel any quicker?

I would lose the ability to grab with my fingertips. Those same strong and grasping fingers had saved my tethered ass in many a rock climb. I prayed they would be equally helpful while I wasn't wearing a safety harness. That decided things for me. I raised my right hand to my mouth and pulled the glove off with my teeth, letting it fall into the alley. The air was cold, but I needed to "see" with my fingers. One glove should be enough.

I moved another foot. Simon moved two. I reminded myself to breathe. It was easy to forget and let the anxiety build up in my stressed lungs.

"I've figured out the timeframe for when you threw in with Moran." If I kept him talking maybe someone would come by and see us clinging like barnacles to the side of the building and call the police. Despite the fear Simon did have key city law enforcement officials in his back pocket, I had a few phone numbers I could call as well. I'd take my chances. "When did you switch teams again and swear allegiance to Ermo Colle?"

"When the money came up to my standards."

"I didn't know bastards had standards."

He waggled the knife back and forth, as if scolding me. "Cannot tame that mouth, can you?"

"Was it all about the money, Simon?"

We were both moving, but he made slightly more progress on me each time.

"Not necessarily money, but financial superiority."

Power was what he wanted.

"Crook, murderer, traitor. Worth the risk?" I passed another window. Locked and lights out. Everyone was likely at the casino.

"What risk? I dispatch you, and I'll be rewarded again," he said. The knife blade flashed in the streetlamp's glare.

"I told you, I likely killed my...your boss."

His face lit up with the worst kind of grin. "Good. I'll get a promotion. I guess I should thank you. And kill you."

"How many others have you murdered, Simon?"

"Not a one. I've only executed offenders."

"We aren't talking retribution for forged art—"

He laughed. "Hardly."

"Then why?"

"The reason..." He sighed. "They worked for the wrong person or couldn't hold their tongues. Or they taxed my patience. Exactly like you're doing."

The corner of the wall was closer. Once I made it to the other side of the building there was a chance we'd be seen by cars driving by, people walking. I had to believe reaching the far section of the building offered an advantage since I wouldn't be rounding the corner backward like Simon. I slid another foot. From the look on his face Simon assumed the same thing I had. At the next window he used precious time to make a one-eighty body reversal. He moved the knife to his left hand to have an easier time grabbing me with his right.

I moved as fast as the ledge allowed. He took several quick semi-long side steps, hugging the wall as he lessened the gap between us.

Another similar move and he'd eliminate any advantage I had.

I scrambled, almost losing my balance in my haste to get closer to the corner. The icy ledge was getting more slippery. The wall was colder here as well. Ice filled the crevices. I looked up. Water runoff drizzled from above. Probably some kind of refrigeration unit. They wouldn't need air conditioners in a Black Forest winter. My right foot—my lead foot—started to slide. I pulled back.

Turning the corner to get into a street view wasn't an option any longer. Time to stand my ground.

I bluffed, "This is it, Simon. No more. I'm taking you with me if I fall. It's going to be much tougher to slice my throat than it has been to take out a forger."

"Why? Because we slept together? You think that meant anything?"

"No, because I presently hate you much more than you hate me. I'll be damned if I let you win this." The baton slid down, and I caught the handle with my gloved hand. Between the wet section of the wall and sheer brick face, there was little to hold on to at this point. There was a thin piece of trim. It wasn't much, but if I kept my weight tight against the building, there might be a chance. If he came closer, I could hit him. Maybe make him fall. Or at least drop the knife. The whiplash would likely send me tumbling with him. My bare fingertips searched for a crack or indention to get a better hold on the trim work. Nothing.

It would have to do. My one chance.

Raising the baton, I got his attention. At the same time, I leaned against the wall and slipped my other hand into the right jacket pocket.

His face hardened. He did a careful lunge and snagged the end of the baton in his fist to pull me closer. I was ready.

My hand came out of the jacket pocket with the travel hairspray. I fired it into his eyes. I let go of the spray and locked my fingers onto the skinny wooden trim.

He shouted, raising the forearm with the knife to shield his eyes. The baton became his lifeline to balance. He tightened his hold.

It was his last mistake.

I clutched the trim tighter and yanked the baton, pulling him off-balance. As he fell, I let go of the weapon. I loved the little beauty, but I couldn't take it home with me. The police may as well find it with him. My leather glove wasn't just pretty—it did a great job at helping obliterate any fingerprints I might have left on the weapon's handle too.

First there was a thud, then a moan, but I didn't look to see. All my attention stayed trained on the open window with light streaming out. No point in risking a fall at this point to see a man lay motionless in a cobblestone alley. The second person I may have killed this evening.

As I crawled back through the window to my room, I heard police sirens coming closer. I wouldn't have to call down to the desk for an ambulance after all. When I could stand safely on the carpet, I looked out the window, leaning to see into the alley. Simon was nowhere to be seen.

TWENTY-TWO

I went to the lobby and sat in the lounge to wait, choosing a chair affording me a view of the desk and front entry. Wishing desperately for my phone and wondering if Jack had taken the burner phone with him or left it upstairs in his room, I decided to go check. In that exact moment, Rollie walked through the hotel entrance.

"Surprise!" His hair was longer again. He'd probably had it pulled back into a ponytail on New Year's Eve. I was beginning to worry about my powers of observation.

He pulled me into a hug. I'd expected someone to arrive. I wasn't sure who, but was glad to see a friendly-enough face. Despite the fact I was still a little cautious about Rollie's alliances after learning so recently Simon's changed as the wind shifted.

They always say there's no honor among thieves.

"You are shaking," he said, frowning. I hadn't noticed, but he was right. He asked, "You are not afraid of me?"

"No," I said, though he wasn't completely wrong. "Too many unexpected things have occurred today. My body is shocked out."

"I come and yell surprise." He shook his head. "*Très* sorry."

"Apology isn't necessary. I had a feeling I'd see someone soon. The police, if no one else."

He grimaced and waved a hand. "The *gendarmes* are gone."

"Did they catch Simon?"

He looked into my eyes as he spoke, and I could see a toughness in his expression to bely his normally bright persona.

"*Non.* My men came to get the car you drove. One of them saw Simon fall. He—how you say? Slipped our net earlier. But you foiled his plan. They saw, but could not get to you to help." He pulled something from his pocket. "They said these belong to you."

My hairspray and glove. I wondered what happened to the baton, if it was covered in blood. Would they have shot Simon from the ledge if they'd arrived sooner?

"Thank you." I held an item in each hand, then wrapped my arms around my torso, feeling a little sick. "Was he...dead?"

He waved his hands. "Simon was in pain. How could he not be?" Rollie shrugged. "Still, he was alive."

"A doctor—"

He held a finger to my lips. "He has been taken where he needs to go. You won't see him again."

I shouldn't ask about him again either, I'll wager. Aloud, I said, "Thank you," as my brain processed options.

He reached into his coat and withdrew a folded piece of paper. It was an airline boarding pass.

"We will go to the room and gather yours and your friend's things. I have a car waiting to drive you to the airport."

"I can't leave without Jack."

"He was...banged up. But he will be flying with you. You'll see him at the airport."

"I need to talk to him first." The desk clerk looked up, and I realized I'd raised my voice.

"*Non,* he—"

"I'm not leaving until I do." I spoke softer this time, but both of us heard the edge in my voice. One part of me was numb, but I felt equally ready to break something—or someone—if any additional interference was thrown into my path. My emotions were all over the spectrum and would stay so until I heard Jack's voice. "I've quit counting how many times I've been attacked in the last twelve hours." I reached up and caught his coat lapels in my hands. "Even by my own late father who I found out was very much alive all these years, and who didn't care that he left me in a financial abyss when he played dead. I'm completely shocked out, Rollie, and I'm not taking more crap. Either tell me how to reach Jack or leave without me and I'll find him myself."

He pursed his lips a moment and nodded. "I must have my phone."

I let go of his coat and stepped aside.

Seconds later I was talking to the doctor working on Jack. The doc tried to put me off, but I was persistent.

"I'll be okay, Laurel." Jack sounded weak, but alive. I knew how little he'd slept and hoped most could be cured with a good night's sleep. Or two. He continued, "I never thought I'd say this, but go with Rollie. He's right. We need to get back to London. Especially you."

I didn't want to ask if anyone had found my father. Or if I'd killed him. Jack's last words decided things for me. We ended the call and allowed the impatient doctor to get back to work. I handed the phone to Rollie.

"I appreciate your help. Thank you."

"*Mais oui.*"

As we headed upstairs, I said, "Please thank your grandfather for me as well. His...little gift...saved my life several times tonight."

"Oh, I am reminded." We were nearing the door to my room, and he waited while I used my key. He closed the door solidly behind us before finishing, "A knife was found when Simon was...transported...by our associates. We've kept it to see if you would like the weapon for law enforcement contacts."

The possibility of matching up the murder weapon with the people who were killed—even a few of them—would help our efforts tremendously. "Yes, Rollie. Having the knife would be wonderful."

"Should I have it sent to your office—"

"No, Simon tried to destroy the place on New Year's Day. Ask someone to get an address from Jack. I'm sure he has drop boxes scattered all over Europe. He'd be best at knowing how to take it in and get listened to. Plus, all the pesky chain-of-evidence stuff everyone worries about."

"You do not."

"I don't want thieves to get away scot free, but I'm always more interested in retrieving masterpieces than leaving with nothing more than the master criminal. I have to ask, was there ever a sword? Or is it one more myth created by Simon?"

His eyes crinkled when he smiled. "*Oui*, the sword. You should forget the sword."

Something told me it was on a wall in one of Moran's chateaus. I said, "Has anyone ever said you answer questions exactly like your grandfather?"

"All the time."

I threw what few things I'd unpacked into my carry-on bag. Rollie helped me straighten the duvet, and the bed no longer looked like Simon tried to kill me on it. We set my things by the door and moved to Jack's room.

He'd unpacked less than I had. I grabbed his razor from the bath and slipped his travel clothes into the unlocked pocket of his bag. The burner phone sat on the nightstand. I added it to the jacket pocket with the hairspray. The burner would do until I got my phone back.

"Okay, looks like we've packed it all," I said. Rollie hefted Jack's bag, and I started to turn out the light. "One more thing. I'm assuming Simon isn't going to be available for trial."

He looked at his watch then back at me. His brown eyes had none of the softness I'd noticed when I'd first met him. "*Non*, there is little possibility. But often families feel better knowing it can be proved who did the crime, even if the perpetrator is already, shall we say, sentenced?"

To death. I hit the light switch, and we returned to the other room to grab my bags and leave.

I checked us out, grateful Jack left a credit card number and I didn't have to play credit line roulette with mine. Rollie waited for me by the front door. At the curb sat a Mercedes G-Class SUV in gleaming ebony and sporting tires with serious off-road and badass weather capabilities. All the back windows boasted blackout glass. I paused. My track record riding in Mercedes vehicles wasn't the best lately.

"A problem?" Rollie asked.

The burly driver's face was set in a frown as he stowed my luggage in the back. Was Jack right? What was I doing getting into this kind of a vehicle with someone who just gave me the coldest look on record when obliquely reporting his associates bundled Simon away and killed him?

Rollie smiled and nodded. "Ah, you are having second thoughts."

Or third or fourth. "I'm kind of losing track on how many people are making decisions for me."

"I could stay here if you would feel more comfortable with only my driver," he said.

Another look at Mr. Burly had me shaking my head. "I think—"

"I had hoped we could talk and maybe if you have questions, I could answer something." He shrugged.

The man knew my weakness, but I wasn't ready to capitulate yet. I stayed silent, hoping he'd somehow sweeten the deal. I thought I'd worn him down when he blew out a long breath. He waved the driver over and said, "Give me your gun."

"Oh no!" I spun around and ran back into the hotel.

"Laurel, wait," Rollie called. He chased me. I pulled on the door to the stairs, and he slammed a palm to keep it shut. He whispered, "Put this in your coat." He handed me the heavy black gun. "I was getting it for you. Not to hold you at gunpoint."

"Oh." That kind of made a difference. At least I hoped it did.

He put an arm around my shoulders and directed me back outside, talking into my ear the whole time. "I wanted you to feel in control. You are exactly right. You have had too many people directing your movements."

We stopped at the curb. Mr. Burly assumed a sentry position, holding open the back door and frowning. I wondered if he was irritated about losing the gun.

Or he could have a resting frown face—or another gun. My

fingers tightened around the rubberized grip. I wished I'd checked if the clip was full.

Rollie stepped aside so I could enter first.

Between the luxury interior and the control panel for Mr. Burly to operate the vehicle after he settled back into his pilot's chair, I figured this model likely ran quite a lot above MSRP. Which wasn't cheap to begin with. The outside may have looked a little Jeep-y, but the inside was first class all the way.

I took the opportunity to open and close my door. To make sure I could. Rollie looked at me and chuckled, but I found nothing funny about any of this. I buckled up and put the gun in my lap, before deciding to put it in the pocket of the bomber jacket to keep it less accessible to Rollie.

He fired off a fast fusillade of instructions to the driver in French, adding Jean-Luc near the beginning, so I assumed it must be Mr. Burly's actual name. I identified about every fifth word. Probably the plan—talk fast to keep me from following the spirit of the conversation. As the car pulled smoothly into traffic, he turned to me. "I think you have some things you'd like to ask me, no?"

Oh, boy, do I. I needed to play this carefully. I didn't know what kind of game Rollie could be playing, and showing my hand did not seem the best response. The look in his eyes earlier, hard as stone, wouldn't be something I'd soon forget. I couldn't help patting the gun.

"Why did you come to London for New Year's?" I asked. "We were really surprised to see you there."

He shrugged in perfect Gallic style. "I was in town. It was an event."

"How did you find us in the crowd?"

"I heard you cry out and recognized your voice. I simply wanted to help."

Right. Suddenly I had an epiphany. "Did you deliver the package to my office from your grandfather, or did you hire someone?"

"How did your assistant describe the delivery person?"

Answered my question. If it hadn't been Rollie, he wouldn't have known I wasn't in the office. It also meant he was still in London when Jack and Scotland Yard thought he'd left. He likely delivered the package to my old hotel too. When I returned to London I needed to check my things for transmitting devices, in case he somehow found out my room number and snuck upstairs. I didn't know why this new information unnerved me more than I already was, but it did. When I saw the grin he shot my way, I knew that he knew I'd figured it out.

"How did you get through customs into the U.K.?"

He made a *tsk-tsk* sound. "Let's not ask boring questions, Laurel."

"I don't find the question a bit boring. I'd wager Scotland Yard wouldn't either."

"I find talk of Scotland Yard boring as well. Let us find another conversation."

Hmm. Must try a less direct route next time. "Was Hamish Ravensdale working for you? Is he the one who signaled where we were at the fireworks display?"

"Good idea to ask about him." Rollie reached behind the seat and pulled a thermos and a wine bottle from a container. "Would you like some refreshment?"

"No thank you. And please don't compliment me one instant and change the subject the next. It was your idea to tempt me into riding along by promising to answer questions, remember."

He chuckled and returned the thermos to the rear area. Following the maneuver, he pulled out a wineglass and set it in his closest cup holder.

Of course, we must have proper stemware for to-go wine. I noticed they were all very deep cup holders in this rear seat.

"I'm glad you mentioned *Monsieur* Ravensdale. He is an old friend of yours?"

"No, he went to school with Jack."

"Ah." He opened the wine and stood it in a small rectangular container set into the floor. "To breathe," he said. He pulled out his phone and flipped screens with his thumb. "I hired several men to follow *Monsieur* Ravensdale while he was in London after receiving several scouting reports like this one." He turned the screen my way and showed me two shots of Simon sitting with Hamish at different café tables, their heads close together each time. Plotting.

"Where and when were these photos taken?" I asked.

"The first is Milan in September. The second is Cannes—"

"In May," I finished his sentence.

"*Oui.* You understand."

Definitely. It backed up my belief Simon was responsible for the Greek's death when I was to pick up the snuffbox at the *castillo* near Lake Como, as well as the forger who was killed at the time of the international film festival on the French Riviera. Which he pretty much admitted tonight when he made his execution statement. "I suspected as much of Simon, but I didn't know the Hamish connection. If the days coincide—"

He spoke two quick dates and more pieces fell into place.

"What business did he have with Hamish?"

"I assumed a connection with you. I saw you talking together as a group at the Florence event."

"I hadn't met him or his wife until that night."

Rollie stared off a moment in thought. "Then I can only assume he works for Ermo Colle. All I know for sure is he was under orders to watch you."

"Weird. You're saying he came up and spoke to us at the Florence event because of me? Not Jack?"

"His history with your friend Jack...it was...convenient?"

A lightbulb went off in my brain. "Putting the question of Hamish aside for a moment, if you had Simon under surveillance in May, you already suspected his change in allegiance before I even got involved in this thing. Why did it take until September before he ran away? Did you tip him off that you'd figured it out? If he hadn't run away, we wouldn't have known he worked for your grandfather and was a traitor to Beacham. By then he really didn't work for your grandfather—he worked for Ermo Colle according to your scenario. Why did he go to Le Puy? Was he meeting you there? Or Moran?"

"Everyone *thought* he worked for my grandfather. Fleeing to Le Puy kept the illusion alive. I had suspicions, but it was complicated."

"You suspected Simon was working all sides. You had the photos and the reports from whoever did the surveillance. You knew you couldn't trust him. Why didn't you out him earlier? Save all of us a lot of trouble?"

He gave a half-smile and remained silent.

I closed my eyes when the impact of the realization hit me. "You wanted the sword."

"He alluded to future things, I cannot say if—"

"But there is a sword. You don't have to confirm it for me to know." I hit the door panel with an open palm to try to eliminate some of the pent-up anger surging through my body. Another masterwork of history and art gone without a trace. Confirmed. One more important item to add to my list of "where are they now?" things to someday try to locate. I didn't even want to tell Jack. He'd likely be more furious than I felt.

Suddenly, two sets of headlights flashed in from the windshield. Jean-Luc cursed and hit the door locks. He started to turn the truck around, but even through the seriously blackened glass we saw two more vehicles join the party and block an exit in the opposite direction.

Automatic weapons and gunfire came next.

I don't even remember removing my seatbelt, but a second later I was in the floorboard. Rollie stayed in his seat. The bullets bounced off the glass and car doors.

"I take it you've converted this vehicle to military class?" I asked. I kept a death grip on the gun.

Rollie nodded, and recapped the wine. "Yes, and I would suggest getting back into your seatbelt. The ride shall become bumpy in a moment."

Jean-Luc cut the wheel to the right, and I learned the true

value of a G-Class Mercedes. We entered a snow-covered field and were a good distance before our assailants got two of the other vehicles off the road to follow us. The remaining two cars stayed behind.

"They will have difficulty catching us, but not impossible," Rollie said, studying the view out the back. "Find another route to the airport, Jean-Luc, in case their luck improves or they call reinforcements."

"What if they call in a helicopter?" I asked.

"*Excellente!* We may also."

Jean-Luc barked out the name Maurice and a roadway number, to which Rollie responded, "*Oui,*" and pulled out his cell. The conversation was brief, but it sounded like we were going to get a new vehicle and driver soon.

"Contingency plan?" I asked

"*Absolutement.*"

"I was kind of looking forward to the helicopter idea."

He threw back his head and laughed.

Poor Jean-Luc kept us headed into the blackness, the headlights bouncing as they showed every obstruction ahead. Our assailants appeared as only bright pairs of lights through the back glass.

One in particular seemed to be having considerable difficulty keeping to the race. Not that it mattered. All they needed to do was follow the tracks in the snow. How many off-road journeys could anyone find roving through the Black Forest on a night like this one?

"Now you understand why we need to get you out of Germany," Rollie said, driving the point home.

I wasn't ready to concede anything. "You picked me up in an armored vehicle. I can't see these particular options as part of a Mercedes sales package."

"My grandfather and I do have enemies. We must always plan accordingly. Tonight...Tonight you must understand you are at risk."

"I get it, Rollie," I said, feeling a little chagrined. He did come to help me, after all. "Old habits for me."

"Yes, I know." He grinned. "Before you ask, I do not yet have word about your—"

"Ermo Colle." I knew what was coming and hurried to stop his words. I wasn't ready to think of the man as any part of my genetic pool.

"Ah, yes, Ermo Colle," Rollie replied, his tone soft. I held my breath. He must have seen I was fighting tears. He clapped his hands and briskly changed the tone of the conversation. "I am assuming these are his lieutenants following us. Which means nothing other than his attack is being avenged, or he remains intent on silencing you."

"I understand why your grandfather warned Colle was afraid of me. The plastic surgeries weren't enough to hide him." I had a much clearer understanding of what Jack had been trying to teach me about the way he recognized people who didn't want to be recognized.

"He is likely to change his appearance again."

Discussion was getting difficult. We hit a particularly savage expanse of rough terrain and hung on. I stared out the windows, mentally helping Jean-Luc drive through the extended rough patch. When the journey settled into a less active state, Jean-Luc nodded toward the rearview mirror and grunted. Rollie twisted in his seat.

"It appears we've lost our entourage," he said.

"Are we still switching cars?"

"*Oui*," Rollie said. "We don't want to break down en route, and this vehicle has been punished enough, I believe. The other two vehicles could have also split up to cut us off somewhere down route. We should not make it easy for them."

No, definitely not easy.

Time to see if he was open for another round of Twenty Questions.

"So, Rollie, if I need to beware of Hamish, is there anyone else I should take note of? After all, I had Weasel and Werewolf chasing me in London, and Jack told me they work for your grandfather."

"Weasel? Werewolf?"

I thought for a minute, trying to dredge up the names Jack gave for the pair. "Fourth? No, Firth. Firth and Marker."

He laughed. "Oh, *oui*, they were keeping you safe. My grandfather was...hmm...giving Simon some rope. Simon promised to bring in the sword, but I was concerned for your safety. My grandfather sent them to protect you."

"They tried to chloroform me on a Tube train."

Another nonchalant shrug. "They are idiots," he said.

A shout of excitement from Jean-Luc directed our attention to the front and the blessedly clear roadway appearing ahead of us in the headlights. In four-wheel drive, the truck had little difficulty climbing the roadbed to get back onto asphalt. I sighed when the shock absorbers again provided a normal ride.

"The palazzo in Florence," I said, working through my mental list. "Was it your grandfather's counterfeiting factory? Or an operation Tony B managed for Ermo Colle?"

I thought I saw a flash of irritation cross Rollie's face, but the light was mostly from the front dashboard, and I couldn't be certain. His voice was pleasant enough when he answered, so I assumed I was mistaken. "Tony B stored some crates without permission. No longer. He has gotten what he deserves as well. Though I personally have no direct knowledge about it."

Yeah, right. He hadn't answered my question either. "The palazzo, was it your organization's or Colle's?"

"Why do you do what you do, Laurel?" He took my free hand. I kept the other wrapped around the grip of the gun. "Works of art are hung in museums like they are items in storage facilities. Others kept packed away and hidden from a lack of space to display the works. No one sees everything all the time, and with more masterpieces protected behind glass each day, no one can peer close enough to notice the difference between good copies and originals."

Meaning he wasn't answering, but in a way he was. I thought

back to the excellent copy of *Woman Dressing Her Hair* I now knew was painted as a copy by Jack's mother. An intentional copy. How it hadn't been a Sebastian original, but her brushstrokes, beautifully close to his method, had confused me as I looked at it.

"An original work is infinitely more than the sum of its parts, Rollie. The heart and mind of the artist is contained in each work, as well as the impressions of their lives at the time. Whether their home lives were happy. If they wanted to leave a message behind to show their children that they loved them. Brushstrokes and paint colors are only one part, but all of it is crucial. No 'good' copy, no matter how well done, can perfectly duplicate the genius and craft of an original artist."

He curled his lip and chuckled, then pulled the wine from the container in the floor. "Let us drink to a successful escape. We should meet up with Maurice momentarily. Correct, Jean-Luc?"

Our driver grunted a response.

I didn't want any wine, but if I wanted more answers I figured I'd better try to finesse things a little.

The wineglass in the cup holder was perfectly intact, making me appreciate the deepness of the holders after our bumper car journey. Rollie poured wine into the glass and handed me the stemware. He reached into the back for another glass. "Go on, drink. Do not wait for me."

As he started to pour a glass for himself, I sipped the vintage. "This is very good."

"*Mais oui.* Only the best." He grinned and clinked my glass.

I drank another sip as Jean-Luc spoke up, asking something about directions. Rollie set his glass into the cup holder and leaned forward to listen.

Suddenly, I was starving. I'd been going out to get food when Simon appeared in the room hours ago, and I'd never eaten anything. All of the subsequent excitement hadn't helped either. The wine had enough calories, and I hoped it would stave off the stomach pangs. Once Rollie and Jean-Luc ended their discussion I'd ask if they had any cheese and crackers in the back. Anything to munch. Another long sip and I finished off the wine, ready for a refill.

The wooziness hit a second later. At first I thought it was from the hunger, until I couldn't make my tongue form words. My vision started to fog. Rollie removed the wineglass from my hand and didn't ask if I was okay. The last thought I had before the darkness fell was, *Jack is going to be pissed off I didn't remember to test the wine with my fingernail first.*

TWENTY-THREE

When I woke up, Rollie was capping smelling salts. We were in an entirely different vehicle with a different driver—Maurice, I supposed—and sitting at the airport. I recalled my last thought before blacking out and promised myself Jack would never learn about this.

The new driver offered a bottle of water. I waved it away, but Rollie showed me the bottle hadn't been opened. "You need to drink something," he said.

I jerked the bottle away from him, poured a capful, and turned to put my nail in the liquid to check. No point letting him know all my secrets. When the color didn't change, I chugged down the bottle. He was right, I did need a drink.

By the time I had my legs again, probable-Maurice had my bags and Jack's checked. He passed me the claim receipts. I slipped them into the Fendi and made myself not think about the fact Rollie could have searched it. Jean-Luc's gun was no longer in my pocket, but the rest of the contents of the bomber jacket seemed intact. Rollie helped me out of the car, telling probable-Maurice to park and wait for his call.

"You could have just told me you didn't want to talk about the setup in Florence," I said, frowning as I remembered what I'd asked him.

He clasped my elbow and steered me toward the electronic doors. "You needed to rest. It's been a long day for you."

"You're saying our jaunt had nothing to do with it?"

I received my third shrug of the evening.

"I never got a chance to ask you anything about my mother," I said.

"I never met her," he responded.

"Doesn't mean you don't know about her."

"Such an excess of hearsay in life today."

Again his words alluded to a better capacity for the English language than he tried to persuade me to believe.

Like any gentleman after he's drugged a lady, Rollie wouldn't let me fend for myself inside the airport either, and he was on hand when I first saw Jack.

I went to hug him, but he held out a hand to stop me. "Two broken ribs."

"The same ones as in October?" I asked.

"No, other side this time," Jack said.

"Steel-toed boots will do that," Rollie said, joining us. "You need to go and check in, Laurel."

I looked at Jack and then Rollie. They both stared back at me.

"Well, I know when I'm not wanted." I headed to the ticket counter, hoping someone there spoke English since my two translators were otherwise occupied.

In the short time it took the clerk to handle my business, the guys seemed to settle theirs. I pretended to search through the Fendi a moment to watch and see that a new conversation didn't start up to run me off again. I walked over and hugged Rollie, thanked him, and said goodbye. There would be retribution for all of this later, especially the drugged wine, but I'd learned long ago to keep things civil until I could most effectively use an experience to the best advantage. Besides, I really wanted Rollie gone and amicability was the best way to achieve the objective.

As he left the gate, I finally got Jack to sit down. His color wasn't good, and I didn't have the strength left to help hold him up. I planned to wait until we got on the plane to hit him with my epiphany.

We had seats in first class. Normally, Jack would have ordered a Scotch before we secured our seatbelts. At least he did the last time he got beat up right before we flew anywhere. This time, he asked for coffee.

"They gave you pain pills?" I asked.

"Yes, some really good ones. Strong."

It was an uneventful flight, and he slept most of the way. This gave me time to separate all the thoughts flying through my brain. He roused about a half-hour from London, and peppered me with questions about what he didn't know and what I did.

"I'm going to kill Hamish."

I laughed. "Out of all I've told you, he's the thing you focused on?"

"I've wanted to string him up for a couple of days. What you've told me simply makes it more appropriate. The question remains, do we trust Rollie is telling the truth? Or did he hire Hamish to intercept you and is covering his arse?"

"A possibility."

Both of us had a clearer idea of the past days' events, and I asked the question I'd been avoiding.

"What about...Ermo Colle? Did I..."

"I don't know," Jack said. "Moran's guy told me the body was gone from the room when he checked. We don't know if he went out under his own power or if someone carried him. Or if Moran's guy killed him or carted him off and was lying to me. I was in quite a bit of pain at the time and may have missed cues for warning me if he lied. Either way, Colle was afraid you would recognize him, and you did. We're going to have to put some safeguards in place. It's too much to hope he won't come after you if he's alive."

Which meshed with what Rollie said. I didn't like to think about what it would mean if he did, or didn't, live. I had a good idea my range of travel might be limited unless I always paired up with someone.

I told Jack about the attempted hijacking on the road, and how Rollie suggested it was lieutenants from Colle's organization.

"You weren't hurt?" he asked, his eyes wide.

"We were in a Mercedes built like a tank. No sweat."

I filled him in on the results of my interrupted interrogation. I didn't tell him about being drugged, but implied Rollie changed the subject each time he didn't want to answer a question. While we didn't have anything to use in a prosecutorial setting, we agreed what he did admit shored up our assumptions.

"One more thing," I said. Touring the cathedral and remembering my professor's discussions about sacred numbers and divine mathematics had given me an idea, and I wanted Jack's take on it. Moran mentioned the numbers changing, and the idea had solidified later in the casino when I started thinking about odds between roulette and blackjack. "I could be completely wrong, but what if all of this is about numbers and odds?"

"I don't have any idea what you mean."

"I've had numbers on the brain today," I said. "We still can't figure out what the string of digits mean that we retrieved from the safe deposit box in Florida, then in the cathedral—"

"The divine number theory," he said, squinting his eyes in thought.

"Right. In the casino, odds of winning, odds of losing, and how much or little the house actually keeps. I began wondering what if we're chasing a numbers thing."

"Like a bookie?" Jack frowned. "Maybe it's the pain pills, but I don't understand."

"Bear with me a moment. What if we stop putting so much time and attention on the forgeries we've discovered and start paying more attention to copies instead?"

"What copies?"

"Any copies of masterpieces shipped into a country as *legitimate copies*. Think about what you saw on the rooftop in Florence."

"The rooftop with the paintings and the guns."

"Yes, and I'm thinking Tony B's crew left the guns without permission. Leading to Rollie chewing out Scarface."

"The palazzo operation was Moran's?"

"Most likely. At least, it's the impression I got. I'm wondering if the rooftop is part of the reason Rollie wouldn't answer me about the palazzo."

Jack's forehead furrowed. "You think Moran was subletting to Ermo Colle?"

I sighed and leaned back against the headrest, closing my eyes for a moment to think. "Possibly. He changed the subject and it seemed more important to do so than when I asked other things. Like how he reentered the U.K."

Yeah, drugging me was a stronger reaction to get away from my questions.

"Plus the whole Scarface argument," I reminded him. "You said yourself the guy had never been associated with Moran before. Why was he with Rollie in Florence? I'm thinking Tony B stepped too far afield this time. Someone needed to take him out."

"You think the Amazon works for Moran?"

I nodded slowly. "Or more likely Rollie."

"You thought she was the motorcycle shooter in France."

I sighed. "It's pure guesswork, but made sense once I learned Rollie was already suspicious of Simon. Besides, the shooter didn't try to kill me, despite opportunity to run me down or take better shots. Scary, sure, but the wound in my arm was mostly messy and not life threatening. If it was the Amazon, and her employer's grandfather showed up, it makes perfect sense for her to leave."

"You were shot."

"I was grazed. The fence I tripped over did almost as much damage to me and my clothes as the bullet. Though, it doesn't mean I think Rollie would be upset if I got hurt."

"My mind is obviously not at its best." Jack closed his eyes. "Exactly what are you thinking?"

I remembered the couple of times Rollie's expressions made me uncomfortable in the level of coldness he projected. Yet he'd been nothing but kind to me. Was it by choice, or had all of our encounters been scripted on orders from his grandfather?

"Rollie's façade dropped a couple of times tonight, and I could absolutely believe him ruthless if the need arose. But I can't see

Moran involved in gunrunning. It doesn't match anything I know about the man. My instincts tell me the guns on the roof were not Moran's."

"Are we back to considering the younger generation overthrowing the elder?"

"I don't think so, but maybe."

Jack raised an eyebrow. "Your instincts again?"

"Hear me out," I said. "I'm thinking Rollie was in Florence in a kind of reconnaissance mission ahead of us, and the place emptied after what he found there. He's not a good guy, but he didn't like what the other bad guy was doing."

"Leaving the two men arguing on the street."

"Possibly?"

"You don't think Junior is trying to take over the throne with a coup?"

Suddenly all the running and bursts of adrenalin caught up to me, and I rested my head on Jack's shoulder as I talked. "Moran told me this afternoon he wants to retire to his vineyard. His whole demeanor said he didn't want to be involved in anything currently going on. I'm thinking he's hanging in until he can comfortably hand the keys over to Rollie."

"I need to look at more connections," Jack mused. "See if I can find alliances to back up any of these ideas. Wait a minute, we've gotten sidetracked. You were talking about something else."

Right, my idea. I started again. "All those copies of the same painting you saw in the crate on the roof," I said. "We haven't seen a half-dozen copies of the scene come in yet. We haven't been looking for it either. Ralf said his cousin was commissioned to make five copies of an abstract, but only put the forger's mark on four. You don't remember if any of the ones on the roof had forger's marks. So..."

Something new tickled my memory.

"What?" he asked. He twisted to look at me "Your eyes say you've thought of something else."

I raised a finger to stop him from saying anything else. There was an idea there, but I had to tease it out. I remembered what Moran told me.

"Moran said all the numbers were changing. What if he was referencing all the numbers of copies coming in with and without forger's marks? When copies are shipped into countries as 'copies,' they aren't tracked. Nothing is thought about doing so. They're copies with no provenance. If they're sold later as originals—"

"They would be discovered because the original is in its normal residence or museum."

"*If* it's where it belongs. What if it's being cleaned...or restored?"

"Like your friend Nelly did as a profession?"

"Exactly. If the restorer is set to clean a masterwork and can plan ahead—"

"Lord, that reminds me." Jack shook his head, then took my hand. His expression had me holding my breath as he spoke, "You have more unexpected work ahead. While I waited for the doctor, Whatley called your mobile. I answered when I saw his name in Caller ID."

"What did he say?"

"The returned tapestry wasn't the original. When it went to the exhibit and was displayed, an expert noticed something and told your clients it was a fake. They went to the Beacham office and concluded the worst when it was empty and the door nailed shut. Luckily, Whatley heard about it and spoke to them. They're expecting your call when you get back."

"Good lord, what do I say?"

"Call Whatley and see what he told them. I wasn't in the right frame of mind to listen to a lot at the time, but once you know what he said you can couch your explanation accordingly."

"Something I don't need on top of a nosy reporter biting at my heels about the break-in."

"I'd forgotten about Ferguson. You're right. Bad luck all around."

"I'll probably need to talk to their insurance adjuster as well."

"Most likely." A spasm of pain flashed across his face.

I sandwiched his hand with both of mine. "Are you okay?"

He nodded, but wrapped his free arm around his torso, as if holding in the pain. "Let's explore this. Keep my mind occupied. If a work is listed as a copy from the beginning, as opposed to an original, a lookalike could be created in a forger's workshop and shipped into the country as a copy with no customs red flags whatsoever. The switch made after the copy entered legally and without scrutiny."

I nodded.

"Still, why kill the forgers?" he asked.

"Simon said they couldn't hold their tongues," I said. "I've been thinking perhaps they were trying the forgers/restorers like interns, to see whose talents were consistently superb and whose weren't. Those who talked were targeted. Also, nerves might be involved. Remember, *il Carver* wasn't targeted until he got suspicious and started hiding out. If anyone acted concerned about the operation or out of character, they were eliminated. Or if they started telling who they worked for. Anything sketchy or worrisome."

"So he killed them for Ermo Colle."

"That's what I'm thinking."

"You think Moran controlled the palazzo where all the fakes were made. I'll wager if we go into the files looking hard for forgers who've recently been in Florence, we'll find a couple of the dead forgers worked for Moran. I'm beginning to think Simon hadn't just switched sides. He was hired to break the competition."

"Definite possibility." I pulled out my phone and added a note with my memo app. "I'll get Nico tracking passport information for the months preceding some of the forgers' deaths."

"What about Ralf's cousin? He didn't work for Moran, so does he skew the pattern?"

"I imagine he was one of victims who annoyed Simon and got taken out due to attitude. He was young. Ralf is cocky, and I can't imagine a Burkhard relative not being the same. Especially one known for being young and successful at what he did. Maybe he talked about the wrong thing at the wrong time. He'd been at a bar drinking with friends the night he was killed, remember."

Jack frowned. "Yeah, but one thing bothers me about his death and Ralf connecting him to Colle. The red hair found on the scene. If it's your assertion the Amazon worked for Rollie—which makes more sense the more I think about it, by the way—what would the reason be for her to kill the young artist? Or is the hair a coincidence?"

The cold hard look in Rollie's eyes flashed in my memory. Moran's words about the killing soon stopping echoed in my ears. I took a deep breath. "Nico said something almost prophetic when you and I were in Florence. While he was drowning in all his and Cassie's research he said this thing was bigger than we'd originally thought. If Rollie found out Simon was executing Moran's forgers, who's to say he wouldn't decide it was open season for Ermo Colle's contractors?"

"So both sides had their own hit squads going after each other's forgers."

"What I'm thinking." I nodded. "And since Tony B didn't work for Moran, he had to be working for Colle. Which explains why the Amazon killed him. Rollie put out the hit on Tony B. That's a project you could take to MI-6, tying evidence of the hits to Rollie and the Amazon to convict for the murders."

"Yes, and with the knife and information on Simon too, we can get MI-6 interested from the turf wars angle. Keep both sides busy while we're working on new angles to stop the heist."

"With luck, MI-6 might even find and share intel we can use. We'll all be working together without having to worry about moles leaking info on where we are in stopping the heist, since MI-6 won't be privy to that information."

"Good point," Jack replied. The PA came on announcing landing preparations. He waited until the speaker quieted before saying, "Back to the numbers thing. Why did your friend Nelly need multiple passports in different names and countries of origin?"

"Damn."

"Don't beat yourself up," he said. "You've filled in a lot of blanks tonight. Your theory about the copies is a good hypothesis and one to research. Who knows where it may lead? We know multiple copies were made, but it's not being done for motel art. Whoever is in charge of this thing, though, I think we can narrow our suspected organizations down to one—"

"I don't believe Moran is totally innocent," I added.

"I'd never presume that," Jack agreed. "As I was saying, this isn't for some kind of cut-rate market. The perpetrators have a more lucrative reason. The guns we found in Florence make it all the more worrisome."

"Moran said something reminding me of it. Something like, 'The easiest or best way to make money isn't necessarily art.'"

Jack nodded. "Yes, if we aren't careful, art may reach a point more for laundering gun and drug money than for true connoisseurs to add to collections. It's probably not as big as Hollywood would have us believe, but it's a known concern."

"Makes me more prone to thinking Moran is behind the copies after all," I said, chuckling a little. The question Rollie asked me about my motivation for trying to catch them put point to my thought as well.

"Imagine the satisfaction of getting the worst bad guys to pay millions for copies of art worth practically nothing. All to launder gun money. I'd think it was karma except every time a painting goes for an unheard-of price, it drives up the price for everything else. Soon, no one will be able to afford good art."

"Yes, looking closer at the copies is an angle we've virtually ignored up to this point," he said. "While we may have taken the long route to get home, the journey was definitely worth it."

"Cassie and Nico should have a field day with the idea of crunching numbers nonstop."

"Just know, if they don't want to do it, the whole numbers thing was your idea," he said.

I slapped his leg. "See, this is why you don't have a dedicated team like I do. You're a chicken. No one wants to be led by a chicken."

"You admitted you're a wimp," Jack said. "A chicken and a wimp. I'd say we make a good pair, as long as you qualify your wimpiness as only relating to cold. I doubt Simon would ever call you a wimp. Or your father." He yawned.

"If they can," I said.

"Don't think about it too much," he warned. "You did the right thing."

Jack's car was still in my hotel's garage, and he stayed with me from the time we left Heathrow. I had a feeling he was doing it simply to keep an eye on me. From his coloring, I wasn't sure he'd be much help if anyone crossed our path along the way. "You're not going to drive while you're on pain pills."

"Believe me, there is no longer any pain medication in my system," he said, holding his side as he spoke. "I'll be as careful as any little old granny until I get into my flat. Then I'm going to sleep for a week."

"You're sure you don't want me to drive you?"

"I've been knocked around much more than this and successfully drove myself home."

"Yeah, but that was when you were younger. You're what..." I thought of the roulette wheel. "...thirty-two?"

His frowned deepened, and I didn't think it was from the pain. I knew for sure it wasn't when he said, "I know what you're hinting at. I haven't forgotten what I said."

"Good, we won't have to talk about it."

Go ahead, pull the other one, Jack.

TWENTY-FOUR

Instead of a week, Jack called the next evening, surprising me out of a funk I'd let myself fall into. Cassie and Nico were even deeper in their researching in New York, and had a few leads to check out. I'd started my day apologizing in person to the owners of the tapestry we now knew was fake, and spent an hour with their insurance appraiser giving what info I could without risking our mission. Then I spoke to the head of the Beacham legal team in New York. A part of me wished I didn't know Simon was dead, so I could track him down again and kill him myself.

To make matters worse, my new pet reporter learned I was back in the U.K. and phoned on my way back from meeting the insurance underwriters.

"Hallo, Lincoln Ferguson here," he greeted. "Remember me?

I was glad he couldn't see my eye roll.

"Yes, of course I remember you, Mr. Ferguson," I replied, striding quickly across a zebra crossing with a midday crowd of Londoners.

A horn honked at someone behind me, and he asked, "Have I called at a bad time?"

"I'm on the run between appointments." I laughed, trying to keep it light. "Pretty normal for me. I'm rarely working quietly behind a desk."

"Exactly the kind of detail I'm interested in," he said.

Damn. I couldn't win. I took a deep breath. "Really nothing interesting, I can assure you, Mr. Ferguson."

"Call me Linc."

I moved out of the walking masses and over to a quiet corner park. "I don't want to sound rude, but I'm just back into the country and I have a full agenda."

"Wanted to see if we could meet. Tea, beer, wine, your choice. You know, a pre-interview interview sort of thing. I have some questions."

Exactly what I was afraid of. "I'm sorry, Mr. Ferg—Linc, but I really don't have time at the moment."

"With your assistant gone and all," he said.

My antenna went to the stratosphere. "You do your research."

"Just my job."

I forced another laugh. "Well, I'm currently trying to do mine, and I don't have enough hours in the day as it is. How about I call you when I see a break in my schedule."

"Brilliant," he said, and surprised me by winding things up quickly. "I'll look forward to it. You can reach me at—"

"The number on Caller ID?"

"Correct."

"I'll make a note of it," I said. "Thank you. Have a good day."

"You as well."

I wasn't optimistic.

The rest of the day was spent in my hotel room on a tedious succession of phone conversations with contractors and building permit supervisors, trying to get the office repaired. When Jack rang, I jumped at the chance for dinner out. I was puzzled when he said to wear a warm coat, but assumed it was a hint he wanted his bomber jacket returned. I spent a half-hour cleaning stains on the leather and rubbing it with oil, feeling pretty proud of my work when I finished. I washed my hands, grabbed my leather coat and the Fendi, and left my hotel room with the jacket left draped over the desk chair. I forgot it. Accidentally.

We met near the Tower complex on the river walk along the Thames. It was one of my favorite haunts in London, and I assumed it was why Jack chose the spot. I was wrong about that as well.

A half-hour later we were cruising the Thames, alone on a lovely launch with our own captain to pilot the boat and a waiter on hand to whisk away each empty dish and refill our glasses. Light jazz played softly over the speakers. Our view from the middle of the river showed London glorious, as the city was lit for the unending night under the navy blue sky. We dined on superbly grilled salmon and vegetables covered with a fruit sauce I would have eaten by itself. The bread was like a first dessert, but the caramel creation at the end topped it all. He brought wine for me, a marvelous white, but his glass stayed filled with water.

"Jack, this is fabulous."

"I wanted to change the memory of our last date along the Thames," he said.

"Well, this certainly does it. An amazing end to a pretty boring day."

He looked pretty amazing too. I'd expected poor wan Hawkes, but twenty-four hours of sleep obviously did good things for him. The waiter came and removed the table, shifting it to the back corner of the boat. Jack stood up and offered me a hand.

"Boring days are good," he said. "We've had more than our share of exciting ones in a row lately. I fear they aren't over yet."

"I think I can forget excitement for...well, this evening." I pointed to the padded benches along the side. "Do you want to sit over there?"

The waiter removed our chairs.

"Or we could dance," Jack said. "Remember, it was my punishment."

"Oh, I think you've been punished enough lately, but I'll take a few spins around the deck with you."

I realized why the music had been slow tunes all night. Mind, I wasn't complaining; the ambience was lovely. A few minutes of cheek to cheek, and he was whispering in my ear. Memories of growing up, coming to London with his mother to see exhibits at The Tate and the National Gallery. I listened, taking in the true tone of his anecdotes, drinking in the intoxicating smell of him, and saying a silent prayer he was back again and almost in one piece—and I hadn't lost him.

The thought about my mandate made me cringe a little, and I was about to tell him I'd changed my mind when he said, "I'm going to break a few laws telling you this, but yes, I'm sort of with MI-6. At least, I work with them and they work with me. Chiefly, I'm with the Home Office."

I pulled back in surprise. "Ohmigod, Jack. I can't believe you said that."

"It can't be a shock. You'd figured out most of it."

"No, I'm not shocked at what you said. I'm shocked you finally told me." I returned my head to his shoulder—the one without the broken ribs underneath—and said, "But how is the Home Office connected to art? I thought it was all caught up in immigration and visas, drugs and counter-terrorism. Stuff along those lines."

"As we discussed on the plane, more and more art is being tied recently to drug and gun money. It's all a question of security and law and order," he explained, his voice remaining low. The information went into my ear and not any farther. "My position was created to act alone. To get me in places a unit couldn't. To determine what was a threat and what wasn't. Different people know me with different histories. Some rather colorful histories, by the way. My connection to the art world through my mother gives me more insight, and my ability to recognize faces adds to my purpose. The only problem I ever have with the job is the inflexibility of the ranks. But I haven't let it hold me back. Much."

I laughed. "I'd say not. There is one more thing I do want to know."

"Just one?"

I grinned. "When we went to Le Puy and you left me in the hotel. You said you were going to Geneva, but there's no way you made the trip and back before I saw you again. Why did you lie? Or why not tell a better one?"

"My god, you're still thinking about that?" He laughed.

"It bugged me." I slapped his shoulder.

He winced, but it was only for show. I knew how to bring pain if I really wanted.

"Well?"

"I did go to see Geneva. An operative who goes by the name Geneva."

"You lied to bug me."

"I obfuscated."

"You lied." I waited a beat then said, "What does she look like?"

He grinned. "You know I got to the church in Le Puy ahead of you. What do you think?"

"Okay. Good answer."

The wind rose, and a thick dark lock flipped onto his forehead. I used fingers to comb it back. He smiled.

"So," he continued, "I'm relatively trustworthy, as long as you remind me—which I am positive you'll do. My life is basically jumping from one mess to another, all in the service of my country. As I mentioned yesterday on the plane. It was yesterday, right?"

I nodded. "And you jump into messes in the service of a certain impulsive blonde when she does things you tell her not to do."

"I wasn't going to say it, but now you have—"

I cut him off. "You think I'm a mess, huh?"

"You misunderstood—"

"No, I didn't. You said you jump from one mess to another. Since you've told me this when I said it was the only way I would consider—"

"Does that mean you're considering?"

I stopped dancing and wrapped my arms around his neck, locking my gaze with his. I saw how much darker his teal eyes were than normal. "Quite frankly, I can't imagine two people less suited for each other than we are. We get into absolutely fatal predicaments together, and—"

His eyes widened. "The only reason we're both standing here is because the other was there as backup."

"You didn't let me finish." I ran my fingers up the back of his head, and he pulled me closer. My words had a shaky quality, and I knew I'd better get what I wanted to say out quickly. "We may get into messes together, but we can get out of them better than anyone too. The reason we are least suited also makes us best suited."

"I agree."

I had to look away for a moment. Stare at the lights on the Eye before I continued. My eyes met his again when I could speak. "We've solved the forger murders, found out we don't have to worry about Simon anymore, figured a way to tap into law enforcement help without showing our hand, and we have a new hypothesis to try to prove or disprove in regard to the full reach of the forgery operation and its leadership. But our to-do list isn't done yet."

He lowered his dark brows. "What are you driving at?"

"What I'm saying...is..." I took a deep breath. "I'm *considering* more of us, with this new segue into trustworthiness on your part. However...we both know I have an impulsive nature. You've pointed it out more often than most. Until we at least get this case solved, we need to ask ourselves if even considering this is too impulsive on both of our parts."

"How would you feel if I said yes?"

Pressure built in my eyes at the thought. "I'm pretty sure I'd be unhappy."

"What if I said this instead?"

Our lips met and he gave me the kiss we'd both missed on the stroke of midnight at New Year's. Fireworks exploded the entire time, but we were the only ones who saw the show.

RITTER AMES

Ritter Ames lives atop a high green hill in the country with her husband and Labrador retriever, and spends each day globe-trotting the art world from her laptop with Pandora blasting into her earbuds. Often with the dog snoring at her feet. Much like her Bodies of Art Mysteries, Ritter's favorite vacations start in London, then spiral out in every direction. She's been known to plan trips after researching new books, and keeps a list of "can't miss" foods to taste along the way. Visit her at www.ritterames.com where she blogs about all the crazy things that interest her.

The Bodies of Art Mystery Series
by Ritter Ames

COUNTERFEIT CONSPIRACIES (#1)
MARKED MASTERS (#2)
ABSTRACT ALIASES (#3)

Available at booksellers nationwide and online

Visit www.henerypress.com for details

Henery Press Mystery Books

And finally, before you go...
Here are a few other mysteries
you might enjoy:

FIXIN' TO DIE

Tonya Kappes

A Kenni Lowry Mystery (#1)

Kenni Lowry likes to think the zero crime rate in Cottonwood, Kentucky is due to her being sheriff, but she quickly discovers the ghost of her grandfather, the town's previous sheriff, has been scaring off any would-be criminals since she was elected. When the town's most beloved doctor is found murdered on the very same day as a jewelry store robbery, and a mysterious symbol ties the crime scenes together, Kenni must satisfy her hankerin' for justice by nabbing the culprits.

With the help of her Poppa, a lone deputy, and an annoyingly cute, too-big-for-his-britches State Reserve officer, Kenni must solve both cases and prove to the whole town, and herself, that she's worth her salt before time runs out.

Available at booksellers nationwide and online

Visit www.henerypress.com for details

MURDER IN G MAJOR

Alexia Gordon

A Gethsemane Brown Mystery (#1)

With few other options, African-American classical musician Gethsemane Brown accepts a less-than-ideal position turning a group of rowdy schoolboys into an award-winning orchestra. Stranded without luggage or money in the Irish countryside, she figures any job is better than none. The perk? Housesitting a lovely cliffside cottage. The catch? The ghost of the cottage's murdered owner haunts the place. Falsely accused of killing his wife (and himself), he begs Gethsemane to clear his name so he can rest in peace.

Gethsemane's reluctant investigation provokes a dormant killer and she soon finds herself in grave danger. As Gethsemane races to prevent a deadly encore, will she uncover the truth or star in her own farewell performance?

Available at booksellers nationwide and online

Visit www.henerypress.com for details

MURDER ON A SILVER PLATTER

Shawn Reilly Simmons

A Red Carpet Catering Mystery (#1)

Penelope Sutherland and her Red Carpet Catering company just got their big break as the on-set caterer for an upcoming blockbuster. But when she discovers a dead body outside her house, Penelope finds herself in hot water. Things start to boil over when serious accidents threaten the lives of the cast and crew. And when the film's star, who happens to be Penelope's best friend, is poisoned, the entire production is nearly shut down.

Threats and accusations send Penelope out of the frying pan and into the fire as she struggles to keep her company afloat. Before Penelope can dish up dessert, she must find the killer or she'll be the one served up on a silver platter.

Available at booksellers nationwide and online

Visit www.henerypress.com for details